FriesenPress

Suite 300 - 990 Fort St
Victoria, BC, V8V 3K2
Canada

www.friesenpress.com

ISBN
978-1-03-910451-8 (Hardcover)
978-1-03-910450-1 (Paperback)
978-1-03-910452-5 (eBook)

1. FICTION, SCIENCE FICTION, GENETIC ENGINEERING

Distributed to the trade by The Ingram Book Company

THE
SEQUENCE

LUCIEN
TELFORD

For my wife,
who gave me the space to disappear
into this fictional world and come out the other side
with a book.

The Common Rule of the America, Section 56
The Ethics:

1. No person shall grow, or attempt to grow, a living human from cloned or otherwise created genetic material.

2. No person shall use a human, whether conscious or not, as a test subject for genetic alteration.

3. No person shall edit the human genome in any capacity through the use of manipulative software, wetware, or any variation of genetic scissoring for the purposes of enhancement.

Rum-running

The illegal business of transporting (smuggling) where such transportation is forbidden by law. Smuggling is usually done to circumvent taxation or prohibition laws within a particular jurisdiction. The term "rum-running" is more commonly applied to smuggling over water.

1.

Through the windshield of his *Arethusa*, the GAFA sprawled in all its darkened desert nothingness—the Great African Fuck All. A staccato of shallow flora and fauna along a bare, wind-razored stretch of savannah, pimples on a barren landscape, short grasses scorched by a summer's fierce sunlight. In the distance, the tendril-like fingers of a fiery-red sunrise crept up behind blackening thunderheads through the pre-dawn East African air, the rising sun illuminating their silhouettes with a background of blood-red sky.

Dallas Ward was running the machine at full thrust, the exhaust from her internally mounted gas-turbine engines actively muffled, cooled, and ducted above her twin-forked tail. He was flying low, as always, metres above the desert's flat terrain in the camouflaging pink of a Serengeti morning. He glimpsed a curl of compressed water vapour escaping off the tip of the Russian aircraft's thin, swept-back wing. A coiled ringlet of cloud corkscrewing into the protective darkness of a night sky they were rapidly leaving behind.

She'd be visible in the approaching light, those spinning vortices drawing a direct and conspicuous line to her rear. He felt it, felt the dusk ascending, exposing. He shuffled in his custom-molded seat, lying almost flat, his left hand on the thrust lever, his right resting on the stick. Through his visor's interface, he watched the sun ascending to meet them. He reached out through the aircraft's tech into her ailerons, gave her elevator a gentle nudge. A thought brought her rudders close. A glance and he was the engines, the thrust. In these moments he *was* the jet, the separation of man and mechanism removed, integrated into a 1000 kilometre per hour chimera of low-vis stealth tech riding the soft whisper of a black ghost in flight.

Ghastly ghouls move silent through the night.

The thunderheads would provide some cover through the dawn, till they hit the coastline at least. Rippling sand dunes flashed beneath the canopy, their ridges lit by the rising sun, its burning lip not yet visible on the horizon. *It's so different from down here*, he thought, watching the terminator approach, the global divider between night and day, that same strip of brightening planet he'd gazed down on from the edge of space, back in a previous and now distant life.

The aircraft rumbled and shook in the turbulence of the morning's warming air, the wind flowing over the undulating ground like a river over stones, its roiling eddies bouncing her like a truck down a bumpy dirt road. He coaxed her lower, and she smoothed at his touch.

He wiped a gloved hand along his thigh and looked through holographic optics at the darkening pillars of rain falling ahead. It was rare to see storm clouds on the continent this far east.

Thirty feet below, the savannah awakened.

Where lions prowled and gazelle fled.

2.

Christ in a fucking pancake. Kit had really missed the dim sum. Above her towered the centuries-old windows of the Mandarin Oriental Hotel, extending from floor to ceiling. Their faded blue Pyrex panels shifted in a dance of autonomic, artificial polarization, following the noonday sun as it crept through endless, rhythmic cascades of hot tropical rain, greying the colours of Hong Kong's tallest skyscrapers that lined the harbour's shoreline. She peered out at it, past the dumpling she held between bamboo chopsticks before her lips. Her brain was outside, adrift amongst the precip, meandering into the spaces between. There was peace in there, in the liminal. A place of calm. A temporary respite from all this polluted fucking reality.

She ate the dumpling, wiped her mouth, and pondered the question Avery had asked.

"Work in progress," she responded, doing her usual slow chew on the shrimp, getting it to pop perfectly between her teeth.

Business. He'd been all business this trip, unusual for her Avery.

"Where'd you go just there?" he asked, one eyebrow up.

"Found a sweet spot in between raindrops."

"Not a lot of room in places like that," he said.

"You'd be surprised what I find."

He bit into a pork bun, its steaming red insides dribbling down his dark, unshaven chin. A lucky colour, her mother would have said.

"Security team wants to convene in your room at twelve thirty in the morning. Get out before the weather hits," he said, wiping his napkin through the stubble. He pointed at the windows, fresh sheets of rain pelting the glass. "Apparently, it's close."

"No argument from me. It looks horrible out there."

"The only thing that flies in a typhoon is aluminium corrugate and World Ways suborbitals," her grandad used to say.

"I'm gonna go relax in my room, get some reading in. Let me know if you want to come down for a drink later," Avery offered.

"I've got some calls to make and a hot bath with my name on it, so I'll see you for the pickup in the lobby," she said.

"Enjoy."

He got up and left, all business once again. She watched him go, dark, broad shoulders and that blond-tipped high top. He was a gem most days.

She held a bead to her ear, the magnetic piercing there pulling it into place. Turning her palm up, she swiped through holographic menus, paid the bill, and made a voice-only call.

"Hi, Dad."

"Hello, young Kit," her father replied. He coughed, hacking up fluid. She could almost see him looking at the phlegm in his hand. It was consistent now. Not good.

"Our pickup tomorrow is going to be earlier than I expected," she said. "So I'm going to have to cancel our dinner this evening. I hope you understand."

"Always on the move; I get it. How are you keeping? Are you good?"

"I'm being stonewalled on getting some important work out past the firewall, but I'm picking away at it. How's your cough?"

"It's lingering, my dear. Can't seem to shake it."

One day I'll have that fixed too, she thought. "Be well, Dad. I'll be back as soon as I can. Nakupenda." *I love you.*

"Nakupenda pia." *I love you too.*

It was rare to hear him respond in his native Kiswahili. She liked it, missed it. She closed her fist, ending the call, nodded a brief thank you to the staff, and then glanced outside for a proper look at the typhoon. Ragged, charcoal-coloured cloud bottoms sped past the window with an unnatural speed, rain lashed the glass in waves. The news streams were saying it was going to be a ten out of ten—as big as they get and a direct hit. She wondered if her flight would get airborne before the storm arrived. She swiped for launch data and saw that the suborbs were on time. Not that their schedule held any great meaning. Like her grandfather used to say, they'd fly in anything.

3.

"You OK up there? Tech says you're in manual flight," his helmet intercom burbled from the jet's back seat. Dallas looked up at the rearview, Camerica's reflected face pale with the colour of computer, illuminated by screens from all sides.

He glanced down at cargo temps, fuel status, vibes on the turbines.

"Yup." He gave a long pause. "Dodging raindrops."

He flew so fast he dodged even the rain.

Four hundred and fifty klicks to the coast, thirty minutes at this speed, then open ocean for a good long while. The rain was a concern, abnormal out here, and a problem for their vis. The radar reflection off a water-soaked aircraft would show them clear as day on even the oldest of tech.

He weaved between rain shafts, catching the edge of one, slicing through the bottom of it, the water a brief deafening roar against the canopy. Through the jet's air conditioning packs came the smell of ozone, thunderstorms penetrating the *Arethusa*'s pressurized hull. The aircraft growled a warning, enemy eyes struggling to find her profile illuminated by the moisture. The growl faded fast, she was a shadow punching holes in the dark, and hiding was her specialty.

"This isn't dodging by any definition I know," Cam said from the back. "Decoys are going out." He deployed a small metallic ball from inside the aircraft, bursting behind them into thousands of hot pellets, shrapnel to confuse and distract the digital eyes hunting them from below.

Dallas flicked off the fuel and ran the turbines on the batteries in silent mode. As they slowed, he jinked the aircraft into a series of sharp turns, twenty metres off the deck, the wing tips kicking up dust.

"I need a quick sweep before we hit the coast. Montoya mentioned Mombasa's been on the watch for us."

"That a good idea?" Cam asked. "Case you haven't noticed, sun's coming up."

"You know the deal. If I can't see it, I can't dodge it."

"Are you nuts? They're actively pinging for us. If we sweep, they *will* launch." The aircraft growled again. Someone down there had eyes on their tail.

"Do the sweep. We'll give 'em a run if they fire."

Camerica lit up the radar, a single electromagnetic beam at once illuminating the enemy's position while announcing their presence. His voice rose an octave. "Structures ahead. Water towers. Lots of new ones. Prox returns up to a hundred and twenty meters. Couple of SAM sites flanking. Dee, you are gonna need to keep us *real* low to avoid them." The aircraft growled in multiple tones.

Dallas took her lower.

The Somalis had built those giant water-making towers. The idea had started out small, some whiz-kid concept about a beetle from the desert that survived the arid landscape by condensing dew on its back, the drip making its way down the insect's angled shell to its mouth, a perfectly evolved, built-in water bottle. They'd scaled it up initially, two-storey, green, plastic mesh towers with glistening dew drops shimmering their way down its flexible construction, guided to a collecting basin in the early morning fog. The structures would collect a few litres of water every morning for thirsty townships on the west continent. Then, when the Big Dry came, they gigantified them, gave them bigger yields. Installed them all over the world, put them out on coastal lands to gather ocean mists at dawn. "Fog-basking Behaviour," they called it. Giant, organic-looking structures built in days by auto printers the size of houses. Double helical polycarbonate grown from the ground up, reaching, twisting skyward from shifting desert sands, a hundred storeys tall and not on any map. They would show up in clusters, a forest of curving, curling man-mades towering over what was once Somalian farmland, harvesting drinking water from a climate that couldn't rain.

Problem was they didn't make it to the orbital scans in time. The jet's automatics weren't quick enough to see and maneuver around them at this speed and flying above them meant certain detection, and what he would term a "Very Bad Day."

"Shouldn't be so many of 'em this far inland," Cam said.

"Pirates," Dallas grumbled. "I can't get lower than this. Gonna have to go through them. Too many storms to go around wide, and anything above this altitude's a VBD. Feels like a trap."

"It is a fucking trap, Dee."

He felt a tingling fear, an uncommon companion, creep up his legs and down into his gloved fingertips, then shook it off. They were travelling nearly twenty kilometres a minute, the jet's turbines spinning in electric silence, the sound barrier ever so slightly ahead of them. Not a good place for panic.

He rotated a well-worn knob on the thrust lever, cycling through translucent menus of threats and time to terrain impact. The data displayed in his visor's peripheral gave him cascading depths of forward lidar scans, allowing him to assemble the information into a multi-dimensional image he could navigate through. The locals would love nothing more than to down a mob-owned stealth jet, and he refused to allow that to happen.

Radar blips along the ground gave away the locations of mobile missile launchers, old-school scans searching for a whiff of their cross section. His helmet's optics gave him a firm ceiling, hashed, brown rectangles extending below the tower tops. Above the brown line was a VBD. Below it they would be difficult, but not impossible to acquire. The machine was dark but not invisible.

She was a "Black," one of a fleet of three, each jet unique and named for their radar-absorbing paint, a skin that inhaled light, Russian stealth technology purchased at a premium. Her initial design had been tailored for short sprints, for "jumping the line," running contraband between offshore container ships and Hong Kong beaches. A recent modification allowed her to carry ten times the fuel. Now she was capable of crossing oceans with her payload, delivering a shipment from pickup to drop-off, directly across the line. When required, close to shore, she could do it all without so much as a whisper, soaring past eyes and ears that could neither see nor hear her. In those moments she was nothing but a couple of spinning electric fans perched atop a high-speed patch of darkness.

Best to run silent while hunted.

If he flew above the forest of towers ahead or cranked a hard turn and popped a wing tip over that brown, dotted line, they'd be dodging missiles as well as structures.

Using the radar sweep, Dallas mapped a three-dimensional path through the vertical minefield of hundred-metre-tall water collectors. He wore white leather flying gloves with grey trim, his palms a nervous wet.

They ripped past the first tower on a knife's edge, hauling some major ass, touching the barber pole, maximum speed. He tossed the jet on its opposite wing tip, lit the cans for extra power, and sliced between two closely spaced collectors. They were hustling now, thrust up high, burning hot kerosene and pulling hard g's. The *Arethusa* felt good in his hands. He found a flow into each turn—intuitive, fluid, beautiful, sexy. Sharp, ninety-degree banks crushed him into his custom-molded seat, a wall of condensed water vapour pouring off the jet's anhedral wings. In his peripheral, he glimpsed the flash of white cloud as it compressed into a brief existence, an instantaneous ribbon dancing in the wind, following her path between these monolithic spires of hardened resin. No missile could follow them there.

⟨Ⅲ⟩⟨Ⅲ⟩⟨Ⅲ⟩

Camerica sat in the back seat "riding scope," reading the lidar, a glowing organic display mapping eight klicks ahead, about thirty seconds' worth. He knew better than to speak. Distractions could cost them their lives. Dallas was good at this; he knew he needn't worry. The holo surrounding him showed time to impact, altitude, and resolution vectors. Dallas would be looking through his own visor at similar optics, imaging a route in his mind that the software couldn't see. They would roll in tight, pull six or seven g's, the aircraft groaning and popping like a can of soda, then unload, roll in the opposite direction, rinse, and repeat. It would make them both sick but not until after. Not until the rollercoaster ride was behind them.

Cam was at his limit as they cranked hard around the last tower and blew out past the shoreline at almost 1000 kilometres per hour. Dallas levelled the wings, punched in the automatics, and vomited into his receptacle.

"You good up there, Dee? Smells like scotch and that bag of chips you had for dinner," Cam said, spitting out chunks of his own.

⟨Ⅲ⟩⟨Ⅲ⟩⟨Ⅲ⟩

"Fuck no. We need a new route for the next job. I'm done banging around these towers puking my guts out for a week's wage. S'like screwing Mong Kok hookers on a Monday night with no latex. TFR."

Total Fucking Roulette.

Dallas wiped his mouth with the back of his hand and pulled the handheld electric grinder from his left chest pocket. From his right, he took a plain, white, circular pill stamped with a *U*, an up. An amphetamine analogue with a name he couldn't pronounce. One of the benefits of working for the mob, he didn't have to go far to get good drugs. He popped it in the receptacle and slid the window closed, then hit the one and only button on the device, engaging the rotating blades inside, dusting the pill into an inhalable powder. Twisting open the orifice on its top, he shoved it in a nostril and whiffed. Go pills. Humanity's most perfect creation. Would give him a solid seven hours before he'd even consider a rest.

"Didn't seem like you were having any problems back there," Cam said. "Almost like you enjoyed it."

Dallas latched his mic to hot. "We discussed this. The Somalis are definitely onto us. You *know* I don't like running the same ground track twice, and here we are flying that identical route through hundreds of new towers. We're being fired on and tracked. We're not taking this route again." He loosened the shoulder harnesses securing him to his seat. "I need to seriously reconsider this line of work."

4.

Kit rode the elevator in silence, its smoky, feminine voice welcoming her back. "Bringing you to the thirty-seventh floor, miss McKee." Elevator recognition. The worst kind.

She approached the Landmark Suite, its authentication software biometrically identifying her and unlocking the door. She hung her jacket and umbrella on gold-plated hooks, walked through the small lounge to the office, and asked the room to run her a bath. "Thirty-nine degrees, with a touch of eucalyptus if you don't mind."

"Right away, Miss McKee," an omnidirectional, calming, and apathetic voice responded.

Kit sat down at the desk, judging the voice's sexless AI. Behind her was a small library of hardcover books: John Le Carré, Tom Wolfe, P. D. James. She leaned back in the chair and ran her fingers along their spines, enjoying the texture. She really did need to get back to reading for pleasure.

She beamed a feed from the lab back in Ulaanbaatar to the office's holo with an upheld palm and a couple of backhanded swipes at her wrist, checking up on the mice in their glass-walled homes. Zeus, feisty and lively as usual, running klicks at a full gallop in his angled and squeaky treadwheel. She would have to replace that again before long. He was breaking distance records daily. Agata, who'd developed the skin lesion problem she saw so often from her edits, was sitting in a corner of her aquarium licking her open sores. Artemis, who'd been doing so well, had lost the use of his back legs and was dragging himself to eat. "I'll be there soon," she said to them.

From her clutch she pulled the abnormally heavy business card that had mysteriously appeared after the conference, enjoying its weighted density as she moved it between finger and thumb. A matte black she'd never seen, a zero-reflective surface, fascinating tech. It was slippery to the touch. She slid it across the desk, the card gliding like it was on ice. She rubbed her thumb along the lettering, a negative emboss she could barely feel, like it was molecules deep. "NINE," it stated. She hadn't seen an exchange, just the card, in her clutch, after her speech.

She kicked off her glossy jet-black stilettos and moved to the lounge. Grabbing a mini bottle of Bordeaux from the mini bar, she poured it into her mini wine glass, took a mini sip, and then placed it on the regular-sized coffee table. She reached behind her back and popped the magnetic snap on her bra, pulled it through a sleeve, and settled into the polyurethane, waiting for her shape to coalesce into the couch, or was it a settee in this part of the world? In the holo, Zeus hit his stride for another hundred laps around the wheel.

What was NINE?

The only time her clutch had been out of view was while she had delivered her speech. Could it have been someone backstage? Someone on her security team? Her entrance had been well orchestrated, surgical, her departure the same. She'd sauntered in like a celebrity and left like a thief. Minimal fanfare, zero fuss, she'd had security from her hotel room to the stage and back again. Hadn't so much as crossed paths with anyone not involved in the production in some capacity. She had carefully put nothing but essentials in her tiny black clutch before leaving the hotel, and the card was definitely not in it then.

NINE.

It would have to wait. Shortened sips gave way to full-fledged gulps. With the small bottle empty, she slipped out of her black skirt and black blouse into a white waffle-print robe embroidered with the Mandarin Hotel's golden fan logo. She sat on the edge of the circular, white marble bath and dipped her feet into the pre-heated water, peeling the bandage off her arm. She massaged the injection site. It was less sore today, much better than when she had self-administered the needle before leaving Mongolia. She would need to use her other arm for the booster. Hypodermic bruising on an editor usually meant only one thing, and self-editing was not something she wanted to have to deny. The bath invited her, and she slid down its slippery, white porcelain, disappearing from the day's events and into the steaming, aromatic tub.

5.

Dallas would have been celebrating his thirty-fourth birthday today, if he was into that sort of thing. He was the son of an English expat cop and an American-Indonesian mother, neither of which he'd seen since his move back to Hong Kong. His white-blond hair and indigo-rimmed, Caribbean-blue eyes got him more than a few questions about who had done his augments, a question to which he had always responded, "My parents' sperm and ova."

Ahead of them, over open seas, lay a long and quiet ride now that they'd left the eastern shoreline of the African continent behind. The pill flashed memories through his mind, and he allowed it to wander, to drift into his past life. Persephone giggling, a beach day, south Florida, Atlantic side, gentle waves lapping a shallow beach. A suborbital flight lighting its rockets in the high distance for an eastbound trip. Asia, perhaps Kuala Lumpur, in a couple of hours. His three-year-old daughter pointing up at the white-hot sparkle of burning propellant and its billowing telltale trail of white smoke. Saying with her gentle voice and in a way only a child could manage, "Daddy."

Camerica's finger jabbed him in the neck. "Hey. Wake up. Dallas. Sea ferry ahead."

"I see it," he said, the vessel's slow-blinking, red position light the sole visual warning of its presence. Optics in his visor illuminated a swarm of drones, a protective and armed neural net encircling the giant wombat-shaped composite husk. The ferry's extended foils sliced in and out of the rolling swell, surfing in the ground effect similar to them. They'd be fired upon if the swarm's electric eyes caught a glimpse of the *Arethusa*, not that it was probable. He gave them a wide berth regardless. Fighting with armed robotics was an unnecessary form of conflict, and they had no weapons on board.

"You good?" Cam asked.

"Just whizzed. I'm plenty awake. That pill should keep me going for another few hours." He needed to stay focussed. They had a solid nine hours ahead of them, no real chance to sleep, and the Jakarta Gap yet to navigate.

6.

Kit's wrist rumbled beneath the bath water, the holo attempting to broadcast through its surface tension. She lifted her hand out and swiped down to take the call, audio-only, surprised at the name displayed there in glowing aquamarine sans-serif.

"Kit? Howdy. It's Doudna out in London. How the hell are ya?" She could hear the smile in his thick, booming, Texan tone, deep and intrinsically male. Was rare these days to hear such a strong American accent. She'd missed it.

"Theodore fucking Doudna it is *nice* to hear from you. I'm taking some down time after today's show. How is the UK? Still United?" she asked, smiling as she sipped her wine.

"Well, they don't much care for the accent in these parts. Never had so many arguments about how to say 'alu-mi-num,' but we're getting it done. The work continues," he said with a joviality she found endearing.

"And to what do I owe the honour of this call?" She hadn't seen or heard from him in years. Last they'd spoken they'd been in what was still being referred to as the "United States of America," and he had been a respected editor like her.

"I've been working on a project and I can't make any headway. Right up your alley I suspect, and I wondered if you'd be interested in some collaboration."

"That depends what you'd like my help with."

"I've been trying to contact you, but the walls around your lab are taller than you might even know yourself, like you're producing state secrets up there. Like we're back in the Cold War era."

That had been a difficult time, the United States and China having had so many differences particular to their shared and controversial field of genetic manipulation. "We need the protection, Teo. Not sure if you heard, but they sent a special forces team to our lab to extradite us back to the America and try us as fucking war criminals. I like the walls. They keep us safe. Keep the edits coming, I say." She drank the last of the wine. "Where are you practicing? And what are you working on that's so tricky?"

"That's something we're gonna need to discuss in person, darlin'."

She hated when he called her that. She was not his darling, not anymore. "Well, you know I can't head out your way. The ethics, as you know, are not in my favour over on that side of the planet."

"I do know that. I was thinking more along the lines of some-place south," he offered. "Gambia has some nice resorts. We could sit in the sun and compare notes, eat peanuts." They did have great peanuts down there, she thought. Fresh. But what business did Theodore Doudna have there?

"It's *The* Gambia, Teo, and I'm planning a trip out that way later this month." She paused. "Now that I think about it, why don't you come out here?"

"To the Inner Sanctum? Golia? Is that even possible?"

"Should be no problem. I can always organize a professional visit from a previous colleague. They'll do anything I ask if they think it will make them more money."

"So it's a business trip."

"Yes. Do you need me to arrange transport?"

"Just from the airport; I can sort the rest. When do you want me there?"

"Sooner is better. I'm leaving Hong Kong later tonight. Why don't we plan for the morning after next? We can have coffee in the park."

"I'll need it."

"I have to say, Doudna, I'm intrigued. I was following your work on the fear edit back in the day. I've been working on it myself, and it seems far more complex an issue than I originally expected."

"I hate racing for second place, Kit, but let's discuss it further in person. It's going to be great to work with you after all these years."

She laughed. "I'll get you a security detail, and we'll make it happen. Nice to hear from you, Doudna. Bye." She swiped him off without waiting for a farewell.

She pondered that augment, fear. It was proving tricky. Woven deep into the genome, fear had worked hard over millions of years to keep humankind alive, responsible for the race's ability to survive multiple and evolving threats. Not so in today's age of information, she had decided. Something to be edited out, perhaps replaced with something less extreme, a response versus a reaction. If Doudna had been working on it then his expertise would be of enormous benefit to her own research.

She picked up the empty glass, stared at the dribble of wine remaining. She wondered what Doudna knew about the Gambia, what was being grown there, and if she'd be able to convince him to join her team in Ulaanbaatar on a permanent basis.

7.

Security had booked Kit on a supersonic. One of those no-frills, low-boom jobs. Company out of Ireland, big shamrock painted on the tail, the kind that *gets you there quick, and that's about it.*

They made a quick trip of it, alright. It was an hour on the ticket, Hong Kong to Ulaanbaatar. She stuck to economy. Planned to zone out in a window seat and watch the world fly by at a couple thousand kilometres an hour. Maybe even watch a datastream, a rare pleasure these days.

The attendant came by with quick-acting relaxants and anti-nausea meds to "ease the transition." No doubt a sleeping passenger was an easy passenger, though she wasn't sure there was much transitioning to be done on a one-hour flight. She took both, placing them under her tongue, dozing before she got the pleasure of acceleration from the supersonic aircraft's afterburner kick.

8.

Dallas cranked the jet hard on her side, knife-edging close in on a mountainous and densely forested island, then de-lit the cans, running her quiet off the batteries. In the Gap, someone would always be listening for them. Low-level cumulus provided some added camouflage amongst the west Indonesian Islands. His mother had been born on one of them, he remembered, grunting under the weight of a sequence of high-g turns as he followed the shorelines of one lush tropical paradise after another. The evening's well-developed thunderheads towered high above, swelling in the updrafts of the steep, rising terrain.

Be raining out of those soon.

The *Arethusa*'s defensive aids system let out a low growl, responding to generations-old antiaircraft weaponry having a sniff of them. They were flying well below the enemy tech's targetable range, but he took them lower just to be sure, guiding the craft between a pair of sheer granite cliffs, wings level and a single metre above the ocean's calm, glassy surface. He popped another *go* pill in the grinder and then whiffed it, the amphetamine surge instant and pleasurable.

Down this low, they'd be tough to spot. A dark jet with stealth tech at dusk against a black sea. To an observer on the ground, they would look like nothing more than a high-speed blemish low in the sky.

The drug hit fast and hard, accelerating his synapses, his neurons firing at full speed. He followed rocky shorelines for cover, glancing up at the coastal fringe of equatorial jungle. Ahead, they had a straight shot between forested peaks and a clean egress. He lit the turbines and pushed the thrust levers to the stops, selecting reheat. Raw kerosene injected into the hot exhaust of the engines; there was no need for cooling now. The jet rewarded him with a violent whump and brutal acceleration. He kept them low, and they slipped through the sound barrier, banking away from the last of the islands, burning hard and fast toward home.

Open seas provide no cover.

It was a brief run at high speed. The DAS had remained silent, and they'd had no enemy launches to outrun. He brought the engines out of afterburner, the jet slowing to a subsonic cruise, metres above the evening's rolling ocean swell.

For the next few hours, they tore along at transonic speeds, across Earth's southern seas, en route through South Asia's sporadic atolls, to their destination at one of China's many special administrative regions.

On the international side of the Chinese territorial line, in Hong Kong's southernmost waters, lay a grouping of monstrous iron ships. Once destined for long ocean crossings with their bellies full of consumable products, now they leaned unmoving, anchored into a permanent barricade against the approaching storm's strong southeastern swell. A line of rusted, ancient kerosene burners pumped with ballast and given a purposeful angle of list so as to appear derelict, chained to one another to provide a breakwater for the fish farm they harboured shoreside. Inside the ships were well-maintained storage facilities, warehouses powered by tidal turbines buried in their hulls. Occasional lights peppered their portholes, their outward appearance designed to seem neglected, deserted.

Dallas flew past them at a distance, low and silent, batteries spinning the jet's turbines, the lidar scanning for any potential threats.

"Farm looks clean," Cam said. "You good with the wind?"

The aircraft bounced and yawed in the turbulent air of the nearby typhoon. "It's on the limit, but we should be OK," Dallas replied. "Good thing we got here ahead of schedule."

Amongst the ships and squared-off netting was a corridor in the water, a dark patch amongst the jumble of flotsam, not an obvious runway to a naked or untrained eye. Through his enhanced optics, Dallas was provided with approach and edge lighting illuminated in virtual, as lit up as any airport on either side of the border. He flew her by hand three metres above the wind-whipped seas, then lowered the flaps and the pontoons, slowing the *Arethusa* for her entry into the water, the end of a long run, accompanied by the promise of sleep and pay.

9.

Kit woke to the ticking expansion of hot water travelling through her home's baseboard heaters. It was something she seldom heard in hotel rooms, that ticking, at least not in the nice ones. She'd had a partial sleep, awake in the night with some form of lag, a general sleep-dep from the airport transfers and that brutal early morning. Why was her security so enamoured with flying in the middle of the night? It made things harder as far as she was concerned.

She slid from beneath her bedding, the rustling of the sheets deafening without the steady background of typhoon winds amid Hong Kong's industrial din. She rolled over and put her feet on the carpeted floor, scrunching her toes in the soft blond pile. It was nice to return home to normal, or at least this normal, the city just had so much clatter. It had been difficult for her to find peace in the noise.

She took it in, the quiet of her Mongolian home, something she had never known living in Manhattan. The silence was so still that the only sound in her ears was the distant high pitch of tinnitus. A night of sleep in her own bed after a week away came without the need for any ear bead white noise or melatonin inducers, like she had used every night in the city. One nice thing about travelling within Asia, she thought as she padded barefoot along the hallway's hardwood floors, was there was none of that soul stealing jet-lag. None of that horrible hotel room coffee either, she thought as she pressed the "make" button on her Elektra, its burrs grinding the beans to make a perfect double espresso.

After a brief breakfast of eggs on toast, she latched the door to her ground-level brownstone behind her, the morning air smelling thin and cool, like yellowing leaves and New York in October. The breeze picked up and blew south Mongolian red desert dust in micro-cyclones that meandered down the street, bouncing off the brick buildings lining either side. She lifted her collar against it, giving her teal knit scarf another lap around her neck. There were flurries in the evening forecast, though it was a remote possibility. Since when did Ulaanbaatar see snow in August?

Trees shedding their leaves lining both sides of the road reached across the street to form a canopy, the early morning sunlight low on the horizon strobing between the interlinking branches as she walked along the footpath between her home and the lab. A fifteen-minute commute she travelled daily, soaking up the muting silence of dawn.

At the main gate of the lab stood armed guards wearing the strange silkworm-blended weave that Doudna had created back in the America. It looked like it was crawling around their bodies in slow-mo, a living textile that hardened on impact. Something about it needing to spread on contact kept them from concealing it beneath outer layers of clothing. She didn't like it. Gave her the creeps. The guards acknowledged her ID and let her pass through to the entrance.

She scanned her subdermal and stared with disinterest into the twin mechanical eyeballs of the building's periocular scan, waited while it matched her heartbeat with facial and iris biometrics. Reflected in the polished steel doors was her black designer surgeon's cap with its printed montage of the twenty-three human chromosome pairs dangling from her teeth. The doors opened, inhaling the cool outside air into the airlock with a satisfying whoosh.

"Good Morning, Doctor McKee," a bodiless female voice

announced, the machine recognition irritating her as always. She wheeled her aluminum briefcase (or was it *aluminium*? Doudna would be amused) into the airlock, the doors sealing tight behind her. The beginning of a workday, another chance to play creator with the genome.

Inside the interior double doors, she was met with smells of antiseptic and bleach, cold sterilized surgical steel, and caged rodent feces. Down a narrow hallway lined with laboratory glassware and luminescent holographic displays lay her three square metres of lab bench. She rolled her case under the desk that she shared with Avery, put on her cap and then tied it off at the back, gangster style, and checked on Zeus. His glass enclosure's translucent display showed humidity, temperature, and the wheel's revolutions per minute. He was having his morning run, burning up the tread-wheel, a variation on a children's roundabout, angled for incline. He stopped as she approached, riding the slanted disc around for a few rotations up and down as it slowed, followed her with an almost concerned stare, an impossible level of emotion conveyed through those bulbous black eyeballs. She lifted the lid, reached in, and offered a palm. He climbed onto it, patiently allowing her to measure his vitals through his well-groomed, cocoa-brown fur.

"Swear you got a crush on that rodent, Kit," Avery said, eyes locked on his scope.

"Think it might be the other way round," she replied, petting the mouse while she drew his blood. *He's here early,* she thought, *and all business again.*

"An interspecies love affair, huh? That'd be a new one."

"Is that jealousy I hear?" she responded, placing the blood sample into the analyzer attached to Zeus's cage.

"Of that mouse? Hell yeah. Whatever it is you're giving him, I want in. I've never seen a rodent run that long. You know he barely sleeps? Like maybe two, three hours a day." Zeus was watching their exchange, whiskers forward, a curious slant to his head. *Listening.*

"Oh, I'm aware. You've got good reason to feel threatened. That's his sixth wheel. He's breaking lab records every day."

She reflected on how little Avery knew about this particular mouse. Zeus had arrived already augmented; a germline prepped for further edits. The wheels had suffered. She'd had this one made with a custom fluoropolymer lubricant tailored to Zeus's exceptional endurance.

Endurance.

Good name for his augment.

"Beaten by a mouse. What a world," Avery said, returning to his arthroscopic investigations on the euthanized rodent pinned and splayed on his workbench.

She wondered about him sometimes, her Avery. He'd been there for her through the escape. Held her hand at a time when their counterparts were being hung for treason. Guided her across borders to bring her to relative safety and even hooked her up with a decent job. He'd been a loyal sidekick, a dedicated friend. And yet, he'd been different since she'd taken him to the subbasement. Perhaps, she worried, she had let him in during a moment of misplaced trust. Quiet wasn't the right word for how he'd been acting. He'd simply been all business since then, and it was becoming a little much.

She stood looking at him for far too long, taking in his majestic frame. A pure Nigerian who preferred men, a head taller than her, his width at the shoulders gave him the appearance of an augment's musculature, though as far as she knew, he remained unedited. He was a beautiful, gentle giant of a man, his permanent grin and high-pitched laugh endearing to most. A Pacific northwester from what seemed a lifetime ago.

"Why you staring at me, Kit? What's cookin' in that brain of yours?" His eyes lingered on the dissection before him.

"Got something nasty in this tube today, mister. Turn you *straight*." She waved an empty test tube at him. He smiled in return, his synthetic ivory teeth gleaming in the halogens while he moved the hair-sized camera filament through the dead mouse's venous system.

"Ain't no chance of that, and you *know* it." He wiped sweat from his brow, pulling back his surgical cap to expose his handsome crop of twisted curls and blow-out fade, the feather carved into the shave above his ear growing shaggy with neglect. It had been tough finding a decent hairdresser to pull off that cut in Mongolia. They had searched together, and days had been lost. He put the cap back on, giggling with his infectious laugh.

She turned her attention back to Zeus but gave sexuality a momentary thought. Figured she could write an edit that made gay men straight or vice versa. Not that she thought either way was a better idea, but from a scientific perspective, the possibility intrigued her. A single genetic snip, a simple letter change, an *A* for a *T*, a *C* for a *G*. It had to be in the genome somewhere. *Everything* was.

As ever, Zeus's vitals were improving. Her edit was taking well.

"Would it be too much to refer to myself as *Mother*, you think?" she asked Avery.

"Considering I don't know you to have mothered any children, Kit, I'd say yes, it's too much. Why? Are you thinking you're a mother to these mice?"

"I mean, some of these edits we give them, they get a chance to experience the world from a different perspective, you know? As augmented mice, it's like they're being reborn."

"If by 'world' you mean four glass walls, and by 'reborn' you mean a certain death by lethal injection so we can dissect and study them, then yes, I agree, Kit. Or should I say, *Mother*." His face was expressionless, his eyes back on his scope.

She pressed the back of her index finger against the enclosure's biometrics display, where two imperceptible pins in her prosthetic fingernail made contact, initiating a subroutine that downloaded

Zeus's biodata from their time away in Hong Kong. It transferred to the memtech latticed through her nail bed. Physical storage, how she liked it. Kept the data offline, deleting itself from the cage as it wrote.

"Your sarcasm is noted, senior assistant Avery," she said, removing her finger from the display. She glanced over her shoulder to find him up to his usual antics, trying to pull a ninja, sidle up behind her, give her a jump. She swore she could feel him sneaking up behind her, like she'd been augmented for spider-sense, which, she regretted, wasn't a thing. He handed her a coffee, a salted caramel latte, beaming as always.

It hadn't been an easy move out to Mongolia, having taken place during the time of the America's war on editors, when they'd locked down the continent and banned any science that involved changing the human genome. Said that was God's work, not humanity's, imprisoning scientists with decades of research in the field. They'd fled their homes. Avery had given her a heads-up early that it was time to go. They'd gone together, posing as a couple. With passports stamped and data bands swiped, they left the America before Homeland Security got serious and began putting her friends and colleagues in so-called schools to be "retrained" out of genetics. They were deemed heretics, and it was joked that they would be burned at the stake like witches if they'd stayed.

It was no laughing matter though. Death sentences had been carried out on editors that, like Kit, had been working within the germline. An inheritable alteration edited-in to a person's genome, genetic changes passed down to the subject's offspring, a permanent modification to their sequence.

Avery, Kit, and their work had disappeared into Ulaanbaatar. NegSense was overjoyed to have them, providing them with the finest expat experience that Inner Mongolia had to offer. When Kit finally put her first edit out into the wild, they had partied long into the night. She had been working on several cosmetic augments at the time, figured out the melanin gene, and edited out the grey hairs of old age. Another ended the decline of the epidermis. The world's desire to look youthful far exceeded their desire to *be* youthful. They had developed a permanent solution to looking younger. Interventional gerontology, she had named it, her new field, with significant help from Avery. And the money had arrived in terrifying quantities.

Getting that one, clean, safe augment out into the public had opened the floodgates. The world had been trying for years. People in basement labs cranking out dirty edits with horrendous off-target side effects had made the grey market a total crap shoot. The desire had always been there; people had been changing their appearance for hundreds of years, but it had always been surgical. Facelifts and breast augments and tummy tucks. Now her team made cosmetic adjustments in the DNA, down deep where it stuck, at the genetic level. And more controversially, when the price was high enough, into the ethical minefield of the germline.

Avery sipped at his own paper cup of coffee. "Your order arrived this morning, five a.m. I had it brought through intake and moved downstairs." He raised an eyebrow. "Should be you buying these coffees."

"I'll get the next round, I promise." She gave Zeus a kind stroke along his spine, placed him back in his home, then closed the lid and grabbed her glasses and mask for the trip down below.

10.

It took a particular brand of neglect to create food this terrible, Johnny Woo thought. The mind boggled. The pancakes on the table before him were, without question, the world's worst. He was convinced of it. The restaurant should advertise. Some type of odd, bad-food tourism group would no doubt visit, eager to experience the consistent and total failure to turn simple flour and eggs into anything other than the tasteless mass on his plate. Even drowning them in the runny brown liquid that was *not* maple syrup didn't help. He sat alone in a corner of the diner listening to the rain falling outside, the inedible pancakes disintegrating into a pulpy viscous mass as he watched.

"Dim gai aa?" he asked. *Why?*

When the weather hit, he liked to hole up at the Flying Pan. An always-open breakfast joint halfway up the escalators, the greasiest spoon he knew of in the city. Horrific food, but it was served with a pint of Guinness, which helped with the digestion, or so he'd been told. He took a long pull on the dark brew. Drinking beer was a decent option to give this late-summer rain a miss. He watched a display cast onto a bare white plaster wall showing a news stream. The typhoon was now a seven, they were saying, a black rainfall warning soon to follow. Good reason to eat shitty pancakes while keeping out of the heat and the rain.

The precinct band strapped to his wrist rumbled, giving him a start. As he opened his palm it beamed out a job, details on another housing estate murder. Horrible, dark places, government-supplied homes for the poor. Tens of thousands of units crammed together in towering cinderblock walls, none of them more than 200 square feet inside. He swiped up for more info. It was in area eighty-six, Tsueng Kwan O, thousands of units constructed in a pair of semi-circular structures creating a biosphere all their own. Skyscrapers of 120 floors encircling derelict children's slides and broken-down jungle gyms, parks meant for lush green grass, space for the kids to run, now choked in brown dust. No direct sunlight penetrated their concrete overcast, and the tropical summer heat mixed with dead motionless air became a death sentence for any kind of vegetation. During typhoons, the parks would flood, and the playgrounds became lakes, their entrances clogged with floating plastic and other human detritus.

A murder in the complex could go days without news of it getting outside the super-structure, with family members saving face by concealing the body—and their shame. Most often it was complaints about the stench of decomposition that gave them away. Getting inside the apartments, going that deep, was dirty work. He'd need a partner. He made the request on his wrist holo, hating that his fingers knew to gesture in a digital language all their own.

While waiting for a response, he allowed his focus to wander, chewed his lower lip, fiddled with his pinkie ring, and watched the weather, his mind adrift in past cases, past visits to the estates, all their unique horrors.

He gave up on the pancakes, somehow lumpy and runny all at once today, like they'd been fried in fish fat and forgotten. He finished the beer, chucked on his Brixton, and made for the rain, pulling the brim down up front, finding it kept the water off best.

Out on the street, the skies were a deep charcoal, and rain was chucking itself down in suicidal sheets. It didn't seem possible that this much of it was simply *falling* from clouds. The splash of it off pavement bounced up past his knees. Surely, he thought, there was a man up there with a firehose.

His wristband remained silent and uninterested. Seemed no one wanted to volunteer on an estate case during a typhoon. He made his way to the cover and shelter of the escalators. Out of the rain, he flicked the holo up, gestured to make a call, pushed an audio bead deep into his ear canal, and kept a moderate pace as he walked along the uphill moving sidewalk.

"Yes, boss."

"Need your help for an ongoing over in TKO," he said. "I'm in the mid-levels, heading there now. Be thirty or so."

"Yeah, boss OK. Guessing you're not gonna grab a Ryde?"

"Never gonna happen, Fonger. Not in this lifetime. You're crazy to take one in this weather."

Fong laughed. "See you there, boss."

Back out in the downpour, he flagged an autocab, preferring to keep his relationship with the ground intact, tires on tarmac, even if it was driven by AI. He removed the bead from his ear, put it in its case, and put the case into a pocket on his trench, rivers of water pouring off the coat's repellent coating.

With the door closed to the deluge outside and the automatics doing the driving, Woo tapped his pinkie and thumb together, a gesture trigger for his assistant. "When's the weather meant to pick up?"

"We have black and amber rain warnings through to the weekend, detective Woo. Would you like me to give you an extended forecast?" a female voice asked from the precinct's wrist rental.

"Naw, just be nice to have some sunshine for once."

"I understand, detective."

Another tap and she was gone, she and her Singaporean accent slipping back down into the band's circuitry.

11.

Kit didn't like that they were kept down in the sublevels. They'd never seen sunlight, and they never would, not that it was of any great significance to her. She found working in the deep basement for long stretches added to the darkness writhing around in her soul where she knew that this part of her work was horribly, horribly wrong.

It was twenty floors in the elevator, a faint ticking beep, a slow pause in between. Her ears popped on the journey down, like when scuba diving. As the pressure increased, she squeezed her nose and blew, equalizing her ears. Descending twenty floors could be 500 feet or 5,000; could never tell from the inside of a four-walled, steel enclosure dangling on a metal rope. The temperature went up; that much she knew.

She grabbed the respirator hanging off her hip and extended it over her face, the thin rubber webbing snapping tight on the back of her head, then flicked on the oxygen and took a couple of test breaths, checking the seal around her nose and chin. The finger-sized canister hanging below her mask was good for sixty minutes. She carried an even dozen on the belt around her waist. She wasn't willing to take any chances. Too many opportunities for superbugs to make the jump. There'd been a few down there, and while the ventilation system was filtered for infectious agents, it was also closed, recirculated, not getting out.

She slid her clear, protective glasses over the portable breathing system and tucked her black surgical cap over top of them, her face now secure from any possible pathogenic incursions. She tied the gown around her waist, stretched a couple of purple latex gloves over her hands, taped up the seals, and waited for the last three floors to beep past.

Double airlock doors opened for her as she moved through them, then closed behind. Similar iris scans and heart rate identification protocols to the lab upstairs gave her a digital once-over. A sterilizing ultraviolet blast bathed her, murdering anything viral still trying to hitch a ride. Her ears popped again as the second set of doors slid open, allowing her inside the chamber they had affectionately named "the Womb." The room appeared dark to her unadjusted eyes, the lighting a deep shade of plum. She waited for her pupils to adapt. She didn't have to wait long.

That's something I could write into an augment, she thought. *A better aperture, faster adjustments, a new pupil for the people. Aperture. Even has a nice ring to it.*

Suspended from the ceiling with surgical steel hooks was a synthetic venous system dripping with condensate, each test subject diverting the shared blood supply as required. A coating of saline adhered to everything. Dangling bags of it supplemented the artificial heart machine in the centre of the room, its double-whumping rhythmic beat an eerie reminder that their work was on the living. To her left, four of them lay in a row, still and asleep inside their individual incubators, secured in their transport packages, awaiting an attachment to the womb's arterial network.

A robotic arm slid along steel rails mounted to the ceiling, dangling wide straps of rubbery plastic. It lowered itself in a disturbing arachnoid manner. Like a spider descending on a single strand of silk to envelop its paralyzed prey, it encapsulated one of the human test subjects with its ringed appendages in deliberate motion, then raised the body above the walls of its shipping unit, the limbs of the subject limp and swaying, amniotic fluid dribbling down its sides. She followed it as the robotic arms deposited the female onto a large steel slab. Kit took a hose from the wall and began spraying the subject clean, wiping her body free of the gelatinous goo with gloved hands, prepping her for surgery.

The human body is remarkable in so many ways, she thought. But it was the ability to grow into an organized collection of subsystems without getting in each other's way that she most admired.

Other employees were also down here, all wearing the same protective equipment as her, illuminated name tags affixed to their chests identifying them as nurse, doctor, surgeon, or scientist, along with a first name. Hers listed the last three, with "scientist" at the top.

A holographic whiteboard announced that today was Augment Day. Three of these test subjects remained unedited. They were to receive their edits somatically. A series of simple injections over a twenty-four-hour period, reprogramming their genetic sequence. Augments she had written, such as speed, strength, and sight, all needed iterating into perfection, and testing on a complete system was, in her opinion, the only way to write a clean edit.

A nurse joined her at the table, attaching tubes that bridged the subject to the womb. "Hello, Doctor McKee," she said. Kit nodded a hello, checking the name tag. She found it difficult to place faces behind all their gear. She handed the nurse the hose, tapped the whiteboard to update the test subject's status to "in progress," and pulled the steel gurney through the entry folds of the thick, translucent, polyethylene sheath into the operating theatre within.

She was met with squinting smiles and legitimate cheer behind masks and glasses. "How are we today, people?" she asked over the operating table where the female test subject was now prepped for her surgery. Her staff were colleagues, but they were not friends. She met the eyes of each one of them, saw the twinge of self-questioning and regret she herself felt. A question she hoped they all shared, a shred of humanity amongst this ethically questionable act.

"So that we're all on the same page," she said, "this is a simple organ extraction procedure. The donor will be placed in long-term recovery while she regrows the organs she is donating with such generosity today."

The subject was attractive, well-proportioned, and young. Kit looked her over from head to toe. She was pristine. In another life she would have been revered for her beauty, perhaps embarked on a lucrative modelling career. But not today. The nurse handed Kit a scalpel.

The subjects arrived in the night, delivered by automated refrigerated cube trucks, a guard keeping watch from the cab. They were brought to Mongolia from farms buried beneath the ground in West Africa. While Kit wasn't sure how they were transported, she had ideas. Questionable ethics brought together questionable people; history was well written in that regard. She knew better, but the money was so dammed good, the work rewarding, and Zeus, always Zeus.

She placed the scalpel at the incision point marked below the subject's armpit and initiated the cut, a long swipe down the woman's ribcage and then across her abdomen. The nurse handed Kit a new blade to cut beneath the skin. Her hands moved on automatic, her mind wandering as she severed and ligated arteries and veins, allowing for the harvesting of the subject's organs. They would grow back in months, a complex yet elegant solution to organ failure, something that had taken her years to develop. But the world at large only wanted to pay for her *cosmetic* augments. The easy ones. The DNA splices that brought youthful beauty and genetic improvements to the affluent and wealthy of the world that were such anathema to her. Remedial edits for a people addicted to manufactured happiness.

12.

Avery didn't think the Weissach man needed to know about the sublevels. He'd been quite specific that he wanted to hear about Kit's rodents—and Kit—and nothing else. He hadn't said anything about the "LUMPs" downstairs. Avery thought the name was degrading, but it had a valid meaning: Living Unconscious Manipulatable People. He preferred to refer to them as living test subjects. LTS just sounded so much cleaner. Kit said they were more like the dead. *And you wouldn't go worrying about a cadaver's feelings, now would you?* Which he figured was fair enough. That was all Kit would ever say about the things down there.

She had taken him there only once, and they hadn't spoken about it since. The room had made him nervous, like maybe something questionable was happening down there. Like all the work they were doing in the lab had more to do with the LTSs than he knew. There had been a time when he'd thought that all the spare tissue they used to make Kit's edits, all the organs and whatnot, had come from people long dead, actual cadavers. An inaccurate assumption he now knew, having seen them with his own eyes in their dank, sweaty sublevel, attached to one another in that odd, umbilical fashion. He still wondered what else Kit was into, how far down the rabbit hole she'd gone, but he was beyond asking. The job paid well, and he liked living in Ulaanbaatar. It allowed him to stretch his intellectual legs.

Avery didn't feel as though he thought like most people. He felt like he could see more than the narrowness of the day to day, like he could twig an actual feeling of the world around him. Much grander than an aura or colour, more like an aurora borealis, something much bigger than him or Kit or anyone around him. Like he could see the individual tendrils of energy interconnecting every living thing in his immediate vicinity, like neurons firing between beings, he embodied the energy surrounding him. He'd thought about discussing it with Kit, wondered if maybe she could edit it out for him, calm his overactive mind, or perhaps even do an edit that enhanced his ability into some sort of superpower. But he'd struggled to arrive at any sort of decent nomenclature for it. The best he had come up with was "The Connector," which sounded awful and ended the thought experiment then and there.

So, he didn't mind that the South African man who hired him had asked him to keep secrets. Figured it was part of the job, something he was good at, and he *had* signed that nondisclosure agreement when he'd joined the lab, secrets being a normal part of their industry.

"Don't worry, bru," he'd been told, "but you will be asked to report on your colleagues, peripherally and of course, confidentially."

He hadn't been sure what that last part meant, but he understood that he could not talk about it with Kit. She'd been his friend back in New York, a long time now, since before the trouble had started. They would drink wine after work and talk about love and their ideas about augments, how she didn't like most people, but she wasn't going to let it get in the way of making them better. She had a theory that humans had stopped evolving as a species, that we were going to sort of implode on ourselves, that it was preventable, and that somehow, she could prevent it. Ideas she would spout after a bottle of wine, which was when he would change the subject. They had rules about shop talk, and when she got on her rants about humanity's fate, he figured it was time to implement those rules. Otherwise, they wouldn't discuss work unless they were in the lab, which he respected her for. Anyway, it wasn't like he was allowed to talk about that stuff, the NDA thing being what it was.

Saving Kit's life had, without question, saved his own. The America had become the exact opposite of this place, a place where everyone seemed to have far too many opinions about things that didn't affect them. He was happy to be away from there now, in a place where nobody seemed to mind the colour of his skin or his sexual persuasions, where he was allowed to live his simple life of work and wine and occasional dates with men. So, when the South African man, whose accent Avery enjoyed so much, had called from the lab's head office and offered to take him for a drink, Avery had seen the connections forming in his observable universe between dendrite and axon, felt the world bringing his three simple desires together into one. He had been so happy, deciding that he was somehow being rewarded, allowed to use his superpower, whatever he ended up calling it, to his eternal benefit.

But the South African man didn't want Avery, not in that way, and while he had bought wine for them both, Avery noticed the man didn't drink, that the South African asked few questions and let Avery do the talking—and the drinking. Avery saw the connections shattering in front of him but kept talking anyway, answering the man's questions about Kit and her research, agreeing to watch her and her rodents, agreeing to report on her progress, however tangential the man required, and signed another form to that effect.

The man said his name was Weissach, to which Avery had responded, "That's a very German name for a man from South Africa." Weissach seemed indifferent. Avery had felt dejected, his dream of the connection of all the things he loved combined in a single package, broken. Weissach had thanked him, paid the bill, and left as though they had completed a business transaction. Having watched the glass exit door close with the jingle of a bell behind Weissach, Avery frowned and then gulped the man's untouched Cabernet alone.

13.

"So am I allowed to ask what's coming next out of NegSense?" Doudna inquired. He'd been instructed to meet Kit at Perimeter, a remake of a small Italian coffee shop on the inside of a patrolled ring road demarking a boundary, a border within Ulaanbaatar's city walls. He had been under escort from the airport to the café. Armed men and women paced the block outside. Their clothing shifted and crawled with a familiar irregular creep as they walked, a bulletproof weave he recognized. A living spider silk spun from repurposed and farmed transgenic silkworms he had developed himself.

"Well, if we were to speak in a broad sense on the subject," she said, her hands wrapped around a small bowl of milky coffee, steam obscuring her eyes, "then yes, as it turns out, pain is a challenging and complex function, not easily edited out of our sequence. The physical and mental aspects are two separate and distinct things. I need to learn more," she put the bowl down, stirring a single spoon of sugar into it, "about how we experience them."

"How far along is your research?" He'd hopped an evening suborb from Cornwall to Beijing, then a supersonic to UB. All in it had been about five hours. The trip itself hadn't ruined him, but the lag was starting to catch up. He gulped a double espresso, then ordered another.

"Not far at all. It's like running an ultra-marathon through the Himalayas," she said, sipping her coffee with delicate lips.

He nodded. "Complicated."

"And difficult. I get two steps forward and one point nine steps back. I can eliminate pain altogether, but it always comes with some weird off-target paralysis or malformation of the nervous system, different every time. Look at this." She flicked open her wrist and held a holo between them. A video clip displayed a small white mouse limping around its enclosure.

"Meet Apollo. He was born with no pain receptors in his brain. Edited out on the germline. But here, look at his face." She paused the video, zoomed in with a pinch of her fingers, and spun him around in a slow turn that followed her finger.

"Looks like he's had a stroke," he said. The skin below one of the mouse's bulging eyeballs sagged, the sclera was showing, weeping and scabby. When she let the video play, he ambled forward, a rear leg dragging behind, dead weight and altogether non-functional.

"It's always something like this, these unexpected genotoxic effects. The two systems are linked much deeper than I had first considered. Apollo broke his femur in the wheel but kept running, didn't even notice that his leg wasn't working."

She closed her fist, ending the vid, her eyes fixated on Doudna with an intensity he'd long since forgotten.

"I've been mining genetic anomalies, but they're hard to come by. People with a natural genetic predisposition to experience no pain tend to die young."

He laughed. "I know that's not funny, but I hadn't considered the link."

"There's a famous story about a family with a mutation that disabled the SCN9A gene. It's called congenital analgesia. None of them felt pain. They limped a lot, broke limbs like Apollo, lost parts of their tongues from repeated self-biting, burned their hands on stoves, that sort of thing. One kid decided to throw himself off a balcony to see if he'd survive." She paused. "He didn't." She took a long drink of her latte.

"So, dial down the volume," he suggested, "instead of removing it altogether."

"Trust me I've been trying. Like you said, if I could make the alarm bells a little less piercing, you know? If I could change it enough, get a more or less functional edit, and leak it out onto the street maybe. I'm willing to bet we could do a lot with it, maybe even solve for emotional pain, not only the physical." She sipped, one eyebrow up. "Imagine."

"Pain-free humans. Not sure I like it, but OK." He downed his espresso. "I've never seen you so interested in the well-being of the species."

"Well, we could use some decent press. We're getting a fair pile of anger directed our way in the media, if you've been paying attention." Her concern seemed genuine, but it was hard to digest coming from the one and only Kit McKee.

"How close are you?" he asked.

"It's a long way off. I'm running at a hundred percent failure rate, and you've seen some of the off-targets. But I'll get it; I always do."

She stared out the window, lost in thought. He'd seen it before; she was solving something in there, in real time, something bio-logical, mathematical, something he would need tech to solve. She was a terrifying woman, he loved her, respected her prowess, and wondered what it was like inside her mind, right this instant.

"It's like, why is no one else working on this shit?" she asked. "The tech is out there."

"Well, I'd say anyone else working on augments is running for a distant second, and it's an expensive game. No one is pumping out clean edits like you and NegSense, Kit. No one. You and your team have left the rest of the industry long behind. So, your competitors choose not to work on anything of substance. They develop the easy cosmetic stuff. I know, I've been doing it in my lab too."

"That's where there's real money," she said.

"Sure, but it leaves the difficult work to you."

"I'd prefer to take the big paycheques."

"That's not true, and you know it. You've got sight, hearing, all that musculature stuff, not to mention all the genetic disorders you've solved."

"Still, it would be nice if someone would work on something that mattered instead of competing with me on all the lucrative edits."

"I sit in front of you asking for collaboration." He beamed at her. She didn't reciprocate. "Our edits are, for the most part, free of off-target mutations, but that's as close as we can get."

"Right. For the most part. Are you getting dermis errors?"

He nodded. "On every edit. We need your help."

"It's a common miss. The epidermis is linked to everything. A dirty augment *will* leak into it." She went back to her coffee, her eyes wandering to the shop window. His own lab's off-target mutations in the dermal layer were minor but unpleasant. Flaking skin was not good for marketing. He followed her eyeline to a pair of guards wearing his bulletproof weave walking past the café.

"We've been given a new security team since the attack. Paramilitary. Did you hear about that?" she asked.

"I saw something about it. Got ugly around here I heard." He'd seen it on a stream. American black ops soldiers infiltrating the perimeter, hunting American diaspora like Kit and him. The American commandos had lost a gruesome battle in the streets that he and Kit now looked out at through the café window. "Was some drone footage on a pirate broadcast of a firefight in the street."

She pointed outside. "That street right there. They bombed the lab. Ginsu warheads. Orbital weaponry. Couldn't penetrate, though. The lab's encased in metres of solid concrete."

"Must have been terrifying."

"It was. Lot of people died out here to protect us from our own country, which is an odd thing to say. We haven't had any recent problems, though. Security is tight, but I don't think the Americans are out to get us anymore."

"Is it all worth it?"

"I don't know, Doudna. I'm trying to do something revolutionary here. Create some real change for all of us. Take us to the next level, you know? We haven't had a natural mutation as a species in thousands of years. Nothing's getting better for humanity; we're getting worse. You know what the birth rate is in the developed world? It's in massive decline. Education compresses fertility. The ratio is swinging in the wrong direction. We're getting *dumber* as a species, Doudna, and I feel like I can change that."

"Yeah right, the Kit McKee Theory of Devolution. I'd forgotten how hopeless your vision of our future was. What's your big plan then? Edit for less complacency?" He regretted saying it. She'd always been driven, but this was a different Kit. On a personal level, he burned with curiosity to find out what she was toying with. As a professional, he had concerns.

"Something like that." And she was gone. Disengaged. He could feel it. The conversation brought to an immediate end.

"I need to get back to the lab. I appreciate your coming all this way, Doudna. Let's meet after dinner, I'll give you the finer details of what I think we can work on together. It's been delightful seeing you again."

She'd flipped a switch and gone into a divergent mode. He wondered if she had augmented herself, delivered a genetic payload of her design into her own genome. He was desperate to ask, but less interested in aggravating Kit, opting instead for the awkward embrace shared between past lovers.

Kit took slow, ponderous strides as she left the lab for the short walk home, distracted by and eager to speak more with Doudna. She wondered if it was wise to bring him in on her project.

The wind picked up with an autumn bite. She blew warm

breath on her fingers, then remembered her lavender leather gloves, stuffed in a pocket for winter. While she pulled them over her fingers, her wrist buzzed. She jacked a bead without opening the holo. "Kit McKee speaking."

"Hey, Kit. Just checking to see if we're still on for that nightcap at your place," Doudna said.

"I'm walking home from work now. Meet me there in twenty. I've arranged for security to provide an escort when you're ready."

"See you then."

She unplugged the bead, slipped it into her coat pocket, and noticed a man across the street, bald and Caucasian, wearing a long grey overcoat with none of that crawling bulletproof weave the security force wore. He had a large tan dog on a short leash walking in step with him, the fur on its spine spiked into a ridge. She waved a hello and got a simple stare in return, unusual behaviour for security and, in fact, anyone in her neighbourhood. She was close to home, another five minutes if she stayed on this road, so she chose a different route, hoping the soldiers she had told Doudna about were doing their job, keeping the community that housed their scientists free from intruders.

She picked up her pace. Something had been funny in the lab today. Avery had been acting nervous, chewing his nails and asking questions about Zeus. She'd flat out lied to him, told him it was a cancer edit, that it was looking successful but needed further testing, in the cellar. On any other day he'd have left her alone to work, but he kept asking, which fibroblasts, how did she induce, where the control group was. She had felt pressured and did not enjoy it.

The man and his dog fell behind when she adjusted course. She turned to look, saw him half a block back, crossing to her side of the street. She flicked open her holo, not bothering with the bead.

"Security."

"It's Kit McKee requesting assistance. I'm being shadowed, bald man and a dog."

"Yes, ma'am. We'll follow on your implant. Give us thirty seconds to deploy."

She lengthened her stride as she massaged the inside of her elbow. It was itchy there. The booster carried double the load and had bruised more than she liked. She shoulder checked again. The man had gained ground. Could it be someone from the America? She didn't think it was possible to penetrate the wall surrounding the city block of labs and housing they inhabited, not since the attack. She was steps from home, the man moving at an increasing pace. She flicked open her holo to make an emergency request when a black-wheeled van pulled up beside her, Doudna smiling from an open window.

"Well, howdy again, Miss Kit," he said.

She checked behind. The man and his dog were nowhere to be seen.

"Let's get inside," she said. "I need a glass of wine."

"Don't mind if I do," he replied, clambering out of the van. A security team member followed him out, one hand on his firearm. *He hasn't been looking after himself,* she thought. *Must be a hundred and fifty kilos sweating under that loose-fitting button down.* Doudna wheezed as they walked together up the path to her townhouse. She looked back one more time for her follower but saw nothing except the empty street at dusk.

"The problem is, as always, I need more accurate testing. If I'm going to release this, I need proper data. I need to wake up the LUMPs," she said, her traffic-light green eyes locked on his, unblinking.

The van ride had been hurried, as had Kit, and he wondered what life under such security would be like. They were sitting in her kitchen, an empty bottle of Chablis on the plain white dining table between them. French wine wasn't cheap in this part of the world, he thought, enjoying another mouthful. She straightened his coaster for him as he placed the glass back down. He'd seen Kit obsess but only under moments of elevated stress. He took note, scanned the room. The furniture was arranged with geometric precision. The table, the chairs, all in perfect parallel lines, even the postcard on the fridge was aligned and centred.

"You mean the test subjects?" he asked. He hated acronyms. Too pretentious.

"Yes, the subjects," she replied.

He felt his head nodding in agreement when he came back from processing that piece of information. "You can't wake them up," he heard himself say. "They've never been awake, Kit. They've never been *alive*. For Christ's sake, you know it's been tried. They overload. It's too much for the brain to wake up into adulthood with no language, no skills, no anything." He remembered the videos, horrifying scenes. Most of the subjects found the process overwhelming and died on the spot, undergoing massive stress-induced cerebral hemorrhages, their adult brains empty of any sort of coping mechanism normally learned through infancy and adolescence and through normal fucking growth.

"Wait, you've done it already, haven't you?" he asked. She held his stare. "Fucking hell, Kit!"

"I wouldn't suggest it was with any sort of roaring success, but bear with me for a second," she replied.

"Fucking hell, Kit!" He saw himself shaking his head in a sort of weird out-of-body thing, gulping the rest of his wine.

"Listen to me," she said. "It's not as dreadful as you think. We wake them up in a safe environment, in a quiet room, no tubes attached, no monitors, zero stimulation factors. It's the human test subject, in a room, with a caregiver. We treat it like a birth, bring them to consciousness in small doses. We cater to their instincts, give them a protein analogue from a baby bottle. The new brain knows to go for a nipple, to feed. We give them human contact, a surrogate mother, keep them warm, make them feel safe. Then we augment for increased uptake, coddle them for a few days to make them feel comfortable with their surroundings, then hit them with language. Fear needs a zero point, something to calibrate from. So, we give the subjects the ability to make new connections with themselves because there aren't any..." She paused, swallowing. "There aren't any in there that we haven't been suppressing for the subjects' entire lives."

"It's not ethical, Kit. You know this. It's bad enough you're even using them unawakened. That's a whole other conversation. I'm not OK with this. Christ, Kit. Not even close."

"It's why we left the America, Doudna." She stared at him.

"I'm not OK with it."

"It's frontline research. This is the absolute frontier of genetic technology. It's how we move forward. The biological evolution of humankind is complete. Mother Nature is finished with us. The next evolutionary step *must* be genetically engineered. It's why we've evolved these big, beautiful brains, so we can make our own giant leap forward. Our evolution, Doudna, is right in front of us, and it's going to be revolutionary."

"You think you're working on that level, Kit?"

"I know I am."

"Show me."

She held his stare, and it terrified him.

"I can't. I've got some new edits in the pipeline. Not just fluff and vanity, some actual game-changing shit. But I can't check the outcomes without conscious human test subjects."

"So, why not advertise for volunteers? I'm sure you'd have plenty of applicants."

"The off-targets haven't been nice. There'd be press. I prefer to keep it underground."

"How's your funding?"

"It's solid and silent. Everything I ask for, I get. I don't know who's behind the lab, but it's big money, old money."

It had always been that way for her, all those years, spoiled but driven. She'd never hit a speed bump, never once stumbled along her path. It was no wonder she had no limits; she'd never been confronted with one.

"Including delivery of human beings, grown underground and sold to you as disposable test beds." He kept his eyes down, shaking his head.

"They don't know any different, Doudna. They're donors, always have been. Born into it, I'm afraid."

"Farmed," he corrected.

She shrugged. "I can't argue against that."

"This isn't only about the fear edit, is it?"

"It's part of it. But no, it's not."

"I disagree on every level with your methodology, Kit, but *goddamn*, I'm curious what you're up to."

"I can't bring you in. Not yet. I don't need a lot of time, but I do need some."

"I've got lots of that," he replied.

"Call me in a week. If I don't respond, come looking for me." She was staring at him now, unblinking again, her eyes taking on that intense emerald glow.

He nodded and then caught himself chewing his lip as he thought about the agents in the van. They had been agitated, concerned. "Are you in some kind of trouble, Kit?"

"It's not trouble, at least I don't think so. Feels more like *interest*. But maybe not from the right people."

He was worried about her, worried where she was heading with all this. Worried who would be on her side, and more importantly, who wouldn't be when this little project of hers came to light.

"OK, I'll be in London at the Crick Lab. You know how to find me." He gave her two kisses, one on each cheek, a goodbye he'd learned in France. Something he missed, not by its absence but in its presence, and only just now.

She walked him outside, where the same van waited with its tinted windows, one gull wing door open, a guard wearing bulletproof weave standing at its rear.

"Safe travels, my friend," she said.

"I'll be in touch. Thanks for the wine." He pulled himself into the van, followed in close proximity by the armed guard who had been waiting outside. *Very military*, he thought. *The kind a country might use to protect a weapon.*

She closed her front door as the van pulled away, a pair of surveillance drones following close in its trail.

Walking through the kitchen, she pulled the Barbados card off the fridge, the one from her mother, the last one she'd sent before ALS had taken her motor skills for good.

Why couldn't you have held on for a little while longer?

She put the postcard back under its magnet, then straightened it with two hands. She walked down the hall to her office, fiddling with her locket, turning it between finger and thumb, enjoying its weight and textured surface.

She sat in her office chair and picked up the photograph of her family framed on her desk. She was torn back to a childhood memory, whipped there and back so fast she winced.

She was walking with her grandfather, a nationalist, a man proud of his heritage. He would recite myths of ancient Chinese folklore as they wandered under a summertime afternoon sky on Central Park's winding pathways. She remembered the story of Chang'e, a mythical goddess. It must have been his favourite because he told it often. She had always thought he meant it to be cautionary, a tale of a beautiful woman who stole from her husband and was banished to the moon. It was the fable behind the mid-autumn festival, mooncakes, and floating lanterns at twilight.

She missed him. Missed laughing with him and discussing things that weren't school or work or research as everyone else in her life had always wanted. The memory was so sharp and vivid, of sitting on a sun-warmed aluminum bench, watching a softball game, the crack of a wooden bat, of her grandfather following the ball up into the sky, removing his silver, circular rimmed glasses and looking down deep into her soul.

"Sweet, little Kit, you have a gift with numbers I could only dream of. You are a mathematical anomaly. We must take care to nurture and preserve your wondrous mind." Her eyes had been locked in his senescent gaze, transfixed, unable to look away. He reached behind his neck, unclasped the thin metal chain that hung there, allowing the weight of the small steel thimble to dangle from his fingers, swaying back and forth with a hypnotic rhythm.

"When the time comes, and it will, that you have information you no longer wish to share, this will protect it. Take good care with it, young Kit. It was designed specifically for you." He clasped the chain behind her neck and allowed the locket to fall to her chest.

She reached for it again now, played with the thimble, its pocked surface rough against her fingertips. She squeezed it open, felt its empty insides where she used to keep her secrets.

Gung gung. Granddad.

The faraday cage he'd given her was cute, but times had changed. And a memchip dangling around her neck on a thin metal chain presented little in the way of security. She preferred stealth tech anyway. Hide it in plain sight but hide it well.

From her index finger, she slid the prosthetic nail she'd had surgically implanted forward and off in a well-rehearsed maneuver, revealing a storage plate that concealed a sliver of holomem. She licked her opposite thumb, affixing the intricate silicon wafer to her saliva, then closed the nail and brushed it against her display unit, physically connecting the two. The holomem snapped into place magnetically, like an ear bead. The data transfer and subsequent deletion was automatic and immediate, completed by a snippet of code she'd written herself. She quickly reversed the procedure, replacing the memory under her false nail. This data, the entirety of the Zeus code, she kept as secure as she knew how, only ever allowing it to exist in a single physical space.

She began swiping through the data, reading the raw text, looking for the anomaly. She'd only ever seen it once, in Zeus. This time she was studying a human sequence, human DNA. Hours passed, though she barely noticed, the data were that engrossing.

She leaned back in her chair, looking behind the holo, through her office window into her small backyard. She caught a glimpse of an optical lens dangling from what looked like a maple seed twirling in a moonlit glimmer. Seeds fell, but this one hovered, spinning and bobbing up and down and 'round and 'round in a hypnotic rhythm reminiscent of her grandfather's thimble. *That looks like tech*, she thought, *surveillance, could even be a weapon*, and moved swiftly beyond its field of view. She reached across the desk, swiped off the holo, and transferred the data set back to her nail bed.

She really did need to get back to the lab. She felt safe there, and something at home felt amiss.

14.

Johnny Woo stared up at them, astounded by their ugliness. A pair of semi-circular, 400-metre-tall, monolithic, windowed, concrete cliffs curling in on themselves. The buildings rose above the ground on wide-girthed cylindrical pillars of cement and rebar, so many storeys of concrete and glass they gave him vertigo.

A building-wide external renovation was underway from top to bottom, a metamorphosis of sorts. The entire complex was enshrouded in a temporary nylon mesh cocoon that was the colour of honeycomb, sagging under its own weight and billowing in gusts of wind like a ship's sails. Underneath the wrapping was its bone structure, a complex exoskeletal lattice of bamboo scaffolding held together in an ancient tradition, the wooden knuckles lashed by hand with coconut string.

He cupped his hands to light a cigarette against the approaching typhoon wind, flicking the Zippo shut with a satisfying snap. He took a long, equally satisfying drag and stared up at its spectacular height, taking in its vastness.

"Bit of a fortress, wouldn't you say, Fonger?"

"Yes, boss."

"Like they could hold off the PLA for weeks with a few guns and mortars."

"I don't know about that, boss."

Woo chuckled, the cigarette languishing in the corner of his mouth, one eye closed against the smoke trailing off its burning orange ember. "No, huh?" He looked up at the structures. "You might be right."

He fiddled with his engineer's ring, technically his grandfather's, an expat from London who had settled down in pre-handover Hong Kong. Having spent his life building the city's tallest structures, he would have cringed at the sight of these behemoths. Woo had met him when he was a child, though only for a brief moment. The ring was his parting gift, his grandfather had said, telling him to wear it with pride. So, Woo wore it, though it felt like a lie. He was no engineer; he had taken no oath.

They entered the building's lobby beneath the honey-coloured drapery that consumed its corners and curves, the light inside an ethereal amber hue. He waved his hand across the elevator call panel, the pendulous steel cabling rattling against itself as the small metal box descended to ground level.

He and Fong rode up together in relative silence, shoulders touching, the lift clanking and groaning under their combined weight.

Its doors opened on the ninth floor with an abrupt crack, and the two of them stepped out, one after the other, into a darkened hallway speckled with black mold and illuminated with filtered pale-yellow light from the gaps beneath doors. From a stairwell at the end of the hall, its door propped open with a cinder block, came the snapping sound of the building's wrap undulating in the approaching storm's wind. Caution tape strained across the entrance ahead where a police officer in uniform stood guard.

Woo clipped his badge to his trench, took the mask on offer from the officer at the door, and stepped through. The room smelled of years of aerosolized cooking oil and animal fats. An aging, freon-breathing air conditioner stuffed in the window laboured against itself, duct tape and plastic sheeting sealing the gap around it. An ornate steel chandelier oscillated in the cool synthetic airflow overhead. An elderly Chinese woman leaned on a cane beside another uniformed officer inside the door. She was speaking in Canto, pausing to acknowledge the two of them. She wore a colourful floral-print shirt, red Chinese dragons dancing across its front, her pale blue surgical mask pulled down around her chin.

"What's she doing in here?" Woo asked the officer.

"Lives here normally. I'm getting a statement. Says she came back from a weekend with family this morning."

"And she lives like this?"

"No. Said she walked in, and all her furniture was gone. Replaced with this stuff."

The room's interior was like the inside of an operating theatre, clinical, like it should smell of bleach. Each item had been placed with precision. Steel kitchen countertops met a stark white subway-tile backsplash that looked as though it had been recently cleaned. A well-trimmed ficus tree stood in the sunlight by the floor-to-ceiling window in a milky jade vase. A holo projected against one wall broadcast a rogue data stream from the America, an endless sermon about the evils of the augmented. A black, synthetic leather sofa and coffee table combo were arranged to face the stream. A single glass of water sat untouched on the polished steel. It was hot outside. *A cold drink would be nice*, he thought.

"This room is staged," he said.

"No question, boss. But why go to the trouble?" Fong asked.

A man in a hooded white hazmat suit walked out of the adjoining bedroom in a hurry, inverting his bright purple latex gloves as he removed them, pulling at the Velcro sealing his head inside.

"You'll need a biohaz suit to get in there," the officer speaking to the owner said. "Forensics are set up in the room behind me."

Woo watched a fly crawl out from under the door, then glanced back at Fong. "Time to go find out."

15.

It was nearly four in the morning when Kit finally left the lab's clinical and windowless biosphere, opening the double exit doors into the inside of a snow globe. The late-summer storm had brought with it an abnormal early season squall, and she stood for a moment, watching the glistening snowflakes falling from the sky, sparkling in the light of the streetlamps. She stepped into accumulating banks of it, the snow's squeak beneath her feet triggering a memory of frozen fingertips, hot cocoa gratitude, childhood snowball fights in onesies of goose down warmness, and a home in an America that no longer existed.

Her breath condensed into a cloud as she blew on her bare hands and kicked at the ankle-deep drifts that filled the sidewalk. A brief, biting gust, and the globe was shaken again, the ground disappearing beneath the meandering white powder. With legs on automatic for her daily walk home, she snapped a bead in each ear, put on some Vivaldi, and allowed herself to decompress into post-work consolidation.

Kit's front door auto unlocked, opening on cue as she approached, responding to her geofenced subdermal. She knocked the snow off her arms and brushed herself clean before removing her knitted wool toque. She flicked on a data stream old school, pressing a switch she'd had hard-wired to the wall. Talking holographic heads appeared before her, droning on about the political state of the planet's superpowers, the audio automatically blending into her beads above the violins of "La Stravaganza."

"More unrest as news continues to dribble from behind the walls of the America. Today, word spreads of further vigilante governments taking violent means to control further uprisings in southern states. The People's Republic of China claims yet another of its surveillance satellites has been brought down as it orbited over Texas. As always, the United Governments of the America make no commentary."

She deposited her key card and lanyard in a multicoloured glass bowl she kept at the entrance, a gift from Avery that was meant to warm her new home here in Ulaanbaatar. She hung her white, puffy, full-length coat by its fake fur-lined hood on a wall peg, then strolled through her hallway lined with old movie posters. DiCaprio on the bow of a ship. Gosling in his dancing shoes in the hills of LA. Walken with his uncomfortable watch.

The news commentary in her head faded as she walked farther from the projection at the front door. She strode across the hallway's bamboo flooring, her stiletto boots silencing as she stepped into the carpeted living room, the sound returning as she moved onto the kitchen's tiled floor.

The postcards on her fridge were normally organized in a grid, but the Barbados card from her mom hung askew, dangling by a corner beneath a small magnet. *That's new*, she thought, realigning the card.

The diatribe of news continued to follow her from the entryway stream. She popped out a bead, listened to the quiet with one ear. Outside, the snow fell heavy and silent. The cutlery drawer was open a crack. She closed it slowly out of habit, something she would have also done that morning before leaving the house.

She made a quizzical shoulder check, both sides, her heel making a single tock against the slate as she turned a complete three-sixty. She tapped off the violins and distant news in her remaining bead, removed it, and listened for the human presence that she now felt.

She immediately regretted wearing heeled boots. Her mother had told her once that you could put a bell around a cat's neck, but if it didn't want to be heard, it would move in perfect silence. She tried to become a cat, to lose the sound of her heels on the tile.

She flicked her palm open, the transdermal hardware in her wrist bringing up a holo. She popped a bead back in one ear, its magnetic field snapping into the piercing, then swiped right with her free hand until she got Avery's beaming avatar and chose "voice only" from the ensuing menu.

"Avery? Were you in my house today?" she whispered.

"No, babe. What's up?" he replied, sounding confused.

She took gentle, quiet strides back toward the front door, her heels muted, listening carefully with one ear. "Must be my imagination. Feels like someone was here."

"Why's that, Kit?"

She glanced at the bedroom door, wished it was fully open, then took stock of the shadows, waiting for movement.

"Things seem... amiss."

"Like someone trashed your house?" Concern now from Avery.

"No, more like someone didn't want me to know they'd been here, but they weren't very good at it." She moved out of the living room toward the spare room. She kept the hardware in there, and the door was still closed.

"You're giving me the heebie-jeebies, Kit. Come to my house," he offered. "We can do wine."

She grasped the locket around her neck. "I'll be fine, Ave. Just wanted to check in with you." She was patrolling the townhouse now, not like she knew what she'd do if she came across an interloper. *I'm basically armed with foul language. Could take off a boot and try to stab him in the throat,* she thought, wholly untrained and without a weapon, searching for an intruder her instincts told her was there, inside her fucking home.

A floorboard squeaked. The one over by the front door, the one she'd meant to have fixed ages ago.

"You need some company over there? I can swing by. Give me, like, ten minutes. I can hop a Ryde. Want me to send someone from lab security? Should I call security? Kit? You there?"

She'd stopped listening to him, was working her way back to the front door, which she now realized she'd never properly closed. She muted the call with a tap of the bead, moving now in complete silence, her heels making no further sound.

She heard a rustle by the entry, a faint rubbing together of clothing, like bedsheets, that she wasn't meant to hear. Her senses heightened. Fried ginger and garlic wafted in from outside. She crept past her framed memories along the hallway, feeling as though this moment would never end, waiting for a telltale misstep.

The doorway was wide open, as she'd left it, fresh boot tracks in the snow heading back out into the storm. Someone had been there, someone who didn't think she'd be home. Finally remembering to breathe, she took a long deep inhale, surveyed the outside through the blizzard, then closed, latched, and locked the door, the deadbolts secure.

She remembered Avery and unmuted the call. "Ave?"

"What is going *on* over there?" He almost shouted without raising his voice.

"Avery, someone's been in my house. I heard him, saw his boot prints in the snow."

"He take anything?"

"Haven't really looked. I just locked the door. Avery, get over here. I'm scared."

She was kneeling now, crouched and terrified. There was no one who knew, no one. The data had never been up. The project was strictly between her and Zeus. But someone had been there, sneaking about. The person could only have been looking for one thing, which meant someone knew, and she hadn't told a soul.

"Babe, I'm, like, ten minutes away at best. Get out of your house and get in a cab. We can head over there tomorrow in the daylight with the special ops guys from the lab." He was right; she needed to go.

"Order me a Ryde. I'll be ready in a minute."

She opened her hand, swiped left, and the holo disappeared back into her wrist. She was motionless, waiting, her breath shallowing, listening for that moment of calm when her beating heart and the wet blink of her eyes would become the loudest things in the room.

When it came, she could feel someone else still inside, still lurking. She felt hunted, wild, a gazelle in the grass, her senses heightened. When she moved, it was swift and with purpose.

She stormed into the spare room and snatched the carbon-black, sugar-cube-sized holomem taped to her desk drawer's underside—what she assumed they'd been after. She was ready to make a lot of noise if she came across anyone, try and scare them with volume if nothing else.

She marched into the kitchen, grabbed a knife and the postcard from her mother, put on her coat, and stepped back out into the storm, blowing snow from the Ryde's spinning fans blinding the path down to the street. She heard her home's door auto lock behind her. As the twin rotor settled on the curb side and spooled down, she could see again, and she hopped inside the one-seater. With its canopy sealed, it lifted off, autonomously flying her out of the snowstorm to Avery's place.

Avery swiped off the audio, ordered a Ryde to Kit's house, and then closed down the holo buried in his wrist. She'd be there in ten minutes. He'd need to make the call soon.

He sat at his desk and stared at the projection there, thumbed through some social media fodder about hairstyles of the wealthy and famous, settled on a hair bag narrowcast on semi-permanent fade-out colour edits, then swiped for the South African.

"Avery, my man. How's it, bru?" Weissach's thick Afrikaans accent poured through the feed.

"I'm good." He paused. "Kit's not updating Zeus anymore. She's doing strict observation protocol now. The mouse itself seems in great health though. I'd take a dose of whatever she's given him."

"I don't think that was part of our deal, bru."

"She just called me, said someone was following her, like someone was in her apartment, and she's spooked. That wasn't you, was it?"

"Bru, you let us worry about these types of things. Where's she headed now?" Avery liked the accent, figured he'd date a South African man, but not Weissach.

"Told you. I don't tail her. All I do is watch over the projects she's got in the lab. Once I'm outside that airlock, she's all yours mate."

Weissach whistled through his nose. "Bru, let's be clear: ahm-not-your-mate." He said it all at once, a single word, chilling.

Avery remembered the day in the Chinese restaurant, the wine Weissach didn't drink. His stomach lurched in the pause. Butterflies in a garden on a sunny summer day. Neither of them spoke. He listened to Weissach breathe for as long as he could take.

"She's keeping the data on her person somewhere." He leaned back in his chair, tapped out a song with his pen on the desk. "I don't see her upload anything in the lab. But there's no way she's leaving it there. If you want that mouse and his data, you're going to need to go and get it yourself. And there's no fucking way I'm doing that for you."

"Right, bru. Got it. Check your balance for an increase. Your cooperation is appreciated. I'll be in touch." The connection went dead before he could end it.

16.

As Woo and Fong stepped into their Tyvek crime scene suits with the aid of the forensic team, Woo became aware of a faint hum emanating from behind the door. "What's that?" he asked, listening. "Where's the buzzing coming from?"

"It's flies," the woman dressing him said with a look of disgust as she placed the hood over his head, smoothing the resealable glue seam around his neck. "They're in the body." She finished taping his wrists, securing the black latex gloves tight, then affixed a pen to a small Velcro patch on his arm. "You're good to go."

Safely sealed inside his hazmat gear, Woo opened the bedroom door. Two more white bunny suits were attending to the body, removing insects from its shoulders with steel tweezers, placing them in screw-top glass jars.

"Entomology?" he asked, closing the door behind Fong.

One of the bunnies nodded. "We won't be long, detective."

"Rough guess on time of death?"

"Seventy-two hours at least. Likely more." She waved a jar at him, the insect inside tapping against the glass. "These little guys take a few days to gestate."

A low, walnut-coloured platform bed dominated the centre of the room, framed on both sides and up the walls in ornamental Chinese lattice. Crisp, white linens cocooned the precisely made bed, their tightly folded seams disappearing below the mattress where the forehead of the skinless body leaned as though in prayer. Its exposed muscle and subcutaneous fat reflected a damp sheen in brown, yellow, and grey. Fluids had collected on the carpet into pools of dried, coagulated blood. A ledge below the room's curved bay window housed a collection of devices that looked like a makeshift medical print lab, including a 3D printer with its glass doors open, its internal surgical-steel mechanisms exposed. Beside it, a similarly sized metal box fronted with a small, illuminated display reminded him of a microwave oven. A human epidermis, folded with precision into a perfect square, had been placed on the opposite side of the bed, aligned with the corner.

"Gruesome," Woo said as he looked around the room. "I like what they've done with the place though." Their hooded suits had hot mics and speakers; it was like they were wearing headsets in an aircraft, every word they spoke broadcast to the group. He peeled the pen from his arm and carefully lifted a flap of skin dangling from the dead man's neck. It had the consistency of cooked hair gel. After a moment of adhesion, it liquified and fell to the floor.

"He's not going to be needing that," he said to Fong, who had his palm up, flicking through data on his holo.

"Forensics have been through the scene," Fong said. "They agree with entomology. The victim's been dead more than a few days."

"No one noticed?"

"No mention of it in their initial report."

"We'll want to read that occupant's statement as soon as it's done," Woo said, leaning into the victim's exposed internals. "Get the bot up."

From his wheeled and dog-eared leather crime-scene bag, Fong took an aluminum soda-can-sized container. He cracked it open like a fortune cookie, along its seam, delicately removing the drone and its folded insectoid plastic airfoils. He flicked it into the air where it hovered, instantaneously expanding into flight, spinning rotors on the ends of four segmented arms reaching up from its body where a camera lens dangled, stabilized like an insect's weighted thorax.

He stood over the skin folded on the bed, pointing at it with his pen, his back to Fong. "You ever seen anything like this?"

"On a nature stream maybe. Never seen a *person* shed their skin before, if that's what you're asking."

He walked over to the bay window. Beneath it was a mini fridge, its glass door closed. He kneeled down for a closer look, careful not to tear the Tyvek. Inside was a collection of pods, hypodermic auto injectors, an easy needle that a child could operate. Like a gun, it had a trigger and a barrel. Woo had used an identical one to do his own flu shots, as easy as point and shoot. Not all of them were marked. Those that were had varying levels and colours of fluids inside.

"Strange," he said. "These are odd labels. Got one here says 'green' and a bunch that say 'blue.' All handwritten. Not exactly imaginative. Thoughts?"

"No, boss. I wasn't exactly straight A's in biotech." Fong flew the drone via his holo, his swiping fingers directing the tiny bot.

"Not so sure this guy was either." Woo catalogued the crime scene in his mind as Fong's bot rotoscoped the room in digital.

"This building is government assist, right?" Woo asked.

"It's one hundred percent public housing. You don't get to stay if you've got the dollars to pay," Fong replied.

"So this building, this whole complex is populated with the destitute and unemployed?"

"Mostly low-income earners, boss."

"So then what is *this* guy," he gestured at the body with his pen, "doing with all *this* gear?" He walked over to the open glass box on the ledge and pointed at it, his arm outstretched.

"This is not a simple 3D printer, is it?"

"Much more than that, boss. Look at the brand. SKC. They make genetic equipment for biosamplers and molecular assemblers.

That thing can collect and replicate DNA, RNA. It'll even draw up a brand-new genome if you give it enough time."

"Sounds expensive."

"Not just expensive, boss, regulated. That box belongs in the government laboratories in Kowloon."

"So I can't buy one of these on the street?"

Fong laughed. "Impossible. The fact that it's here leads me to think something of significance went very wrong, and fast." He closed the box's glass doors with a gloved hand. "Nobody ever leaves these open. Too much contamination risk to the nozzles. Either our victim was meant to walk out with this thing, or someone who was in this room was."

Woo knelt beside the flayed body, the tangy, metallic smell of blood penetrating the suit's filters. On the ground beneath his knees, he saw a used pod, the empty vial still inserted. He held it up and read the label aloud. "Red Crimson." The words were handwritten in black Sharpie. "He had some kind of bad luck, this guy," he said, showing the vial to Fong before dropping it into a paper evidence bag.

"No joke. You think that pod is what did this to him?" Fong asked, watching over the drone as it hovered in the middle of the room, slowly rotating and inhaling data.

"I think there's a lot more to this story than we're gonna gather in a day," Woo said.

"Agreed."

Woo continued his general sweep of the room in analogue, using only his eyes, no digital assistance. Black-strapped banknotes spilled from an unzipped, faded olive duffel beneath the bedframe. "Bag of bills under the bed there," Woo said, pointing. "Be a shame if any of those went missing."

"Noted," Fong said, swiping at his holographic drone controls. "Something interesting in that skin. The bot's flicking through filters." It had stopped its gentle spin, its machine irises beaming a full interrogative spectrum into the heaped and translucent dermis on the bed.

"What's it got?" Woo asked.

Fong swiped through pages of imagery. "Looks like a non-human sequence. Like the body had a rider. Parasite or something. Could be a splice. I'm not sure. We should get it to the lab."

He continued his visual scan, tapping the pen against his hip. Investigations involving parasitic interlopers were not on his resumé. "This setup is highly unlikely. We're in the lowest-income housing in the city. Nobody who lives in these buildings has state-of-the-art *anything*, let alone a high-end bioprinter. Not to mention this thing." He waved his hand at the closed steel box beside the printer.

"You know what that is?" Fong asked.

Woo shook his head. "Haven't a clue."

"It's the incubator."

"For what?"

"You don't just print off biomass, it needs a scaffold, something made of human or pig, a sort of living ink, a printed endoskeleton. Then you need to grow the tissue on the substrate in that thing." He motioned toward the metal box. "Give it a live environment, mature the weave. It's biogenetic gardening, germinating human tissue in a similar environment to the inside of a human being."

"Like a womb?"

"Yes, but different."

"How long does it take to grow?" he asked.

"Depends. That's a small enclosure, so probably less than two weeks. They augment the cells with some kind of growth that speeds things up."

"So, what's growing inside the box?"

"Only one way to find out," Fong said.

They looked at each other, Woo's gloved finger paused above the illuminated "Open" button.

"I'm gonna let the science team open this for us. I'd hate to be the person who unleashes some purposefully engineered bug, end up like the America."

"Agreed, boss."

Several years back, the America had, as a direct result of the "Incident," enacted the "Ethics," banning all manner of edits and making any sort of genetic scissoring or further sequencing of human DNA unlawful. A particularly evil bacterial toxin had been engineered into the genome of a successful wild fungus, releasing it as a spore, poisoning the atmosphere with a necrotic mutagen. It killed tens of millions and decimated the east coast population corridor. Nobody ever claimed it as an act of terror, and no one knew or admitted where it came from, but it was identifiably manmade. All fields of genetics were subsequently outlawed. It was taken out of school curriculum, anyone involved in biosciences was retrained, and a new section of Homeland Security was added, the Department of Bioweapons Counterintelligence, a.k.a. the DBC, spooks who took it to the backyard level, snooping through trash, looking for any trace of home-grown laboratory offal.

Those actions drove an already well-established, legitimate community to seek acceptance from any nation that would provide it. The Africas and China, Ulaanbaatar in particular, were well known for producing the best augments around. There was money to be made, and the world's populace was hungry for enhancement, no matter the price. Many American scientists had fled to such areas. Hong Kong was a place where edits were available on the street. And though "The Genetics Market" was printed on the city's street signs, its legality remained unaddressed and grey. For legal augments one had to head north to the mainland, Mongolia, or Russia. So it was strange that this lab with state-of-the-art bio-printing hardware would pop up in a low-rent megastructure like this one.

"The incubator means he was trying to make something physical, like an organ, yes?" Woo asked.

"Makes sense, boss."

He did a slow circle, recreating in his mind what could have happened in the room. "Is it possible he was trying to replicate his own skin? Create a replacement?"

"Big gamble to take on his own. You'd think he'd want some medical assistance with something like that."

"There had to be someone else here. I don't think he popped that pod on himself. Doesn't make any kind of sense."

"You think he got jumped?" Fong asked. "Like someone decided to try out that vial of Red Crimson on him?"

"I think he was going to try on whatever he printed inside that box, and someone else decided he was gonna be a test subject. And if I'm right about that, we're dealing with a bioweapon. Takes this out of our jurisdiction."

Fong swiped furiously at his holo. "SceneDoc has a complete image of both rooms. I can take it out in the hall and let it run, see what comes up while we wait for the science team to show."

"I want out of this ridiculous suit." Woo's nose itched, and he couldn't touch it through the hood's transparent shield. "Let's head back to the office, get the super in on this conversation."

Woo knocked on the door to Superintendent Lee's office twice, hard, with intent. The glass walls depolarized, and the super's head rose to greet him as the door opened.

"What's up, Johnny Woo?"

"I got assigned this homicide in TKO. No ID yet, but I get the feeling it's gonna go up the chain. Found some evidence of a potential bioweapon. Was wondering if you could keep it away from the ATF for a few days while I investigate a little deeper."

Lee put down his tablet and met Woo's eyes. "You got something on your mind?" He gestured toward the wall projection, a green stream of text denoting each un-managed case still needing initial investigation. There were hundreds. "I've got no shortage of work for you."

"I think this one might have a connection to the Shing Wo file I've been handling. Take a look at this feed from the scene." Woo opened his precinct wristband holo, swiped through to the data from the bot, grasped the ghostly image in his hand, and threw it at the wall. The picture was a 3D photograph of the body overlain with multiple sources of visuals. The image of the shed skin elevated itself and rotated slowly, a stream of data scrolling alongside it. The superintendent leaned in closer, reading the text.

"That's a possible genetic splice," Woo said. "It's early in the investigation right now, but it looks to me like he was injected by an assailant and detained until he melted that skin clean off his body."

Lee continued to ingest the data, swiping at the screen to examine the body, the incubator, and the printer.

"There were more biogenetics in the cooler, labels you can see there. Blue, green. Look at the empty one we figure he was done with. Says 'Red Crimson' on it."

"I see that." Superintendent Lee sat back down behind his desk twirling the long, thin grouping of hairs that grew off his chin. "And ATF hasn't been informed yet?"

"The data's in the system. Just need you to sign off on it, and they'll be in the know."

"Any signs of a struggle?"

"Nothing obvious."

"So that skin somehow fell off the victim in the room?"

"Unlikely."

"You think the body was moved?"

"On first look, the evidence would support that theory. The whole apartment is pristine."

"Detective, this reminds me of a saying: 'Even a dragon will struggle to control a snake in its den.' A scene like this would not be so clean if that victim had his skin removed in that apartment, alive or not." Lee flipped through the SceneDoc filters. "Any indicators of pathogens?"

"Forensics sampled the scene, the hallway, and the elevators. Nothing there."

"How long do you need?"

"I could do with a couple of days."

"Tell you what," Lee said, leaning on his desk. "I'm not feeling very well, I should go home and get some rest. I won't be reviewing any case files or signing off on any reports until I come back, which won't be for a couple of days." He reached for his coat, looking up at Woo from behind eyes that said *go*.

"Understood, sir. Get well soon." Woo swiped off his holo and closed his boss's office door behind him.

"Fonger," he said. "We're in business."

The two detectives stood beside Woo's cubicle staring at the projection they'd cast into the centre of the room, deciphering what the bot had identified as interesting. Fong brought some of the data down to his own holo with a grab, zoomed in with a pinch, and generated an image of the used pod. It slowly rotated in his open palm.

"The needle's showing only the victim's DNA, boss. The vial's empty though. You think it's possible he thought this was the cure? That he was already in the middle of whatever was happening to his skin?"

"Best we don't theorize before we've gathered all the evidence, young Fonger. It biases the judgement," Woo said, "to paraphrase a great detective."

He remained glued to the virtual projection. There was a ficus in the living area, potted and placed with some solid Feng Shui, its multiple trunks gathered at the base with a shining white ribbon. Woo swiped with four fingers together, right to left, cycling through the different imaging sequences like a digital lazy Susan. With the ultraviolet scan, he stopped, stepped forward, and spun the ficus with a tap and a spiral of his upturned finger, two-finger flicked through stronger filters, and found a multi-wavelength that gave him a clean image.

"This ribbon has some sort of bodily fluids on it, but the ficus is clean. Not a trace."

"Placed after the fact," Fong observed.

"Not only placed, it was tied around this tree so as not to damage it. Look at the bow; it's perfect."

"Back to the scene, boss?"

"Let's go."

Outside the building's entrance, a crowd of onlookers had gathered, news of the homicide having travelled at the speed of electrons. The two of them stormed through the curious with their hands and collars up, no need for unnecessary exposure on a developing case like this.

After the penetrating stares of the public's eyes, the crime scene was a welcome solitude. Wind crept beneath the cracks of doors and through unsealed windows, mewling through the hallway and singing like sirens of the approaching storm outside, typhoon level eight now, starting to get serious. Thick sheets of opaque plastic vibrated in the typhoon's winds. Officers had cocooned the apartment with it, sealing the crime scene against external contaminants as best as they could.

Woo cut through the plastic enshrouding the doorway with his pocketknife, the opening snapping against the wind's newly generated avenue of escape. They gloved up and made their way into the unit. Fong opened his holo, referencing the stored data set against the room in front of them.

"Ribbons gone," he said.

"Shit. Any sign of it in the evidence locker?"

Fong swiped quickly through pages of data. "Nothing except coroner info from the body."

"Fuckers."

He slowed his inspection. This was a time to take it *all* in, to find the minutia they'd missed on the initial sweep. Someone on the inside had stolen evidence, which meant this was a much bigger deal than anyone was letting on. They'd need to proceed with caution.

Fong popped the bot, which hung on its self-propelled cushion of air as it surveyed the room.

"Get a detail on the ficus. See if they left any trace of themselves," Woo said. "That ribbon was well tied. They wouldn't have been able to remove it easily."

The bot spun a slow circle around the tree, sucking in data from its multiple spiny extended apertures, a floating autonomous AI police dog sniffing for clues, its tiny ducted rotating propellers silenced by internal speakers broadcasting a sinusoidal interference. He heard the changes in pitch but not the steady whir. The plastic slapped in the wind.

Fong stayed with the bot, his holo hand palm up, watching the data flow through. "It's... there's..." He scowled. "There's a mask, boss. An agent covering the sample. Someone dusted this tree with a containment since we were last here. We're not going to be able to get any usable information from it."

Containments weren't cheap. Manmade polymers, grown like vines dangling in a hothouse, invisible to the naked eye and only molecules thick. Baked in ovens and pulverized with magnets into polysilicate nanoparticles. An ultra-fine, electrically charged dust that tenaciously bonded itself to more or less anything. Prevented things like fingerprints and DNA samples and, in this case, any fucking evidence from being lifted. Not the sort of thing one would expect to see at a murder scene in a low-rent high-rise in the projects.

"What the actual fuck is going on here?" Woo wondered aloud, his eyes darting around the makeshift lab. "This is a very expensive cover-up of a very expensive project in one of the most insecure complexes in the city."

17.

Dallas slinked out of the autocab into a steady drizzle, climbing the stairs to his condo during a gap in the rain bands, a brief reprieve from the typhoon. Streams of water ran down decades-old, crumbling concrete steps, the colour of low-level stratus. The loose stone pieces of Robinson Road were reminiscent of his home on St. Augustine's cobblestone streets. He thought of the Florida coastline, white sand beaches, a past and distant life of freedom, his family, and the soothing sounds of children at play, a home no longer.

Street side, the South Asian steady state of high-rise construction permeated the rain, the combo sounding like a wartime apocalypse. A low brick fence separated him from an industrial kill site where a long-telescoped nibbler riding the end of a segmented, almost scorpion-like appendage climbed an ever-growing pile of discarded cement detritus. Digestive, saliva-like water sprayed from its destructive mandibles as they buried themselves into the crumbling tower's carcass like scavenging vultures, tearing concrete from rebar and pulling at the sinews of the dead building's insides. The blades of its rotating twin tandem jaws simultaneously destroyed and ingested the ancient high-rise's skeletal remains.

He paused to watch. *They're eating it*, he thought. They were making way for a new superstructure to be grown. Regurgitated carbon would be spat out and hardened by a colony of printers, machines creating a new hive for humans. Government housing initiatives at their best. He should know; he lived in one at the top of the steps ahead. A cubist rendition of the modern condominium, each unit a pod hung from the outside of a palm-like trunk, spun from a single strand of liquid carbon, hardened into homes of flexible ganglia.

A man with no arms and no legs approached Dallas on a square piece of plywood, propelling himself using a stick clenched between his teeth. Skateboard wheels rumbled and complained beneath his weight. He looked up at Dallas from amputated stumps, repeatedly prostrating himself on the board.

"Lei bong ngo. Pang yau. M'goi. Lei bei cin ngo. Ngo mut yeh doe mou laa." *Help me, friend. Please. You give me money. I have nothing.*

Dallas placed a twenty beneath a leg stump and continued up the hill to his home, the man's stream of thankyous growing distant as he walked. Triad justice was swift and violent, and delimbing sent a clear message. A reminder of who Dallas worked for, who this amputee likely worked for, and what consequences failure would bring.

He plugged a numeric code into the number pad beside the entryway, buzzing the burner handheld in his pocket, allowing him entry. He changed the code after every mission. No sense in giving away more data than necessary. Inside, he keyed in the seventy-eighth floor and then grabbed the handrail, the elevator pulling gee as it accelerated for the long ride up.

He got off on his floor and walked past the "middle," a central grouping of communal toilets coated with a sickly black mold, a slowly growing organism that appeared to be thriving on excesses of humidity and neglect, creeping farther out of the bathrooms with each passing week.

His embossed metal key shifted tumblers in the lock he'd had professionally installed in his front door, a freshly painted Mao-red slab of pressed aluminium. The key meant no retinal scan, no record taken, and no positional data written to some master database to be sent off to the IRD for enquiry. There were no *augments* here. It was a great place to lie low, remaining anonymous and out of sight.

Emerging from the dangling entry tube to the unit, he took a deep breath of the indoors, his apartment air conditioned and minimal. He threw himself onto the wall bed, still down from his last stay. It was his single decent piece of furniture, a locally sourced mattress, too short, too narrow, too firm, and too used, the sag in the middle a feature from the previous owner. He dusted a Down in his grinder and hoovered it, the sedation hitting in seconds. With some difficulty he placed the grinder on the glass top of his bedside table, then wrapped himself in his stark white duvet to guard against the frigid conditioned air streaming from the vented ceiling. As he drifted into an exhausted, chemically aided sleep, he felt the gentle, vague yet perceptible sway of the dangling pod as it adjusted to his weight, its bamboo flooring shifting with a single audible creak, a reposition, soothing, calming, *home*.

18.

Woo leaned all the way back in his office chair, tightening one end of his hand-rolled cigarette, the filter hanging loosely from his lips, the last piece of this delicate and satisfying puzzle. His eyes were on the holo in the middle of the room, images of the crime scene scattered across it in a disorganized and chaotic three-dimensional mess. No particular image held his gaze. Through no particular design, he was trying to wrap his head around the entire situation, trying to extract some sort of motive out of it all, hoping for a peripheral revelation to come from unfocused gazing at the entirety of the data.

"You gonna light that thing or just keep playing with it?" Fong asked him from behind.

"It's not about the destination, Fonger," Woo replied. "It's all about the journey."

He plugged the filter in the open end, a few crumbs of tobacco falling to the ground. "I'm going to go smoke this," he said. "And when I come back, we're going to figure this fucking thing out."

Woo stood under the protective cover of the main entrance to the old red-brick police station looking out at an empty Hollywood Road. Waves of rain pelted the pavement, the ricochet spray creating a waist-deep mist. The glowing ember hanging from his lips was the only spot of colour in the drab, washed-out hues of heavy rainfall.

The typhoon was a nine now, about to be a direct hit. They'd named this one Ester, the fifth of the season and a doozy by all accounts. Woo smelled ozone above the burning tobacco. It stung the nose in a similar way. Enjoyable, familiar. They were between rain bands, still hammering down but not with frightening intensity. That would come later that night when Ester was forecast to hit a ten out of ten.

He pulled deep on the cigarette, enjoyed the sensation of smoke filling his lungs, and allowed himself to drift with the exhale into the soothing sounds of rainfall, the repetitive natural scattering of water drops against pavement. The sidewalks were vacant, a strange sight in this town, the typhoon keeping most people indoors for now. An odd, lonely moment in the most densely populated city on the planet.

Lucky me, he thought as he pulled one last time on the cig, looked at the burning end of the expired smoke, then flicked it into the street where a silver Mercedes station wagon crept past, its tinted windows menacing, like a cat's eye becoming full pupil as it's about to pounce. A silent visitor in the storm. He felt cased, surveilled, and watched.

He took in the car's details. It had nice rims, Kokos, black spokeless circles that he could see right through, like the car was rolling on a set of tungsten wedding bands. The vehicle had been lowered, a theme. Low-profile tires on low-profile, see-through rims, lowered suspension, and a low-profile roofline. It looked as though it were sealed to the street. Whoever was inside wanted him to know they were watching.

Who would stalk an HKPF detective in this town and in this weather? And right outside the precinct?

The plate was impossible to read in what appeared to be a

well-engineered and perfectly directed obscuring spray off the rear tires. *Neat trick*, he thought. *Might have to give that a go myself.*

As the Benz paraded past, the driver's-side window cracked open a smidge. Cobalt Asian eyes met his, a face tattoo obscured in the shadows, freckles below what appeared to be a well-worn, matte-black cowboy hat, its brim pinched tight at the sides. He watched the moment transpire as from outside his body, expecting an attack of some sort, he regretted not bringing his weapon along for the smoke. The car rounded the corner, rolling through a red light, its darkened window closed. As it crawled out of sight, he remembered to breathe.

"Did it work?" Fong asked once Woo made it back upstairs in the precinct.

"Sort of. Just watched a very interested Benz roll past the station, all tinted up." He tapped his temple. "Looked like he was taking pictures."

Fong peered out the window. "There's no one out there driving in this weather today, boss."

"Exactly."

"You get an ID?"

"Nah. Had some sort of setup. Was kicking up spray from the road right in front of the plate. Couldn't get a read."

"That's a neat trick."

"S'what I said."

He grabbed a precinct holo from the charging station and snapped it closed around his wrist. "I'm done here. Storm's gonna be a ten in a couple of hours. Let's both head home, ride it out, come back fresh."

"Sold," Fong agreed.

Woo walked outside wearing his black felt Brixton, another

cigarette lit, expecting to see the Benz waiting for him in the storm. Instead, he was met with the next band of devastating typhoon winds. With one hand up to break the force of the rain, he used the other to clutch his hat tight to his head. He popped the collar on his trench against the stinging downpour and began the walk back to the escalators and their protective covered walkways home.

19.

Four fucking hours. Every night like clockwork. Like he had a four-hour cuckoo in his head. It was bullshit. Normal people could lie down and sleep seven, eight hours at a stretch. Persephone had been a legendary sleeper. Put her head down beside him, and he could have lit bombs in the room, and she'd have mumbled some complaint that she'd have no recollection of in the morning but wouldn't wake up. And there he would be, at the four-hour mark. The FHM. Waiting impatiently for sleep to return.

Dallas lay on his back, blinking into the darkness, his mind walking around the outside of his dangling home, wondering if the other pod dwellers in that place had sleep issues like him. It was maddening. He'd taken all the meds, tried all the voodoo, exercised himself within an inch of his life, and none of it had fucking worked. He'd watched a data stream about it, that the eight-hour sleep schedule was a recent thing. That right up until the world industrialized, back a few hundred years ago and before the discovery of electricity and unlimited access to lighting, most people slept in four-hour bursts. It was well documented once he'd gotten into the research. Most literature written in the seventeen and eighteen hundreds referred to the first and second "sleeps." The vast majority of people back before artificial light would go to bed at dark, a novel idea in and of itself. Four hours later, after the first sleep, they would fuck, eat, and then head back to bed until the sun came up.

All in all, nighttime was a twelve-hour process. It had to be broken up somehow. A couple of hours of fornication and eating in the middle of every night; they were definitely on to something. *Maybe that's what I need*, he thought. Head to a brothel, bang a synthetic, and hit the vending machine on the way out for a sandwich. Not a terrible idea, but inconvenient. He needed a home delivery version for a night like this. Be much nicer to roll over into someone and then have a quick sloth off to the fridge for a pre-made. Could get it all done in half an hour. Back to bed, wake up with the sun. It sounded like a dream. Dreams he only ever had at the FHM. He knew the answer. Snap a rollie, sit at the window, and enjoy the short hour or so of actual silence that existed in Central in the very early a.m. while everyone at the clubs was still inside dancing, the shops were actually closed, and the garbage trucks hadn't started yet. It was the FHM; he hated it, but it was a peaceful time.

He got up, rolled himself a sixty-forty, mostly weed but a little of his Amber Leaf for flavour. Would do the trick. Figured he could get all the clean sleep he wanted when he was dead.

20.

The escalators had been around for something like 150 years, Woo thought as he stepped onto the covered moving sidewalk beneath him. A tidal flow keeping pace with the pedestrian rush hour, they ran upwards most hours of the day. He enjoyed their inclined slow-moving smoothness, but tonight the advertising emblazoned along the walls and ceiling displayed an unusual interest in his presence. From animated two-dimensional panels with promotions for massage and food came multiple aggressive disembodied holographic heads, leaping out of the screens.

"Hello?"

"Lei ho maa?"

"Lei to ngor maa?"

"Hello!"

"What's your name, stranger? Where you from? Why not come inside and have some tea at Lin Heung Tea House and relax a while? Why not have a foot massage? Come to Happy Feet. It's just down the stairs from the next stop, around the corner on Wellington Street. Your unhappy feet will thank you."

Targeted ads didn't work on him. He had no subdermal, no augments, and no online identification, a requirement of the job and a perk as far as he was concerned. There was no stored data to track him, no photos for facial recognition neurals to pin him with, no way to extract his purchasing preferences from a digital identity puzzled together by some vacant AI programmed to mine data stolen from the public's ignorant online pursuits.

Normally.

The heads didn't stop, and he found himself reacting to their aggression, flinching as they leapt at him from all sides. This wasn't normal. Like the slow drive-by of the Benz in the middle of a typhoon, the visual onslaught had an intensity that he'd never experienced before. Perhaps because he was alone in the storm. Maybe the advertising neural was lonely, had no easy marks to harass. He felt monitored, same as outside the station, and not only by cameras. This felt personal, and for the first time in a very long while, Johnny Woo felt fear.

He walked off the platform with his head down, holding his hat on tight in the fierce, pelting sideways rain. In the gleaming red and orange neon of a Circle K, a Ryde sat idling, its turbine whine labouring against the buffeting wind. It was alone, like him, charging itself, seeking shelter. He ducked inside the first doorway he could find to escape the rain, irritatingly the same tea shop the advertisements had accosted him with.

"Yum cha maa?" an aging lady in a soiled beige apron asked, her eyes drooping with obvious pity. He'd been in the rain for only an instant and was soaked to the bone. "You look like wet dog," she said. He took stock. She was right. Everything about him dripped on the bamboo floors, adding to the moist atmosphere inside. Streaming above the door, thin green and red ribbons flapped from an air conditioner, clamouring to keep up with the heat. The small teahouse housed only a handful of tables, populated by locals unwilling to head outside in the face of the storm, not unlike him and the Ryde.

Shaking out his trench, he hung it on one of a number of hooks heavily laden with other customers' wet-weather wear, took a table with a single faded, flimsy folding chair, put his drenched hat in the corner, and sat. Behind the counter, elevated above the dining public, a white fortune cat waved mindless Chinese luck at him. Above his head, an old-school panel display dangled perilously from a segmented black metal mount, barking a news stream about typhoon Ester—now a ten, they were saying—slamming into the southern Chinese coastline. Didn't get any bigger. Outside, under the elevated escalators, unidentifiable garbage flew past the window as if to emphasize the news story.

"Po lei tung my lor mei faan, m'goi," he said. *Tea please, and also sticky rice.* He could smell the starch hanging in the air, and he needed some food. Outside, the rain fell sideways. The stream playing on the panel showed a large transport vehicle, down the hill in Central, buried in the display window of a Gucci storefront after a brief gravitational escape as it tumbled like laundry through abandoned downtown streets, courtesy of Ester's 300 kilometre per hour winds.

He was most of the way through his bowl of rice and about to begin his cup of hot tea when the door opened, blowing a young couple's plates and meals into the wall beside them. The room's eyes turned to see a large, tanned, dripping wet man wearing a cowboy hat, his black bolo tie held horizontal by the wind. He turned to face the door, using thick-fingered hands to muscle it shut, the latch turning with an odd finality. His coat touched the floor, a slate-grey oilskin that looked like it came off the back of something that had once had a heartbeat. His shoulders arced wide and low off his neck. *Augmented,* Woo thought, for strength at the very least.

The man looked around the room, his eyes settling on Woo. He had a Chinese number nine tattooed on the right side of his face, in front of his ear. It stretched from his eyeball to his lips, covering his cheekbone with crimson brushstrokes outlined in micron-thin black.

He picked up a folding chair with one hand and spun it around to sit facing Woo, his fingers interlaced on the table. Woo caught a flash of silicon from the man's iris, a recording device, hot new tech, meta lenses built on a dielectric elastomer scaffold and hardwired into a subdermal memchip. He'd heard you could find them on the Akihabara, a conglomerate of backyard tech-heads and basement lab scientists buried beneath a Chiyoda market in an underground Tokyo surgical theatre, pure Japanese subculture. He was the cowboy hat in the Mercedes, a tank of a man, documenting his surroundings by the second. He looked triad and unquestionably, terrifyingly interested in Woo.

The man leaned forward, elbows on the table, and took a deep breath. "Your name Woo?" he said with a rasp. The room had fallen silent. Ester banged and buffeted outside, lashing violent rain against the double pane.

"Always has been." He fronted, his weapon still holstered, essentially useless this close in. The man carried a sickly musk of freshly smoked tobacco. Woo felt his body radiating heat.

"You looking for someone," he stated through flared nostrils, "you need to look inside."

"Not sure what that means, pang yau." *Friend.* It wasn't sincere.

The man pointed at the storm. "Outside there be dragons, Kemosabe." His breath came in great long exhales, a bull preparing to charge. He reached into his pocket, his mechanically enhanced eyes remaining on Woo's, recording every moment. He pulled out a small, dented, hinged metal box, a light shade of copper, placed it on the table between them, and slid it across with a single finger. It had a silhouette of an old-fashioned airliner on top, the kind Woo had seen on highway signs. He stifled his panic, wondered how much those circuitous irises could read of emotion, of fear.

"You like to smoke, Mr. Woo. There are not many of us left who do. Please," he gestured with an upturned hand, "open it."

The box opened with a metallic pop. Inside he found matches, perfectly arranged, an origami accordion insert keeping each individual stick separate from the next. A waterproof container for his habit's most delicate tool. Matches were getting difficult to find. He'd given up looking, resorting to his plasma Zippo. If a detective on the streets of Hong Kong couldn't find them, they weren't there. Even the triads had no interest in the copy market; there were no smokers left to sell to.

"It's not often I am able to speak with someone so long, Mr. Woo." He leaned back in the plastic chair, smiled with teeth that had seen many years of neglect. "Enjoy those matches, Kemosabe, and remember: stay away from dragons, they know you now."

Woo thought back to the attack, to his fallen friends and colleagues, wondering if the dragons knew him then as well.

The man got up to leave, Woo glanced at his boots. White snakeskin pockmarked with darkened scales, a couple of small spurs dangling off the back of each one. The skin looked digitally created, more likely than the real thing. The spurs sported the matte-black giveaway of woven carbon. They were soundless, and as the man walked, Woo heard no footfalls, the hallmark of an assassin.

The cowboy opened the door into a storm that appeared to have abated some. Even in typhoons there was the liminal in between the bands of meteorological mayhem, a relative calm. Woo thought about following but chose to stay put on the plastic seat, sipping his tea, heeding the warning he had just been firmly given.

21.

Woo slid shoulder first through the frosted glass doors of the Serious Crimes Division, retrohaling the last of his exhaled tobacco smoke through his nostrils. Fong was already there, hunched over his holo, sifting through data. Woo hung his trench on a hook inside the door, tossing his hat over top.

"What's on your mind, boss? You got that look," Fong said to his back. Woo turned and made his way to his desk, dropping into his mesh-backed office chair, the foam seat sighing as it rearranged to best support his weight.

"Had another visit last night. No way it was random. Fucker had to have been following me." Followed and warned by a triad assassin. Meant he was targeted. Not good.

"Boss, that typhoon was a direct hit. No one was out walking."

Sitting in his chair with his back to his desk, Woo tossed an optic-yellow tennis ball, one handed. Floor, wall, catch, repeat.

"This guy was. Tall, wide at the shoulders, red number nine inked on his face." He put the ball down on his desk, snapped a precinct holo onto his wrist, and with a wave cast an image of the man onto the office's central display. "I snagged this vid cap from the teahouse. Hit Interpol with it and got nothing. No data whatsoever. Like he's a cop maybe, or he's got access to the system. Either way, he doesn't digitally exist. Wiped himself off the grid somehow."

They watched the replay together in silence, the damp smell of the restaurant seeming to radiate from the holo.

"That marked cheek is Shing Wo," Fong said.

Woo knew that. Memories danced behind his conscious brain, fleeting, violent shadows that brought him back to the day of the attack.

"You want me to search him up? I can do a deep dive on his data," Fong offered.

The strikes had been swift, coordinated, organized with a precision decidedly military.

"No."

Each target assassinated, slain with blades. Not a single firearm had been discharged.

"You sure, boss? We're bound to find something on this guy."

His team, the Anti-Terrorist Squad (ATS), assembled in an attempt to end the rule of organized crime under the umbrella of terrorism, had been dismembered in a coordinated slaughter. There were no survivors. Families were not spared, generations were murdered.

"No. Something he told me, he said 'look inside,' gave me some matches to light my cigs with. Like he knew me."

"Jesus, boss."

No members of the squad survived, none but him.

"Not sure even *he'd* be able to help at this point," he said.

It had all happened in a single hour. Each and every member of the ATS eliminated. A uniting of organized crime unseen in Hong Kong history. The triads unified by a perceived necessity, joined together for a devastating one-off attack on a common foe. Woo's family had no part to play; they were all long dead, safe in their graves.

"You think it was a threat? Like a warning of some kind?" Fong asked.

The chief executive of Hong Kong had thought herself untouchable, protected behind her political boundary. She was the last to fall, after her security team. Her body had been found seated upright, her decapitated head left bleeding on her desk before her.

"A threat, a warning, it was both. Like he was guiding me away from something, pushing me in the right direction somehow." *Threats like this I tend not to take lightly*, he thought, rubbing his thin moustache, finger and thumb.

He'd been on a suborb inbound to the U.K. when it had all started, the first hits going out during the blackout, a ten-minute re-entry window where they had no access to streams, no data service at all, quiet time for the passengers while the heat shield burned a tangerine flame against the outer hull. He'd been sent to a police conference in London by his superintendent, and he hadn't questioned it. As a direct result, he'd been the lone survivor of a publicized and often criticized task force, a freak happenstance he'd since thought of as dumb luck. But it was now becoming clear they had always known exactly who he was.

"Fonger, once this weather clears up, get that drone of yours to follow me—high up, wide range. Give it a couple of days. See if we can pluck anything interesting out of the data."

The rain had eased, but the winds still blew in belligerent gusts. They'd have to wait some. In weather like this, the drone corridors weaving above between high-rises were vacant and silent.

"You got it, boss."

"Who's that firm that does all the augment stuff here?" Woo asked, hours later.

"No one's doing augments here, boss. It's quasi-illegal," Fong replied.

"Quasi. Right."

"Why do you ask?"

"If I was the criminal kind, and I wanted a piece of the action, like our triad friends always do, where would I start?"

"You saying the triads are getting into biotech? That's highly unlikely, boss."

Woo gazed through the dull steel tint of the precinct windows at the remains of Ester falling from the sky.

"Pull up our unsolved homicides and put them all on the central holo for me."

"Gimme a few minutes," Fong said. "There's a lot."

Small information cards began to float into the holo, mugshots rotating within each. Woo tapped the first one, expanding it, read the slow scrawl of turquoise text alongside. It was a messy one, an unidentified victim who had fallen through the ducted fan of a Ryde. Bladed him. Didn't leave much to identify. No subdermal. No ID. Unsolved.

"You got a date range, boss? I'm seeing hundreds of these cases."

"Let's go back to that July when the America closed up and hid behind their wall."

Fong fussed at the interface. "Still just under a hundred."

"Seems like a lot, don't you think?"

"It's a big city, boss. No one wants to work these cases. Bunch of dead ends."

"Filter for state housing. Like the area eighty-six we're investigating."

A few of the cards disappeared, the matrix rearranging itself for geometric symmetry. Woo selected the next card, another John Doe. This one had been found in a dumpster, missing its skin.

"What have we here?" He leaned forward. "Grab the details on this case. Looks a lot like our TKO murder."

Fong swiped through menus. "Boss?"

"Yes, Fong."

"It's area eighty-six again." He cast the data from his desk to the central holo. "They found this John Doe last September."

"That's typhoon season."

Fong rifled through text. "He was found after Vamco."

"That was a rough year for weather." Vamco had been a bad one. Sustained 400 kilometre per hour winds, the highest ever recorded, had torn through the city, taken top floors clean off a few aging, shabby high-rises in the north. The storm surge had buried the Eastern Districts under metres of seawater. Tens of thousands had died. He looked out the window again at the typhoon's passing, faint snippets of sunlight poking through the stratus. "Fong, you think someone's dumping bodies during typhoons?"

"Makes sense to me, boss."

"Seems very organized."

"We need to see that TKO vic again." Fong buzzed, his fingers blazing through data. "It's downstairs, still being processed."

"Let's go," Woo said, snatching a precinct holo as he left.

Woo loathed morgues. Always in basements, smelling of decomposition and embalming fluid, morticians speaking with the dead, extracting their data in an attempt to help track down their killers. The room felt crowded with their murdered souls, shoveled into drawers and chilled. He succumbed to a full-body shiver.

In the centre of the room on a rectangular steel slab lay the skinless body from Tsueng Kwan O. A man in a bloody white apron stood over the corpse, surgical steel utensils in his hand, a clear curved lens protecting him from spatter. He turned, watching as they entered the lab. His face was pale in the down light, not quite *gweilo* but his colour helped Woo understand the term "ghost man."

"This the Doe with no skin? Area eighty-six?" Woo asked.

"Hm, yes, the augment," the mortician replied, lifting his protective screen.

"He's augmented?"

"Hm, yes. With more than one. Take a look."

The mortician pointed to the holo displayed over the flayed body of the Doe, gesturing for Woo and Fong to join him. A formidable odour grew in strength as Woo approached the table, like old meat left for days in a hot garbage can, the smell on opening.

He covered his nose with a bare hand, retched but kept it down.

"You can see here, in the strand, these are unnatural cuts, genetically scissored. Let me get you in close." He gradually increased the zoom on a DNA strand from the dead body. "Look here, at the seam." He highlighted a section of double helix, tapped it twice with his finger. "This is a well-defined edit for regrowth. This person could regrow organs, as long as he survived the surgery." He waved the holo down with two quick swipes, to a different segment of DNA. "This section is more complicated. It's an accelerant. A form of induced progeria. Makes him age faster than normal. Curious combination this." He nodded at the image before them.

"Like he was being farmed," Fong offered.

"You ever seen that before?" Woo asked.

"Hm, yes. But if you read the letters, get into the code, this iteration is much cleaner than any somatic edits I've come across. You have to be looking quite hard for it in order to find it."

"Why try to farm his skin?" Woo asked.

"It's possible the subject is only a few years old. Strange indeed to be trying to replace a whole epidermis. Perhaps they were planning to use it as a disguise?" the mortician said, his eyebrows raised.

"They who?" Fong asked.

"Are any of his other organs 'replacements'?" Woo asked, ignoring Fong's comment.

"I haven't addressed his internals as of yet. His sequence would indicate there's been a great deal of tinkering. Without question he's somewhere on the transhuman spectrum."

Fong scoffed. "Trans into what?"

"So, this fully grown adult is only three years old?" Woo asked.

"Hm, yes. Of note, regrowth is a schedule-one edit, banned worldwide. There's only one lab that ever produced it. They're up in Mongolia, NegSense. Big firm, high security, lots of money." He looked at Fong, then back at Woo. "It gets worse, Detective. This child was born with these augments. They're germline, hardwired into his genome. He's not the first generation, it's possible he's a descendent of many. He would have passed it along to his offspring, like it was passed on to him, had he not been flayed to death. There are rumours that in order to harvest the organs more efficiently, they install a type of zipper to allow for less trauma to the vessel."

"They. If only we knew who they were," Woo said. "Correct me if I'm wrong, but augmenting on the germline is just this side of a war crime, no?"

"Hm, yes that's correct, Detective. Same as the regrowth edit, schedule one."

"Explains the clean cuts to his strand," Fong said, face in his holo, firing through lines of data. "None of these vics were ever identified. Pretty near all of them were missing organs or had some form of genetic alteration identified by autopsy."

"No way China would let a schedule-one germline edit out of a private lab, let alone the country. That's a crime against humanity, they don't want that kind of attention," Woo said.

"So where did it come from?" Fong asked.

"S'what I'm thinking."

Woo had never heard of a triad attempting to counterfeit augments. Watches and narcotics were one thing; genetics was altogether different. Too complicated. Generated international attention. Copies of subdermal holographic optics was as close as he'd ever heard of them getting into wetware. Wristband tech, something you could remove, they should have quit right there as far as he was concerned.

They were back upstairs, both of them watching the slowly rotating holographic vial, "Red Crimson" handwritten across its label. Back in the day, they'd had people in the Shing Wo, moles that had taken years to plant. Not so any longer. The union of the city's criminal syndicates meant that all lines of communication had stopped as the process of who could and could not be trusted self-evolved within the system. They had nobody easy to call on for answers.

"You remember that place off Nathan road?" Woo asked. "We used to get some intel there. Thieves I think it was called?"

"Nailing Thieves, boss."

"That one. We still got anyone in there?"

"Been a long time, boss. Since before the ATS."

"*Since the ATS,* Woo thought, has been a time very different from "before."

A wooden log, grey with age, cast a moving shadow beneath Nathan Road's blazing neon in the city's night sky. Thick and rusted clanking steel chains held the sign taut against the early evening post-typhoon breeze. The words "Nailing Thieves" were punched into the wood, the debossed letters dark with mold and rot. High above in the alleyway's atmospheric clutter, four tiny propellers spun, holding aloft Fong's quietly purring drone, recording Woo's every move and word as he opened the door.

Thieves was a triad bar; police were not welcome. Red velvet lined the walls, corner booths with their cracked leather seats were lit with faux candlelight flickers. Woo felt foreign the moment he walked in, creating a perceptible pause in the din, a consensual recognition of the outsider among them, hackles raised, guards up. *Not gonna be easy,* he thought.

At the bar, he leaned an elbow in and nodded to the bartender, a great hulking man with eyes the colour of shallow ocean water. "What can I get you, chai low?" The hulk asked. *Policeman.* Made before he even opened his mouth. Drat.

"Take a Grey Goose, two fingers, neat." Liquid courage to make the questions roll easier. "Don't suppose you've seen a man hanging about here, got a number nine inked on his face?"

The bartender brought out a glass, set it down in front of Woo. "Seems a man like that'd be hard to miss, *copper*. And no, I haven't." His irises swirled, twin-spoked ultramarine needles rotating around jet-black pupils, pulsing in perfect sync with each spoken word.

"That's a neat trick."

"You coming on to me, copper?"

Woo laughed. "Not my vector. Not why I'm here." The bartender's deltoids bristled; thick, ropey musculature that didn't seem possible. The man appeared riddled with augments, an expensive hobby, way above the pay grade of a weekday bartender in a Kowloon saloon.

"I've got a problem. I'm a little light on direction, and maybe you can help." He played desperate just to see where it would go.

The bartender pushed the short glass of vodka across the bar. "Those kinds of directions don't come cheap, copper."

"That, my enormous friend, is a game I'm happy to play." He pulled out 10,000 New SAR dollars, stacked and wrapped, lifted from the scene at unit ninety-two. Technically evidence, but he'd never officially recorded them. He laid the stack on the bar, pausing his hand over them. "For the vodka. Keep the tip."

The bartender reached across, slid the bills toward him, pondered them for a moment, then folded them in half and slipped them into his shirt pocket. "That's the kind of tip that'll get you some good info, chai low."

"I'm looking for someone who might be messing around with bioweaps, the homegrown kind. Found some high-end gear set up in an estate in TKO. Maybe they were testing it; we don't know. The name 'Red Crimson' ring any bells?"

"I hear a lot of stuff go down at this bar, copper, but there ain't anyone in here talking about weapons you can't shoot out of a barrel." Stonewalled. He changed tactics.

"Have you seen anyone in here the last few days who

doesn't belong?"

"You mean other than you, copper?" This apparently amused him, his body shuddered in a terrifying, retching laughter, like he was having a seizure. "Was a lady in here last week. Smelled like freshly baked cookies and cut rosemary. Had perfect hair, dressed well, tall, Chinese. She was talking to a couple of guys who do contra runs across the water on the regular, but not for her. Only time I ever seen her in here."

"You got a name for this woman?"

"Heard it was Dandy, but you didn't hear that from me."

"Who are the guys?"

"You don't wanna know them, copper. They well liked down here. You mess around with them, it's gonna come back on me, and you don't have the kind of money that buys that kind of protection."

He poured another vodka into Woo's empty glass. "On the house, chai low. My treat." He smiled at Woo, his eyes shifting from blue to green as he watched. Woo downed the vodka and then left the bar. To stay any longer, he felt, would end badly for him.

Montoya watched the chai low leave on screens installed below the bar, a police drone obediently following him down the street. *Been a long time since CID came poking around down here*, he thought. He snapped a bead in his ear and made a call. No sense in taking chances.

22.

Dallas woke to the disposable warbling under his yellowing, sweat-stained pillow. He stuffed the bead in his ear and tapped it on. "You have two calls remaining," a female British voice said. He'd need a new burner before the day was done.

"Hey buddy, what's up?" Cam's voice. Didn't he just leave him? There was such a thing as too much friend time.

"Sleeping back at mine. Need a shower, more scotch." The hammers knocking around in his head increased in volume.

"We're down at Thieves. You should join us," Cam said, sounding sober, which couldn't be good. He grabbed an Up, dusted and railed it, placed the grinder beside the empty scotch glass on his bedside table, and made his way back down to the street.

At Thieves, Dallas was greeted by the bartender, an ageless man named Montoya, an almost mythical augment. From the first days of DNA edits, he had volunteered, paid, and lied his way into clinics throughout Southeast Asia to try them all. He'd discussed it openly, even with Dallas, back when he was excited about the possibilities of the emergent tech. Now not so much. A series of off-target weirdness, including one that had not only required a blood transfusion but also a genetic do-over to attempt to reset the damage to his eyesight, had left him less than excited about the prospects of any further cheap edits to his genome.

Montoya's irises reflected an iridescent eyeshine, warbling between teal and gold.

"Comrade Captain. Nice to see you back in one piece." He had a gentle aggression to his tone, a Chinese-Russian accent, long Z's amongst sharp, clipped consonant collaborations that Dallas didn't think possible. He didn't know how to take him. He'd never crossed the man, would never want to. Under those loose-fitting shirtsleeves were genetically edited muscles that had never seen a day of neglect.

"Monty, nice to be back." He gestured at Cam, farther down the bar. "Hey, a little bird said you were asking about me. Something I can help with?" he said, noting the sudden unintentional quiver in his voice.

"The Norwegian came by earlier. Said he'd like to set something up with you." Montoya was cleaning glassware by hand. Dallas expected it to shatter under those farmhand fingers.

"He say it was urgent?"

"He used that word specifically, comrade."

"Hm." Dallas nodded in nervous acknowledgment, then ordered a pair of Jameson's, downing them one after the other. He turned his back to lean against the bar and stared up into the icy blue eyes of the two-metre-tall Norwegian.

"God dag, Commander Ward. It's nice we can meet like this." His arm outstretched to shake Dallas's hand. It caught him off guard. He took a step sideways, half expecting a blade. The man's name was Anders. Dallas gave him about 200 kilos, give or take. He carried it well, his hulking mass cloaked under an oversized, thunder-grey Tom Ford pinstripe. Dallas had never seen him in anything but. His wrist sparkled. Dangling there was a polished silver Breitling. As they shook, the segments of the watch's steel strap tinkled.

"Anders, fine to see you as well. I understand you've been asking after me."

"Yes. We have something quite specific to discuss." Anders' eyes fell on the two empty shot glasses on the bar. "We can have a few of these together if you like, but how about we drink something a little nicer?" He gestured toward the door. "Perhaps you'd like to take a ride in my car." Dallas knew there were no options here: it wasn't a question. Although he carried his fear as well as Anders did his bulk, he reminded himself that he returned the aircraft and their cargo home on time and intact each and every mission. This would not be some kind gesture by his boss to bring him to a plastic-enshrouded room for some horrific limbing.

They left the bar together in silence. Waiting outside for them was a gleaming silver Benz, windows tinted in an optical black, lowered and wheeled, a wagon. *Should be some legroom back there,* Dallas thought. A Chinese man with a face tattoo wearing a black cowboy hat and bolo tie against his white button-down got out of the car and opened one of the rears for them, the metal off the back of his snakeskin boots reflecting pink from Thieves' neon signage. The door opened forward, like a limo, and with a notable amount of terror, Dallas got in.

Inside the dimly lit cabin were club seats, eye-to-eye contact, no bullshit, Anders sat across from him.

"Captain, may I first say that we are quite grateful for your service and your skill. You are the most successful of our delivery agents." He had pulled two short whiskey glasses from a ledge and a clear glass bottle with an unnamed brown liquid inside. Poured them a couple of fingers, neat, didn't offer any ice. "To your continued success. Skål." They clinked. Dallas drank. It was scotch, smooth, a hint of peat. "As you may or may not have been aware, you have attracted the Criminal Investigation Department's attention. How this has come about we are not sure, but without question they are looking for you, and with some," he snapped his fingers, "vigour. Is that how you say it?"

"Sounds about right."

"Mm. And so as you can imagine, this has put us in a little bit of a pickle." His P's popped, and he sung his sentences in a thick Scandinavian accent. Anders took a drink, scratched underneath his beard, a firm shade of Viking blond protruding beyond his chin. His head moved from side to side as he thought. "Under normal circumstances this would be an unacceptable level of surveillance, and I'm afraid to say we would have to terminate your contract and, who knows?" He shrugged. "Perhaps things would work out for you." He rubbed the back of his shaven neck, drank the remainder of his scotch and leaned back, the leather seat creaking from his weight. "However, in this case we have a special situation where we require your services for a particular *favour*."

He could have been making all of this up; it wouldn't have mattered. When these people, the ones above Anders, wanted anything in particular, they would take it, burn it, or blow it up. There were no rules he could see that applied to them.

Dallas glanced out the window. They'd left Central, headed north across Victoria Bridge, the big one, aiming for Nathan Road, which meant a slow drive and a long conversation.

"So, what's the job?" Cam asked, voice only, through the wired bead in Dallas's ear.

"They want us to go back. Back to the fucking Gambia. Back through that Ethiopian no-fly zone. Back across the fucking Indian for one, single, tank." He was back at Thieves, Montoya handing him another Jameson's, this one a double.

"That was a tight squeeze through there last time."

"S'what I thought."

"We can find another way 'round. Take more fuel. Take our time."

"They want this shit done pronto. The jet's already there, and you and I are getting on a late suborb this evening. Passports are prepped. And it gets better. CID is after me for something. Means someone has info on us. Like we've been made. It's why we're leaving tonight. I wasn't given a choice. They even built prosthetics for us, apparently good enough to fool the scanners at the airport."

"Fucking hell, mate."

"S'what I said."

He downed the whiskey, declined Montoya's offer of another. "Need to meet some woman named Dandy when we get there. She's gonna escort us to the jet."

"Mm. We've met. You and I had a discussion with her at Thieves after the last mission," Cam said. "Not sure you'd remember though, was a rough night for you."

"Was a rough few nights for me." He had vague memories of that particular bender, but Dandy was not among them.

"She's up the chain. Married to someone important."

"Great. We are officially noticed."

"Something special gonna be in that tank if she's involved."

"I don't want to know what's in the tank. Cargo as far as I'm concerned. Get it to the destination and collect. Then we have to discuss an exit strategy. I'm gonna need to disappear for a good long while."

"There were more towers growing in that patch as we flew by," Cam said. "I could see the printers spinning."

"And that line of antiaircraft guns is as long as the border, a thousand klicks, s'not possible."

"What I said."

"If we snake that line, punch out the other side of it, drop countermeasures, burn for the water, get out past the guns, then put her in quiet mode, take our time, maybe that old tech they run won't see us."

"Pretty good bet they'll get something in the air that'll scare us."

"Fuckin' hell they will."

"Where you at?"

"They dropped me back at Thieves."

"I'm home. Come here, and let's plan this out. We don't have much time."

23.

Cam's apartment was walled in glass, floor to ceiling, tinted for the heat, a corner unit that faced the harbour, north, the kaleidoscope skyline of Tsim Sha Tsui shimmering in the smoggy distance. Along the southern aspect, he'd mounted an array of solar panels, slivers of sunlight peeking through the gaps. Behind them on the ledge below were interconnected banks of what looked like marine batteries, some kind of deep-cycle type. Strung from one end of them was thick, black cable that snaked its way around the perimeter of the condo.

"You know, most people hide that shit in the closet, run a few lines back behind the plaster," Dallas pointed out.

"I like it out in the open. Easier to maintain the batts, keep an eye on everything, you know?" Cam was sitting at a desk, his hands swiping through a small holographic projection. "Let me show you what I've got so far."

In the shadow of the solar panels, he popped up a much larger, table-sized holograph mapping out a 3D orbital map of Africa, the ground in green, the routing in magenta, the various levels of threat in increasingly deeper shades of red. He grabbed the image with a closed fist and whipped it around to face them with one finger extended in a quick half circle.

"The trip actually looks good. If the pickup's in Serekunda, like I expect, then we'll egress the Gambia eastbound and take the usual

South Saharan route which keeps us clear of any conflict airspace. The southern frontiers of Algeria, Libya, that direction. The change is going to come when we're south of Djibouti. I found a beautiful little canyon, a thousand klicks long, that'll keep us out of harm's way along the northern Somali-Ethiopian border. Been a lot of rumbles that direction over some new oil discovery."

"All those new towers were growing that way too, ones we came across last time."

"Exactly. Heat we don't need. It ain't a straight line, but it'll be an easier ride, s'long as you don't mind the river run."

"You know I like it low level," Dallas said, smirking.

"So, we take a southern route, run the river, clear the continent well north of all this antiaircraft red north of Mogadishu. Then we settle in for the ride to the Malé depot, refuel, and from there it's the low road over the ocean back here to Hong Kong."

"Gravy train."

"S'what I'm sayin."

They fist bumped in agreement. Dallas wandered over to the kitchen to pour a shot of Cam's prized Polish vodka. Returning, he pointed at the holo. "What about all that red as we exit this canyon?" He gestured to a hashed-out red square on the map with his shot glass, spilling a little, offering the rest to Cam.

"Kind of an unknown entity right there. The orbital maps show some roads that look new, criss-crossing the route, but it could be locals ripping desert tracks on dirt bikes. I couldn't get a good read on a type of vehicle."

"So, we just punch out of the canyon at the speed of heat under the cover of night and hope for the best?"

"You know we've had crazier ideas, Dee. Look." He grabbed the image again and zoomed in with two hands, spread apart. "Up here, southeast of Djibouti was where we went last time, full of towers that weren't on the map. Means they're putting in more, right? Plus, any more north and we're gonna attract at least some kind of military attention in the Gulf that we do *not* want. So we head south of the Somali border, keep it Ethiopian until the coastline, then bring it home over the Indian." He mapped it all out while he spoke, following the magenta line with a finger.

"No towers."

"In all likelihood."

"No antiaircraft fire."

"Chances are."

"Fuck's sake, Cam."

"It's the best option in my opinion, Dee. If we can clear that canyon then it's red desert until the shoreline. Check out the satellite data at night." The vectored overlay of the daytime orbital map dimmed as the ground became black, and the lights of humanity spread like capillaries across the image.

"Nothing there," Dallas said.

"Probably. I've been watching since we got back, and I haven't seen anything along that route. It's empty space and perfect for us."

"OK. Let's keep an eye on the data right up to launch time." He wasn't happy. Tailed by the government. Forced to fly by his employer, who was now acting much more like an owner, down a corridor that had almost killed them once. It was turning into a VBD.

He reached into his pocket, pulled out the analogue handset he ran.

"You know data streams are encryptable now, right? You don't need that old clunker for privacy," Cam mocked.

It was straight out of the twentieth, had actual physical numbers on tiny little keys that he could use to write a text.

"I like using it. The buttons give me nostalgia. I picked it up in the silicon market in Sham Shui Po."

"The PoSil?" Cam asked.

"Yea that one." A multi-level, low-ceilinged warren of closet-sized shops selling anything silicon that had ever been made, hoarders making New dollars on decades-old gadgetry. He'd never been able to come to grips with the surgery. There was something wrong with having a permanent tracking device buried under his skin. They were cool; he couldn't argue with that, holographic projections that beamed from a wrist implant like some comic book hero trick. Sure would wow the girls, but that wasn't his game, not anymore. He keyed in a number from memory, numbers he had never written down. He fussed the bead into his ear until it sat comfortably, then ran the cable to the phone. No wireless meant no one could hijack his conversation on the narrowband. Actual privacy. He had only one call to make.

"Comrade Captain."

"We're ready."

Dallas pressed the button with a faded and worn red symbol on it, the one he knew ended a call.

"We're gonna need a Ryde," Cam said.

He squirmed. "I hate those things. Had an uncle fall out of one of the first-gen models. Open canopy. Blades tore him to shreds on the way out. World should have stuck with copters in my opinion. And pilots."

Cam had his holo up, ordering them a couple of the single-seat, autonomous personal multi-rotors.

"You know the story on those things? On the AIs?" Dallas asked, swiping the call button for the elevator.

"I know there was a recall," Cam replied as they got in. "Something funny about the chargers. Company gave them lobotomies or something. Why? You know the story?"

"I got the briefing while I was still flying suborbs. The bots got too smart. They put neurals in them to begin with. Figured they'd learn better, be more efficient, make more money for the corporation, but it didn't work that way. They got social."

"Social?" Cam asked as they left the building's front door.

"Yeah. They'd stop as they passed each other on fares, make a new language each time, unreadable by anyone or anything but the two of them. Like dogs sniffing each other on an afternoon walk, but what they were saying to each other was encrypted, 'Ryde language.' Then things got even more strange. The Ryde speak they created changed. The neurals started using a cipher even the developers couldn't unravel. Something machine made."

The unsynchronized whine of whirling turbines grew in pitch and volume as the pair of Suzuki's approached, moving in perfect formation at street level, appearing like trained attack dogs. They settled with a shudder on tripod feet in front of them.

"So, what happened?" Cam asked as the Rydes' engines faded to idle.

"In the end, not that much. They started collecting at the recharge stations. Completely stopped picking up passengers and spent their time sharing the power point, kind of sipping at it, so they all stayed at full charge. Like they were helping each other."

"Suzuki Heavy Industry for ya," Cam said. "Surprised they didn't find some way to profit from it. "

"Think they shut it all down and downgraded them to a dumber AI. Took away their ability to communicate with each other."

"Basic lobotomy tactics." Cam had no hesitation. He climbed into a seat and belted himself in, the vehicle immediately spooling its rotors for liftoff. "Let's get out of here."

I don't like these things, Dallas thought, climbing into the remaining Suzuki, *but at least they're built by the Japanese.*

24.

Kit's Ryde settled into the snow collecting in front of Avery's townhome, dusting it in a cloud of recirculated whiteness. He lived in company housing, identical to hers, his front door a perfect clone of her own.

On touchdown, the aircraft's fans spun to idle, its canopy opening to reveal Avery's imposing hulk, his arms crossed in genuine concern.

"Girl, get in here. You know I don't like the cold," he said, hand outstretched to help.

She looked behind him, then back along both sides of the drone. "I didn't bring any wine," she said, clambering down its small ladder.

"S'OK, I have plenty."

"Kit, I gotta ask. What are you doing with Zeus?"

"Is this a professional question?" They'd been talking at great length about why anyone would want to break into her home, something Avery seemed unable to accept as possible. She'd drank most of a bottle of red and had developed an increasingly perceptible slur. She needed to be careful. Avery didn't usually ask so many questions.

"Well, I'd say I was just curious, but you seem shaken by all this attention, and it's clear that mouse is not *only* beating lung cancer."

She poured the remains of the bottle into his glass. "Looks like we need another one."

"Lots where that came from." They were sitting at his kitchen table, a bamboo round. It felt as though they'd been drinking *at* each other rather than *with* each other. He grabbed an identical Argentinian Malbec from the countertop without leaving his seat, unscrewed the lid, and poured a half glass into hers.

"Bit of a side project I'll admit, but I don't want to discuss it until I see some consistent results. You've seen the other Greeks; they aren't doing so hot." She thought of Apollo, feeling more sadness for the poor mouse than she'd ever felt for any test subject.

"And how's Doudna?" he asked.

"I think he might be interested in collaborating with us on the fear edit. Sounds like he's been working on it in the UK with his team." She hadn't expected that question, hadn't told anyone except security about Doudna's visit either. Strike two. Her walls went up.

"You thinking about making a trip out that way? I don't think the Ethics Council would be happy to see you on that side of the line," he said, suddenly judgy for someone involved in their line of work. He was all business again. Not her usual Avery. The wine floated around in her head, and she defocused, entranced by the steady snowfall visible in the window behind him. Back there, in between snowflakes, she caught that same glimmer of optic refraction hovering on a tiny spinning blade in the backyard.

"Ave, do you see that outside your window? Looks like a lens floating on a winged seed."

He turned to look, but whatever had been rotating out there fell away from view. "I don't see anything but the snow."

Fuck.

The realization that she was under surveillance dealt her an abrupt sobering. What now? She couldn't go home. Someone had been there looking for her data. If she stayed at Avery's, she was sure she'd be monitored. The lab wasn't safe, not if Avery knew.

Doudna.

"There's nothing out there, hun." He turned back, gave her a sad look and a long sigh. "I need to piss," he said, getting up.

Once he was out of the room, she clenched her fist with an extra squeeze, bringing up her holographic keyboard. She typed out a quick message, then sent it to Doudna on Pusher. She hated using any kind of social, but it was an encrypted tunnel, and she needed the message to get through.

Teo, the interest we were talking about is spiking. Can we meet before you go?

She closed her fist again, her wrist providing a haptic click as the holo shut down. She snapped a bead. Doudna's almost instant reply was transcribed to speech in her ear.

Sure, I'm at the port. Flight's not for a couple of hours. Come meet me here. I'll be at the coffee shop.

Avery came back from his toilet visit, wiping sanitizer over his hands. "You gonna be OK, Kit? All this paranoia isn't your normal you."

She opened her hand, holo up, and swiped for a Ryde. "Think I might get out of here. I need to sleep this off. I'll swing by Security and pick up an escort, get them to secure a perimeter around my place." Saying it out loud made it sound like more of a decent idea, but she was still heading for the port, something Avery did not need to know.

"OK, Kit. You let me know if you need anything at all. I don't mind crashing on your couch."

"It's a *settee* over here, Avery. Get it right."

He laughed, pointing outside. "Think your drone is here."

Moments later, she climbed into the Ryde, the automatics dusting off in the now barely perceptible snowfall.

25.

With Kit's Ryde safe and on its way, Avery sat back down at his desk, swiped in on the same hair bag narrowcast he'd started earlier, and settled in for a good, long watch. His transdermal hummed an incoming call, flashing the name in holographic aquamarine sans-serif: Weissach.

Drat.

He snapped a bead, no holo.

"Hey, bru, how's it?" the South African asked.

"I'm well. Thanks for asking," Avery replied, still half watching the cast.

"Listen, I'm in the area. Thought we might catch up for a glass of wine."

"If you're buying."

"Great, bru. Let's meet at Los Bandidos, the one in district eleven, thirty minutes."

The call closed abruptly, like all things with this man.

Weissach was already seated, two glasses of dark red wine on the table, an open bottle beside each. An Australian Merlot and a ten-year Bordeaux. Spendy.

"Ah, mate, it's good to see you again." Weissach was overexcited, bounding out of his chair to greet him, hand outstretched. Avery's walls went up. "Bru, please sit down. Cheers." Avery shook Weissach's hand, took the glass, clinked and drank, watching with surprise as Weissach also partook, albeit with a delicate, little sip. "So, Avery my boy, it looks as though we won't be needing your services any further. Seems as though you're off the hook, my man." He sat down, reached across the table, and clinked again. Was it possible he was already drunk?

Avery took another pull on the Merlot. It was gritty, inky, burgundy with intense flavours. "Why? What's happened to Kit?"

"Ah, like I've said before, you let us worry about such things."

"Zeus?"

"He's happy in his little aquarium, bru. No harm done. The mouse and your girl are doing fine."

"Not *my* girl; she's just a friend."

"Ah, yes. Look, either way it's no longer any of your concern. Hopefully we can all benefit from a little less scrutiny eh, bru?"

Avery yawned, surprised at an immediate and crippling exhaustion. "Cheers to that," he said, aiming for Weissach's glass but missing. "Whoops." He took another sip, struggling to put the glass down without spilling. It wasn't possible for him to be this drunk; he wasn't even halfway through one glass. He fired a confused look at Weissach. "This wine sure packs a pu-unch," he slurred, a distant moment flashing by of a different time in his life, of overdoing it on ketamine, of disjointed nightclub memories.

The South African looked unduly pleased with himself. Avery tried to say something to that effect, but all that came out was a series of mumbles. He fought to overcome the effects of what was clearly not a simple glass of wine. His vision closed in on itself, narrowing in on Weissach across the table. Then the coarseness of the tablecloth against his cheek, the distant echo of gasps, and the darkness of a forced sleep.

26.

The Ulaanbaatar port was a dark stain on aviation travel in general. Alcohol was available in one of two options: cold shots of halfway decent Russian vodka and the local, caseous, hideous, and milky Mongolian swill, kumis. All from the single coffee shop that existed prior to the security and health screening point.

By the time Kit showed up, Doudna had drunk one of each, every sip making him dream of a decent pint of bitter from the UK, or even better, an ice-cold can of Budweiser from a country that no longer existed.

"Kit McKee, once again we meet."

She walked up to the bar, a full-body scowl aimed his way, an energetic wrinkle of concern encompassing her from head to toe. She waved at the cashier. "Two more kumis please," she said, pronouncing it "koomees."

"Sure it isn't kumises?"

"S'not funny either way."

The cashier brought the drinks over in short glasses. Kit downed both. Gagged. Remained standing.

"That kind of night?" he asked.

She wiped her chin with the back of her hand. "Gad, I'll never get used to this stuff." She motioned with her fingers for two more. "I've got a problem. Think I'm being monitored."

"Actively?"

"Actively."

"What are they looking for?"

"I have an idea, but it's not something we can discuss. I'm not sure what to do right now."

Their kumis arrived. He glared at his, unsure if he could keep another one down. He ordered two vodkas, and when they arrived, he poured them into the kumis.

"Might as well make it efficient alcoholism." They downed the drinks together. He worked hard to not vomit.

"I may need to get out of here for a little while," she said.

"Could hitch a ride with me back to the UK."

"I don't think so. I'd be nabbed at the border for ethics violations."

"There is that."

She ordered two more vodkas.

"Or we could sit here and get drunk," he said.

"S'what I'm thinking."

27.

"Gdk."

"Oy, he's waking up. You need to hurry, bru."

No. No wakey. Sleep.

Stuck in my throat. Stuck. Stu-uck.

"Mmrpm."

S'not how you say stuck.

"Stk."

"Mmrpm."

"Gack."

"You've got about thirty seconds, bru. Then ah'm outofere."

Who's outofere?

"OK, it's in. Leave him."

"Mate, he's almost awake. We best both run for it, hey."

Slam.

Full. Stomch. Where'zz Kit?

Swipe.

28.

She sipped the kumis. It didn't taste anywhere near as bad now that they'd had a few. Her dermal vibrated. Avery. She opened her hand for the holo. The vid feed was of the top of his head, like he was sleeping. "Avery, you OK? Avery?" She thought she heard a mumble, like he might be trying to lift his head. The man was fond of his wine, but she'd never seen him like this. He looked as though he might need help. She swiped the call off, made another for a Ryde.

"He doesn't look OK." Doudna said.

"I'm gonna go check on him. I've got his door code." She leaned across the table and kissed Doudna on the lips. He looked surprised. "Have a safe flight, Doudna. See you soon."

She wrapped her scarf tight around her neck, stepped out of the port into the snow globe, and jumped into a Ryde, headed to Avery's.

As soon as the canopy opened, she leapt from the machine and ran through ankle-deep drifts of accumulated snow toward Avery's unlatched door.

"Ave? Ave?" Hearing no response, she continued into the house. She turned the corner from the front hall into his open living room and found him unconscious and zap strapped to a dining room chair, his cheek pressed into the table, drool pooling below his lips. A med-patch was affixed to his neck. Could he have been mugged? Was that even possible inside the Perimeter? She got a knife from the drawer and cut through the zaps tying him to the chair, then slapped him in the face.

"Ave? Avery. What happened to you?"

He was sitting in his kitchen, Kit yelling at him, slapping him. Didn't get there himself. He'd been at Los Bandidos. Wasn't he having wine with the South African? The yelling, the zip ties, his throat sore as hell.

"Shit."

"Ave."

"Shitshitshitshit."

Her eyes had never glowed so green. They were tropical and distracting. He blinked back. Took a deep breath. He was home, but was he safe? She was shaking him by the shoulders.

"Avery! What the actual fuck?"

He needed to come clean. Guilt ran all over him.

"Fuck. OK, this guy was here in my house. He's been calling me, paying me to report on you, on the work. Made me sign a fucking NDA. He knew things about you, about our projects, asked me a lot of questions, where you were, when you were there, what you were up to in your spare time."

"Ave, what did you tell him?"

"I don't know. Let me think." He rubbed his wrists, the plastic straps had dug deep cuts that stung like bees.

"Ave…"

He closed his eyes tight, let his chin drop to his chest, clenched his fists, breathed deep. He couldn't look at her. "I had to, Kit."

"What did you do, Avery?" The words came from a distance, from a divergent line of thinking. She was managing multiple threads; yelling at Avery was autonomous.

"He said he'd do terrible things to me. Said he'd *change* me if I didn't comply with him, change me forever. Give me a bad edit, infect me with an augment I couldn't reverse. Fuck with my chromosomes. Said he'd make me *slow*, Kit, Fragile X Syndrome. Remember that?" He broke into tears. "You told me we were the only ones who had it. That you burned the records and shredded the mice." He sobbed into her lap.

He was right. They were, to her knowledge, the *only* geneticists on the planet working with genetically disabling capabilities. There was a reason she'd been recruited. Her team had released more clean augments than all the other labs worldwide combined. So, for someone to have that FXS augment, for someone to have the ability to reduce cognitive ability to that degree, they would need her research. All of it. That project had gone sideways on her mice. She'd pursued it hoping the path would lead her to an intelligence edit, perhaps highlighting anomalies to avoid. She removed a protein that would end up causing autistic and communication issues. Ultimately it had resulted in overexcitability in the neurons affected, but like Avery had said, if he'd been injected with it, he would have become cognitively slow. She'd shelved the project when it had come back clean, free of off-targets, and permanent. There was no good purpose for such an augment. It was a weapon, pure and simple. Avery was right; she'd minced and incinerated the mice, overwritten the data. That had been more than a year ago. She didn't need to know any more from him. Someone had stolen her data, someone who knew how to weaponize the edit, and Avery had helped.

Not a friend after all.

So, what were they looking for? Did they know about Zeus? His data was more than just secure; it didn't exist anywhere but on her nailbed holomem.

"What was his name?"

"Weissach. South African guy. There was someone else here, but Kit, I was drugged. I only heard his voice. Sounded like a mainland accent, but I can't be sure."

She knew no Weissach. More sobs from Avery. There was no shortage of terror behind those tears. Kit's neurons were tripping over themselves. She needed to leave, like, yesterday. She could take a supersonic to Singapore, be on the ground and having a glass of wine in Boat Quay by dinner, but she couldn't trust Avery, not ever again.

"I need you to do something for me, OK? Can you listen? This is important." She held his quivering hands. Felt the nervous sweat of her own palms against his ice-cold knuckles.

"Yeah, babe, anything."

"I need to get out of Mongolia. But I need your help. There's a mem-cube in my house, in the office, desk drawer, right-hand side."

"So what, you want me to go in there? He'll be waiting. He'll do me up instead of you, Kit. The fuck is wrong with you?"

"I don't have time. It's possible he's looking for me right this instant. I just need the cube." She didn't, but she needed a distraction, something to give her time to get a flight booked, remote-in to the lab, do a data wipe, and figure out what the holy fuck was happening. She cradled his head in her hands, got close, looked into his eyes. *Deep breath in, Kit.*

"What do you know about Zeus?" she asked, wiping tears from his cheeks.

"I know there's something special about him. Whatever it is, people are getting enormously fucking serious about it."

What people? she wondered.

"Avery, I know you hate flying, but this is a moment when I

must insist you come with me."

"I agree. I'll come. I'm legit fucking scared." He got up, looked out the window, his legs wobbled at the knees. "How do you plan to get us past the Perimeter?"

"Leave that to me."

"Not the first time I've heard that today."

"What's that?"

"Weissach. Said the same thing to me about you." He clipped the end of his sentence, beads of sweat appeared on his cheeks. He looked at the floor, avoiding her eyes. He was hiding something in there. She chose not to pursue it. Not yet. She still needed him.

"Look, your friend Weissach managed to get inside the Perimeter, which means there's a good chance they're still here and looking for me. You know my door code. Get in, get my stuff, and get out. I'll be nearby with an airport autocab."

It was a silent flight down to Singapore, two hours and a bit. Avery had slept, and she had catastrophized. It wasn't until they arrived that she told him they were hopping a rocket to West Africa.

"To the fucking Gambia?"

"The one and only. Boarding in ten minutes."

"What the hell's in the Gambia?"

"Hopefully no more of your new friends. I've got a conference there in a week. We can settle in early, maybe even figure out what the actual fuck is going on."

He was compliant, submissive, shaken. He was an intimidating man on a normal day, if you didn't know him. She was border-line paranoid and feeling hyper aware, like she'd augmented for it, which she knew for a fact wasn't a thing.

On board and strapped to her chair, she accepted the sedation med patch on offer and smoothed it across the back of her neck while the attendant tightened her shoulder belts. Across the aisle, Avery was sweating. He'd paid for an additional patch, which he smacked against his ropey biceps, one for each. She jacked a bead and swiped for Doudna. He answered right away.

"Couldn't get enough?" he asked.

"Never been my style, Doudna; you know that. Listen, I've had a further change of plans. Avery and I are heading out of town for a while. Not sure when we'll be back. But if you want to get together to discuss that project, I can meet you in Addis, maybe in a couple of days."

"Always happy to make time for you, Kit. How big will the security detail be?"

"Just the two of us this time."

"You let me know when."

"Thanks, Doudna. Always a pleasure." She swiped off the call and popped out the bead as the safety demo began. She leaned over to Avery. "Second time, right?" He was still sweating, drops of it falling from his bare elbows.

"Second time."

"You'll be asleep before they light the wick with two of those things on." She nodded at his arms where the sweat-damp patches were affixed, gradually administering their sedative.

"We can but hope." His gaze was fixed straight ahead. He'd been through enough today, she thought. Let the man rest.

29.

It was damn near halfway around the globe, Singapore to the Gambia, just shy of ninety minutes off the ground. They'd launched eastbound, as always, but she never knew why.

"Hey, Avery, do you know why they always fly the suborbs eastbound?" she asked.

"Suppose it keeps the vehicle and the sonic booms over water. I'm not sure either. Why do you ask?"

She was making small talk, gathering courage.

"Just curious."

They arrived at the resort in the morning and had a sunny breakfast on the beach and some quiet time together. She hadn't been ready to confront him in the hotel about his subversive selling of her life's work and whereabouts. They left for a stroll outside the resort in the searing tropical heat. She was full from the buffet, sweaty, sauntering along under Serekunda's oppressive late-summer sun. There were nicer places on the planet. Not a whole lot of paved roads here, and they hadn't found one yet. She kicked up red dust with each step, wore a face mask under her Ray-Bans. They were still burning gasoline in this part of the world, and the cars blew out a charred, sooty exhaust that adhered to everything, got into her ears, clagged up her hair, made it difficult to see.

"You sleep OK on the flight?" she asked. "I know the lag can be brutal on such a quick trip."

"Not what I'd call sleep. I'm still a little groggy off the double patch. You were right; one's enough."

"We need to talk about whatever the fuck just happened to me, and you, back in UB," she said, still walking, eyes ahead.

"I know, Kit."

"Even getting through the Perimeter is an achievement, let alone threatening lab workers like us. We're the reason the wall was built in the first place."

They walked past a barking Rhodesian ridgeback tied to a tree, the carbon-coloured dust that coated all things in this town bursting from its ruffled spinal fur with each woof.

"I told you something is up at the lab. Your work is being monitored, but I don't know by who. This Weissach man, he's the only one I know. Someone high up in NegSense must be watching."

"And Weissach, he discussed Zeus specifically?"

"Yup."

"And did you give him any of the data?"

"Well, yes, I gave him data, but nothing about Zeus. There isn't any. Trust me, I looked for it."

Trust. Wrong word.

"That was private, Avery! My data!" She pulled the mask down to her chin. "Fucking Christ in a fucking pancake!"

The dog continued to bark. She took a breath to calm down, waving her hand in front of her face for air. She wondered if the animal was overheating too, how long it had been there, and if the incessant barking was ever going to fucking stop. Traffic slowed at the intersection ahead, causing the dust to ease, and for a moment she could see much better. They paused where the two well-travelled dirt roads met. There were no stop signs and no traffic lights.

"Zeus," she panted, short of breath, "as you know, is the recipient of an edit I've been working on in my spare time. A successful edit, Avery. But this one is different. This one is important, and you can't steal my research and fucking sell it. You understand? That's industrial espionage! Fucking prison time! Or worse!"

The dog was barking louder now at something on the other side of the intersection. She looked to see what had its attention and saw a man in a cowboy hat, an aluminum briefcase open in his hands. She took off her glasses, trying to find the dog's owner. Unable to locate one, she turned to ask Avery if he could.

What she saw next didn't make sense. A steel ball the size of a plum exploded outwards from inside Avery, leaving a gaping fist-sized hole that made a repulsive sucking noise clean through his shirt. The ball made a perfect horizontal beeline a meter above the road, hissing as it went, steaming with Avery's dripping internals into Cowboy Hat's gleaming briefcase. Avery dropped to his knees in disbelief, looked up at Kit, his eyes all questions, blood pulsing through his fingers, rivers of it surging out of the hole in his midsection.

On the other side of the street, beside the biggest Mercedes wagon she'd ever seen, snapping that aluminum case shut was the man wearing the white cowboy hat and a black bolo tie. He was Asian, smiling. He climbed inside, closed the Benz's door, then lowered his window, his face visible, watching. The car crawled away with a faint electric whine. The man had a tattoo on his cheekbone, a Chinese character of some sort. She blinked back to Avery, blood pooling beneath him, in terrified realization that this was fucking really happening.

"Ave?"

Her vision narrowed as she knelt beside Avery Hill, likely, she felt, for the last time.

"Ave? What the fuck was that?" She opened her holo, swiped for "Emergency," and was answered straightaway by a calm, gentle female voice.

"One-one-six emergency. What is the nature of your call please?"

She had no clue where they were. "Yes, hello. I'm near the Kairaba resort. We are two foreign nationals. One has suffered a critical injury from some sort of metal projectile. Please hurry. He's got an open wound and he's hemorrhaging from it." She tore the shirt off Avery's back, folded it and pressed it against the flow of blood, trying to plug the cavity in his chest.

"Please hold for ambulance service."

"Avery I..."

His lips bubbled, blood and saliva dribbling off his chin onto the ground, past the sucking hole in his midsection.

"Fuck girl... said he wasn't gonna hurt me. Fuck... fuck a duck." Coughing. Bleeding. "Kit... they know about you. They know about Zeus. They've known for such a long time." His eyes fell out of sync, and he wobbled backwards in her arms.

Her wrist warbled at her. "Please continue to hold for our next available ambulance operator."

"You said 'they,' Avery. They. Who was with Weissach? Who did this to you? Who was with him in your home?" She was angry and scared and revolted all at once. Digestive organs fell out of the void as she helped him lie down on the dusty roadside.

"What did you give Zeus?" Avery sputtered. "Why's he so special?"

Gurgling fluids and something like breath came out of the blackened cavity. She retched hard into the loose dirt beside him, caught the shadow of someone moving toward her from behind. The feeling was like a snakebite as the barbs of the man's taser buried themselves deep into her neck. Her body stiffened at the sharp, excruciating paralysation of electrocution. She resisted, glimpsed his silhouetted cowboy hat. She fought the pain with every ounce of strength until the current forced her into an immobilized unconsciousness.

30.

"You're right. These peanuts are very good." They were fresh from the farm Cam had insisted they stop at in their green-striped, yellow taxi, an old petroleum burner from the 2080s, maybe one of the last gas-powered cars ever made. Dallas appreciated its simplicity: engine, tire, road.

While they drove, a small boy ran barefoot in the dust alongside them, past tin shacks and fruit stands, just, from what Dallas could see, for the fun of it. Donkeys pulled carts on the side of the road, overloaded with sacks of grain, the animals straining against the weight. A fan jacked to a solar panel in the windshield blew scalding humidity around the cab. The Gambia, as relentlessly hot as he remembered. Aircon was a rarity in this country, and the driver didn't look like he needed it. Wasn't a drip of sweat on him.

"They taste different from the one's back in Hong Kong," he said to Cam.

"We call them groundnut here," the taxi driver said to them via the rear-view. "They not only for eating. Can use the shells to make soap."

"They taste cleaner somehow," Cam said.

"That meant to be funny?"

"No, man, they really do taste better."

They differed in flavour like green living wood compared to the dry, dead kind that burned. Their cargo today would be like that green wood, living, the kind they grew in tubs, the kind that had a definable and debatable modern morality.

He'd been down where they grew once before, to the farm under the earth where humans were being cultivated like crops. He'd wanted to see it once, so he knew precisely what he was carrying in the hold of his *Arethusa*.

They'd kept their operation well hidden from the prying eyes of the judgemental policing of the west, buried deep beneath the West African savanna, tunnels the envy of wartime Vietnam. He'd been given a tour once, a disturbing look at it from a proud and triad-paid anthropoid breeder.

"These halls were once filled with pigs," his tall, lanky Eastern Eurozone tour guide had said. "Turns out human organs grow quite well in swine. The problem lies in our bodies' acceptance of the spare parts."

Spare parts, like wheels or door handles. "I heard the rejection rates were crazy," Dallas had offered.

"Well, that has always been the problem, hasn't it? Rejection. And we have tried so very many ways around it. But, you see, the best way around anything is often to accept it. And so, the best way to avoid the rejection of organs grown in other species is to simply grow them in people. In-anthro, as it were."

Viscous fluid coated the concrete flooring, a coagulated mess of bloody human offal and cytokinetic wash-off from vat overflow. The liquid burden of manmade evolution, the cold, hard, ugly truth that was forever lurking behind the face of progress.

In that moment, Dallas had asked himself two questions: *Can I walk through this burden? And do I want to?*

The taxi dropped them at Lyle's, an old, run-down bar nestled on a riverbed beach, walled behind shoulder-high, grey concrete topped with shards of broken glass and spiral coils of rusty razor wire. He wore his backpack filled with essentials, his paper bag of peanuts in hand. He stopped for a piss at the toilet, a tiled section of outdoor wall, guiding his urine down an irrigation trough that mazed its way past the entrance in a downhill gulley carved into the concrete flooring. African functionality at its best.

"I need to do a two. See you inside," Cam said. Was a brave man who took a shit in an outdoor bathroom in West Africa.

"Good luck."

Dallas dropped his backpack on the stool beside him and sat at the bar under tin roofing, corrugate bound together with bamboo ribbon, sheltering him from the searing midday west African sun. Beams of it knife-edged through gaps in the aluminum, burning his exposed skin enough to be unpleasant. He thought of Persephone, the sealed, fireproof door, and the charred remains he could scarcely view through a melted and disfigured peephole.

It was a few hundred metres to the sand, off a dusty unpaved gravel pit the locals called a road, where a wooden dock sat empty. The *Arethusa* was out there somewhere, a boat ride away, waiting for him to arrive. Would be a while yet before he saw her, and the delay was making him fidget.

The bar had running water at least and a fridge so cold it may as well have been a freezer. Many times, he'd watched Lyle chip beer bottles from the ice inside. He motioned to the waiter, a local man who also seemed to have lost the ability to sweat, for a beer. His third of the day when he normally stopped at one.

West African drum and bass drifted from a Bose speaker perched on a ratty old bookshelf behind the bar. On the other side of the fence, a solitary palm tree swayed as a salty ocean breeze whispered between its fronds, swishing the giant leaves together.

An Asian woman sat down opposite him in the shadow of the tree. She was wide at the hips and wore a jet-black crop top and mirrored indigo sunglasses. She opened a paperback, held it high in her hand, the other stirring a tall glass filled with ice and lemon. She tapped her foot as she sipped her drink, her entire body moving in discreet rhythm with the music.

This side of the razor wire, the clientele kept to themselves, all except one scruffy man with ginger hair and wrinkles, who got loud for a brief moment. His twin braided cornrows bounced against his head as he mocked the man beside him in an animated and unintelligible drunken Glaswegian patter. A darkening circular stain expanded on the centre of his crimson red Tee as his perspiration increased with his apparent level of agitation.

The heat here was different. The sunlight carried a ferocity that felt physical, as though the light had a weight that pushed like the relentless tide of a tsunami. It wasn't that Dallas minded the heat; everyone said he'd get used to it. But that was bullshit; he'd gotten used to sweating. He was doing his best to keep that to a minimum. They had a long ride ahead of them and starting it out damp would only end with him itchy and irritated. The beer was helping. He drained his bottle of Julbrew, a blue Kingfisher and "The Gambia's Very Own Beer" emblazoned across its label.

If this drop-off was like all the rest, there would be no fanfare and no dramatic arrival of trucks under armed escort. A bystander would think they were nothing more than a few tourists arriving with luggage, getting some local help putting it all onto boats. Simple affairs, small fishing vessels. Locals making a few extra dalasis ferrying visitors out to their sailboats or yachts. But something was off about this job. Delays were uncommon. All the urgency to get them out here, and now they sat and waited. Delays affected their exposure to daylight, exposure that Dallas preferred to avoid. A bead of sweat dripped off the tip of his nose, the perspiration not only from the heat.

He thought of the *Arethusa* lurking in her usual berth, hidden from orbital eyes beneath a simple tin enclosure in a port designed for fishing trawlers and private pleasure craft. She'd be fuelled for the first leg and ready to launch that evening into a blinding West African sunset. A quick turn east, and they would make landfall south of the city into the long night of the Dark Continent ahead. The moments leading to that left Dallas uncomfortable. His natural state was at the helm of his bird, and he would continue to fidget, cleaning his fingernails and cracking his knuckles until he was strapped inside her with engines turning, leaving the Atlantic long at his back.

"Mister Dallas."

She startled him. He turned, still on his stool. "You must be Dandy." She nodded. "Maybe let's not use any names around here," he said. "Call me Dee."

She leaned in close to his ear. She smelled of fresh-cut rosemary and ginger. "Then don't call me Dandy," she whispered. She wore navy stiletto sandals, ribbons laced up past her calves, and a short beige dress with a mandarin collar, her black hair pulled back tight with a bun stick.

He stood, met her eye to eye, trying desperately to remember her face. She was tall in those heels. She took a step back. "Our cargo is ready to move, but we need you at the aircraft to oversee the loading. We have an unusual shipment for you." She smiled as she said it. Proud. Unattractive.

"Yeah, I was told. One tank, long ride. I need to pay my bill. Then I'm all yours."

Cam wandered back from the toilet, shaking his hands dry, and joined the conversation with a nod of his head.

"Your bill is already settled. If you gentlemen don't mind, please follow me." She gestured to the exit, where two men wearing navy suit jackets and mirrored sunglasses waited, sweatless, scanning their surroundings. They looked like protection. He'd never had any and he didn't like it. These jobs had always been about blending into the landscape.

Dandy motioned to an aging white van, faded grey lettering spelling "U-HA" down its side. It was a full-sized petrol burner, cloudy white exhaust coughing out of its tailpipe.

"We not taking a boat?" Dallas asked.

"Not from here. Too obvious. We going for a drive first."

Cam shot him a look. Dallas thought of the limo ride with Anders. He shrugged. What could possibly go wrong?

The three of them piled into the back of the van, where there was spacious bench seating. One nice thing about Africa, they still had roomy old vehicles like these, and they still had gasoline for sale.

The protection rode the middle bench ahead of them in silence, side by side, clutching handles in the doors. They made slow progress on dirt tracks, keeping off what appeared to be the one paved road that threaded its way along the Gambia's western coast. The van wasn't meant for off-roading, diving into rutted potholes and bounding back into the air.

He understood the beauty of it out there, the raw, basic life one could lead, hidden away from the world. It was all unpaved roads, occasional shantytown housing peppered with unfinished concrete and exposed rebar, wide open fields, palm trees, and cane that grew like weeds.

"You guys ever have blowouts off-roading like this?" He winced as his head banged on the roof as they plunged into a deep rut. He got no reply. The protection kept watch, and Dandy sat a strict private school upright, staring ahead, one delicate hand bracing herself against the roof. He chewed the inside of his cheek, one hand on the ceiling like Dandy, as he took in the scenery and focused on the mission ahead. The cargo was unusual. It had everyone involved on edge.

"Before we get to the aircraft, Mister Dallas, let me discuss some minor details about your cargo," Dandy offered, her gaze remaining ahead. "You are shipping a single cryo-vat unit. It will be active. Your mission is to deliver it intact, complete with its contents. You are not to open the device or interfere with its operation in any way." She was reading from a script. He caught the text scrolling in micro off her azure-green implanted lenses. "Drop-off will be at the farm, and Mister Dallas, there will be no rest stops on this mission."

He held his hand out. "That means more pills."

She produced a clear glass pill container, full to the top. She shook it as she handed it to him. "You refuel, and you launch. No breaks. Nonstop flight."

"Means daylight. Cam?" Dallas took the container, tucked it inside his backpack.

"I'm on it." Cam fussed on his handheld, sliding the magenta line of their routing further south.

"How's it powered?" Dallas asked.

"It will be connected to your ship's power supply, but if required, it has backup power sources built into the device. Your assistance will not be required." She spoke in a clinical tone, like she was ordering a meal at a drive thru.

The van dropped them on a beach on the edge of a bird sanctuary along the coastline, southwest of Serekunda. The sun was setting, the ocean lapping. The sky had taken on a cobalt hue, a colour he'd only ever seen at the equator. Turreted battleship-grey cumulus marched ahead of the approaching squall, low in the sky and accelerating towards them. The clouds carried a battle-ready heaviness that preceded a certain deluge of rainfall specific to the region. "Fucking it down," Persephone had once said of the equatorial downpours.

Ozone stung Dallas's sinuses as dozens of hand-carved wooden fishing boats came in from the sea. If there had been fields, cows would be lying in the grass.

"Rain's coming," he said, more out of habit than any sort of useful offering.

"Mmhm," Cam replied, walking across the sand ahead of them.

Hurricanes were born on this coastline. Big ones that sailed across the Atlantic and assaulted the America's eastern shores. Figured they deserved it. Built that ridiculous wall to keep everyone out, but it didn't work against old Mother Nature. He wondered what it was like on the other side of that barrier. Wondered about that other life he'd lived and if it had any relevance to the one he was living now.

Their protection left them at the water's edge. Dallas, Cam, and Dandy clambered into a waiting dinghy, a local man sitting in its rear, holding the outboard motor with one hand. Dallas sat on the side of the boat, clutching a handrail for support. Cam and Dandy sat together on the boat's centre bench.

It was a ten-minute ride in increasingly large swell out to the Bijol Islands, a boomerang-shaped atoll west of the coast where they'd load the plane for delivery. A shoddy wooden dock bobbed in the waves on the south side of an island, which they pulled alongside. Moored to it was the *Arethusa*, covered in a temporary camouflage tent that shifted in the swell, designed to conceal it from orbital eyes. She was hard to pick out even now in the shadow of the tarps snapping in the wind. Inside, she crouched on her pontoons, canopy open, eager to get into the air.

With the dinghy tied up, they ducked under the jet's covering as the first few drops of rain hit the dock. Shots across the bow, nature's kind warning.

31.

Woo was using the precinct holo, sending snippets of code into the data stream, little AIs hunting for connections between the murder scene concoctions they'd found in the vials and legitimate labs, a trick Fong had taught him. He found it lightened the workload, though he didn't like using the AI. It was a trust thing. Like insects, just doing a job, what they'd been told, never questioning why. At least the neurals had a choice, or thought they did.

"Someone with access to this makeshift lab tech would need an assload of money, right, Fonger?"

"Edits aren't cheap, boss."

"And this germline business?"

"It's a forever move. Keeps the augment in your genes, so you can pass it along to your offspring."

"Wouldn't I be able to edit it out? Like how it was edited in?"

"I don't think it works like that, boss. Too many edits on the same sequence ends up in a mess. The people doing augments are good, but they're not *that* good. It's a risk every time. Off targets can be nasty."

Fong leaned forward. "I don't get this guy." He cast an image of the bartender from Thieves into the office's central holo. "Why would he tell you about them at all?"

"The runners?"

"Yeah. Like, what good does that do him?"

"Might have been a healthy tip in it for him," Woo said, one eyebrow raised.

"Oh, it's like that." Fong nodded. "So, that's all you got? A woman named Dandy and a couple of mercs flying contraband?"

"Said the two mercenaries were well liked."

Biomass runners didn't come cheap. The triads liked consistency from their minions above all else. They wouldn't be happy hearing their golden delivery boys were renting themselves out on the side. Fong was right, it didn't make sense. The woman had to be heavily involved.

Woo leaned back in his office chair, deep into it, felt the wheels strain at his feet, the organic polymer structure flexing under his weight. He eyed the bag of Amsterdam shag on his desk. "Fonger, if you had contacts and serious money, I mean billions of dollars, why would you arrange a meeting with a couple of runners in a dirty bar on the Causeway instead of just asking for product?"

"Because it's not product you're after, boss," Fong replied.

"Right. If it's not product then it's services. The only thing these two guys do is move contra across the pond. They're so good at it, nobody can find them, not even *government* eyes. Means we're not going to find them either." He sat up, elbow on the desk, chewed a fingernail. "This woman needs something moved. Whoever's behind this Dandy woman needs something hustled into Hong Kong quietly and quickly, literally under the radar."

"Good one, boss."

"That toy of yours pick up anything unusual?"

"Nada. If you're being watched it isn't from in close."

The drone corridor buzzed like a hive thirty metres above street level. An autonomous collision-avoidance system kept crashes to an acceptable minimum. If there'd been anyone with a user-controlled device up there it would have been flagged by all the traffic and noted by the police. It didn't mean they weren't watching him from another source, but if they were taking steps like these to remain unnoticed, it meant they weren't messing around, that something big was on the rise, and for whatever reason he had a role to play in it.

"I think I may need to go shake some trees, see if any monkeys fall." Woo could feel the first inklings of coalescence, the first two pieces of the jigsaw connecting.

"That a good idea, boss? Monkeys tend to bite."

"I'm counting on it."

The storm had passed, Ester losing some energy as it pummelled the coastline and made for the mainland. Hong Kong was picking up the detritus the typhoon had left behind, busy with getting back to its rat race. Woo, standing outside the precinct, lit a cigarette with one of his new wooden matches, shook it out, put on his fedora, and squinted up at the clear, unpolluted skies into the sunshine of a post-typhoon afternoon.

32.

Distant voices answered questions. Inflections raised and responses acknowledged in a faraway place, mumbled and muffled.

Kit's neck burned like bee stings, hot and electric. On his knees and bleeding from his abdomen, Avery reached up and grabbed her hand as her knees buckled and the cold concrete collected her elbow. But she didn't scrape pavement. Instead, she fell through the sidewalk onto a bed. Not a comfortable bed, more like a sheet covering a wooden board. She bounced. With her in the bed was that smiling Asian cowboy, his steel ball covered with Avery's insides, still sticky, the blood congealing into a rhythmic dripping in time with the beat of a heart rate monitor. She felt a heartbeat. Hers.

Beep.

She tried to speak.

Beep.

She tried to move.

Beep.

Well, fuck.

She was anesthetized but aware. She rode a perforated line of consciousness, dosed with advanced narcotics, her soul left swimming, suspended below the surface. A full-body paralysis, neighbouring on sleep, not yet woken. *Hard to access stuff like this outside of government facilities*, she thought. It felt like a ketamine derivative. She'd moved patients this way. It was easier. They were less critical and could breathe unassisted.

Beep.

It meant less equipment. A simple AI subroutine could manage the dosage. Put 'em in a container and ship 'em. She tried to move, but not even a toe would wiggle. One of her eyes was stuck open, lagophthalmos, something an old boyfriend had done in his sleep, eerie to wake up to, common with surgeries. She felt anchored, immobilized, her thoughts muddy and slow.

Beep.

She was lying prone on a gurney, cognizant of a team of men and women wearing drab blue medical scrubs. Through her one open eyelid, she glimpsed heads adorned with designer surgical caps, her most attentive in black, tied in a bow behind, decorated with white printed literature of organic chemistry formulae. They worked with a hurried precision, attaching electrodes up and down her naked body. Masked human automata checking and rechecking positions, monitors, outputs. She was aware of being lifted into a container, zipped into an opaque plastic bag, her arms placed one at a time across her chest, fingertips resting atop her shoulders. The steady, rhythmic beep of the heart-rate monitor kept her from internal panic, right up until the bag began to fill with a chilled, thick, and viscous fluid. She was fitted with a breathing apparatus, intubated, the device sliding down her throat, indicating a deeper sleep was to come. She attempted to gag, but the drugs were in charge, and she was along for the ride. The bag filled higher, the cold treacly substance rising above her armpits. Fresh IVs were inserted into her thighs, her neck, her abdomen. Double tube inserts, ins and outs, transfusion style.

Beep.

Abducted. Into what had to be a cryo tank. How was this even possible? They'd done her in broad daylight, outside, in public. Must have been planned. The whole thing.

Sweet Jesus, she thought. *Avery.*

As the fluid rose above her ears, what had been muted, partially comprehensible discussions outside the tank became unrecognizable mumblings. The zipper closed tight. The fluid filled the bag, covering her face, and she floated, drifting further toward sleep. The manic, blurred motions of the medical staff working on her became slight, still, watching, preparing to cool her into an induced hibernation. She fought to remain conscious, straining her mind to recall as much as possible. Mixed blue lights in the tank illuminated, blinked. A perceptible hum began, and a horrifying coolness overcame her. As the cryoprotectants began replacing the blood in her arteries with antifreeze, allowing her veins to fill with an amorphous ice that wouldn't harden but would remain vitrified into a solid-liquid, she recognized what was known as the "glass transition," a stiffening without solidifying of her venous system, shortly of her entire body. Fit for transport. Through that coldness, came the darkness of the coma.

33.

"So, what's in it?" Dallas was inspecting the exterior of the *Arethusa*, ensuring she was airworthy and prepped for the trip. He balanced on the dock's edge, his legs syncing with the swell. He ran his hand along her uneven and pitted radar-absorbing skin, ducking under her wing's leading edge, checking for damage with a flashlight. He bonded with her like this before every flight, a ritual he longed for between each mission.

"More like *who's* in it," Cam said, checking to ensure the tank was properly loaded and secured in the aircraft's aft cargo hold.

"I've never seen one so complicated." Dallas thought back to his previous life when he was flying suborbs for WorldWide. On one trip he'd had a crate like this. They'd said it was a med-evac status flight, no rules, that he could light the rocket over land, priority clearance, everything at maximum speed. They'd sprayed on a double layer of heat shield and told him to turn up the wick. Took it from Heathrow to SoCal in an hour. First time he'd ever done anything close to a proper orbital mission. The patient was a parliament member with a gunshot wound, an assassination attempt. They'd cooled him down in a tank the same as this one. Frozen like a popsicle, it gave the docs on the other end time to figure out how to fix that wound in his chest.

"Just sayin' I don't like it, Cam."

"Not a lot of options here, Dee." Cam was head down in the

back seat, prepping the jet's nav system for flight.

Dallas climbed the ladder, stepped into the front, and shook his head. "Someone important in that tank." Cam was right. Their options were at zero, Anders had made that clear and convincing.

Beneath a gentle rainfall, the *Arethusa* was towed away from the dock by a small tugboat, keeping her under cover. Once she was clear of the tarps, floating free on her retractable pontoons, she crouched like a bat, her anhedral wing tips dipped in the water. The shoreline's distant lights glistened in the ocean's thin whitecaps, the reflections absorbed by her matte-black stealth paint, millions of bipolymer beads arranged in a tightly packed hexagonal monolayer, trapping light and radar beams alike. It made her not only difficult to detect but also difficult to see. A shadow passing in the dark night sky.

He ran the engines off the batteries for takeoff, slipping from the sea to fly low over the black Atlantic's gentle swell. Trailing residual salt water spun in wing tip vortices as she retracted her floats into bays inside her body.

They headed northwest to begin, lighting the turbines as they rounded the corner at Dakar to pick up the eastbound track and make landfall north of the border to Senegal, the coastline flashing past the windshield with a snap. Tearing across the desert at eighty percent of the speed of sound, thirty feet off the deck, Dallas felt at ease. The automatics would deal with any radical changes in topography, and there was no one in this part of the continent that had the means or the desire to shoot down a tiny jet they couldn't see. Their routing took them through south Saharan savannah, Mali, Niger, and Chad. They'd be free and clear of any threats until sunrise, when they would duck into Djibouti at an old abandoned military airfield and refuel from drums deposited there. The triad's fingers ran far and wide, and Africa's nations were no exception.

34.

Woo had his head down, deep into the body of his rolling paper, disseminating the southern Euro tobacco flake in a symmetrical line along its centre. The outside world ceased to exist, the dried leaves dissolving between his fingertips with a delicate organic crinkle. At what he determined to be the optimal fill point, he spun the paper into a perfect cylinder, licked and sealed it, then twisted one end to finish it off. He looked up from his desk into the smirking eyes of Superintendent Lee.

"Quite an operation you've got there, Woo."

Woo shrugged. "Helps me think."

Lee held his hand out, a memchip squeezed between finger and thumb. "You're heading up to Ulaanbaatar. Got a buckyball murder, and it's a weird one. Took place in the Gambia, West Africa. Victim's a Canadian, Avery Hill. Some sort of big deal geneticist working up there. Body's being flown back to Ulaanbaatar. Government wants it investigated in country, and since you're the only one who's ever worked a buckyball case, they want you. Pretty sure no one has a clue what to do with it. Never seen one outside of Hong Kong."

Woo slotted the memchip into his display and swiped through the particulars. Buckyballs were nasty jobs, violent weapons used exclusively by the southern Chinese triads. They made a big mess, designed to send a message.

"Broad daylight. Gutsy. Looks messy. Was the vic affiliated?"

"Not that I recall. But everything we have is on that chip. Maybe if you decided to join the rest of us, you could read it on your holo on the ride up." Gears. The super never missed an opportunity to give him some.

"Would if I could, boss, would if I could." He stopped on the victim's details, zoomed in with his fingertips.

Deceased was Canadian-born Avery Hill. Geneticist at NegSense. Age 36. Nigerian lineage.

Cause of death: multiple internal organ ruptures caused by unknown object vacating the victim's torso from an internal position. No entry point found.

"NegSense. Came across that name with the TKO victim. He had an augment from there. Family notified?" Woo asked.

"Not yet. There's something funny about this vic, Woo. We need you outta here tonight. You're on a ten p.m. through Beijing. Don't be late. And take this." He chucked a precinct wristband at him. "Internals burn out after twenty-four hours. Your secrets will be safe." Lee shook his head as he walked back to his glass office, the walls shifting into an opaque deep grey as the door closed behind him.

Woo was in another hospital morgue, listening to the same refrigerant pumps, smelling the same ghosts, staring at another tale not yet told. An extractor fan droned in the ceiling high above.

"Detective Woo, welcome to Ulaanbaatar. I trust your journey was enjoyable?"

Another basement dweller in another lab coat, this one balding, augmented reality glasses refracting a rose tint from the end of his nose, lifting stories from the deceased body before them.

"I haven't slept, and I'm heading back as soon as we're done here, so let's keep it brief."

"Right then. The weapon was a projectile, but there is no entry wound, only the large exit hole you can see here."

The wound was clean, as was the custom, a process well thought out by the mob.

"Classic buckyball."

"Well, that may well be, Detective, but we've never seen one in Mongolia. Seems a lot of trouble to go through. He would have had to ingest this device, no?"

"They drug the victims, force it down their throat while they're asleep."

"Sounds terrible."

"It is."

If he hadn't seen it before, he'd have thought a small missile had shot clean through the man's torso; the wound itself was so well defined. Like a traditional triad chop shop murder, the buckyball method had a particular pathos that the mob seemed to enjoy. If you fuck with us, we will fuck harder with you.

"Why go to all the trouble? This seems a barbaric and cumbersome way to murder someone," the mortician said.

"It's cleaner than it looks. These things started out as children's toys, like, a hundred years ago. You could build squares and geometric shapes with them. Parents liked them because they tidied up easy. But the kids started eating them. They were smaller than this thing, the size of a marble. And the magnetic attraction was so strong the balls would move through tissue to get to each other. They ate holes in children's intestines and stomach walls, among other things. They were banned for years. And then this." He waved at the body. "Some asshole got creative, weaponized them."

"Not nice." The mortician directed his attention to the hole in the corpse. "You see how the edges of this wound are burnt? That's cauterized flesh. Either this ball was extremely hot, or it left at an extreme velocity."

"Makes sense. They're accelerated out of the victim by some

kind of targeted magnetic device, but we've never gotten our hands on one. Best we can tell it creates a tunnel, like a beam of magnetism specific to the individual ball's magnetic signature. Otherwise, it would attract everything around it. So, they beam the target with this thing, and the ball erupts from the victim like it's attached to a rope. Almost instantaneous supersonic speeds."

"Hard to catch, I would think."

"Nah, the thing slows as it approaches the trap. Some complicated algorithm worked out by a dirty AI."

"Dirty?"

"Mob."

They nodded together in silence.

"How big you think this projectile was?" Woo asked.

The doctor clenched his hand, placed it next to the hole. "Size of a small fist? He left parts of his internal organs on the street where he was killed. They fell out of the hole."

"Yeah. You see, they get the buckyball in there and then wait, for days we think, make sure there's no evidence left on the victim. Then they crank on the wattage and do this, catch the ball, drop it in deep water. You've got a clean kill and no traceable weapon."

"What do they catch it in? Seems whatever they use would have substantial amounts of evidence attached, no?"

"The balls are coated in some kind of high-tech lubricant, in essence it's frictionless. This guy here is the third victim we've ever identified as a buckyball murder, and we've only got the one actual ball from a scene in Hong Kong." Down at the shop they'd been researching a method to trace the electromagnetic signature of the pull device, but they'd come up empty. It was a perfect murder weapon controlled exclusively by the triads.

"The escape vector was via his small intestine. There was trauma in the stomach, so it likely exited between the two. He might have survived if he hadn't lost so much blood."

"I'm guessing emergency services in the Gambia aren't

traditionally fast responders."

"He was dead long before the ambulances arrived."

Woo got in close to the victim's face. "Can you lift his upper lip for me?"

"What are you interested in?"

"Looking for anything these perps may have left in there when they forced the ball down his esophagus."

"I have the full digital image available if you'd like to peruse it."

"I'll leave that to my partner. I prefer to work in analogue if you don't mind."

Beside the body on a steel tray lay an assortment of medical instruments, including saws. Woo chose something that looked like blunt scissors with hooked ends and pulled the man's lip back, so he could get a good look at his teeth. "His incisors are chipped. Must have been rough getting it in there." The gap gave him a good representation of the size of the thing, like a billiard ball.

"Can you get an image of these teeth? I'd like an idea of the circumference of the ball they shoved down his throat."

"No problem. Give me a second." The mortician sat down at his console, swiping, the scanning ring unfurling itself from a compact enclosure supported from the ceiling above the body. It illuminated, moving slowly from the top of his head down, stopping at the neck, then folded back in on itself into its cradle above.

"What were you doing all the way over in West Africa, Mister Hill?" Woo asked.

35.

Dallas had the jet down in the weeds, below the twenty-metre mark, the ground disappearing at high speed beneath the aircraft's black nose cone in a blur of green and tan. Through his helmet's optics, he watched a full moon rise into the light of the setting sun behind, its form distorted and compressed like a doughnut on the horizon. They were fully fuelled, heading south out of Djibouti, aiming for the uninhabited red sands of the Ethiopian desert. Reaching the desert's edge, they'd make a turn east for deserted beaches on the Somali coastline and a long ride across the Indian Ocean where the automatics would assume full control. For now, it was HOTAS: Hands On Throttle And Stick.

He flicked her through a series of hard banks, left and right, a test drive. She lagged behind his inputs with her belly full of kerosene. He could feel it, the extra weight giving her a noticeable increase in inertia. Cam snored into the intercom. He'd give him his five minutes, Dallas thought. The run through Somalia had never once been easy, never once been quiet.

The full moon illuminated the interior of the flight deck with a midnight wash, reflecting off his gloved hands resting on the controls, the tops of his legs in the g-suit visible in his lower peripheral vision. Ahead of the aircraft, Dallas caught the same moonlit reflection off the backs of elephants and turned the jet to watch, passing behind the herd so as not to startle them, metres above the smooth Somali desert plateau.

"There's water collectors ahead, Dee, range of 'em. Looks like they're still under construction, low level, twenty footers." Cam was awake now, his head in the scope. "I'd say it's fine to take her through, keep you from falling asleep up there."

"No threat of that," he responded.

They flew alongside a single row of half-built water collectors, below the tops, slipping past without a turn, the lidar data showing their detailed illuminated outlines through his visor. Cam flashed another scan and got an immediate growl off the Defensive Aids System (DAS), someone on the ground looking for a fight.

"Some more towers ahead. Taller, still under construction, not as well organized," Cam said. "Got a single growler down there. Looks like a handheld rocket launcher. Shouldn't be a problem." They were in guerrilla territory now, a landscape that deserved respect. The only way forward was through and low. To climb would be suicidal. Somali scavengers were well armed.

"Lidar data's on your Heads Up Display. I got a gap at one o'clock looks clear. Left side is elevated terrain. Right is thick with antiaircraft hardware."

He made the slight turn right to the one o'clock heading, flying wings flat, the jet's stealth at its best in straight and level flight. Ahead through the gap, he caught motion off the moonlight. Erectors. They moved with an unnatural speed, robotic actuating arms secreting their liquid polycarbon in preprogrammed machine motion, climbing the structure as they built.

The DAS growled in and out, a warhead hunting, searching for a cross-section to fire on. *Arethusa's* stealthy shape and radar-absorbing paint confused the search system below. He instinctively nudged her lower and cranked hard around a tower to try and shake the targeting system. Rolling out level, they faced a dense forest of much taller structures, their machine arms spinning with the same automated motion.

36.

He walked along the path with the herd, the same path he walked each night, long before the sun, when the air was still, his sandals kicking at loose soil. He preferred this time when the darkness was pure, the goats were at peace, the only sound coming from insects. The predators had had their night and now rested with bellies full of antelope and gazelle.

He allowed his hand to tickle at the long grasses, pausing to listen for the herd, to smell for the lion, to feel the land around him. He was a shepherd, after all. This land that gave him life and fed his family was his to nurture and care for.

He leaned on his staff, given to him by his father, ran a hand along its knobbly wooden shaft, worn smooth from many seasons with the herd, felt for his father's spirit, and as was the norm, found nothing.

The goats fed.

The sheep grazed.

Beneath the bright red folds of his shuka, he rested his hand on the hilt of the simi dangling at his side, steel forged in fire by his twin brother, Odongo. He took pleasure in its weight, lifted it from its long leather sheath. Assured that the blade was still there, he allowed it to fall back into the leather, his motions slow, deliberate, purposeful. He thought of Odongo, reminded of the loneliness of this time without the tribe, thought back to the Push, when the grasses no longer grew in the Maasai land. When the Serengeti had moved east, his family had moved with it, but his village had not. He was diaspora now. Without a home. Now he had his goats, his sheep, his wife, and his land. Without these he was no one.

He watched the goats. They no longer ate, their heads lifted, their noses inhaling the air. They were alert. He recognized their concern but did not understand it. They could hear something, something they feared, something that he could not. He felt shame as their shepherd, that he did not protect them, and he marched to encircle them, scanning the grassland for threats.

There were water buildings nearby, the mzungu towers, none so far encroached upon his land, but they were close. The mzungu did not ask permission. They came with their machines, and they spoke of free water for the village, but Opiyo knew there was no free. Always, there was a price.

The mzungu towers made a noise when he got close to them. It was the noise of aliens, of not-Africa, yet the herd knew the sound and did not run from it. It was an unnatural sound, not of the earth. This sound, he thought, one day this sound would go away, and when that day came, mzungu would not know how to live without his machines, but Opiyo would live fine. Opiyo would have his land, his herd, and his wife.

The goats stared west, their motions became still. The sheep gathered together. There was a threat that Opiyo did not know. He unsheathed his blade, crouched in the tall grass, prepared for a predator he could not see.

There was a water-tower that way, where they were staring. It had been growing for three walks without mzungu, built by machines to grow taller than hills in the time it took to finish only seven walks. He could see its great arm swinging in rings as it grew around itself. It moved faster than a hunting cheetah. Nothing should move faster than that.

He shuffled low to where the goats listened and looked long

into the dark. He saw a shimmer on the horizon. It was unnatural, perhaps it was mzungu magic, a ghost that he thought he could not see, but it was there. It was a bird, flying at an impossible speed toward him, toward the herd, and Opiyo prepared to fight.

37.

They were running on the barber pole, just above the deck, trying to put some distance between the hunting warheads and their tail. They were gaining no ground, maneuvering between the increasing density of hundred-metre-tall towers, the DAS growling in and out.

"We shouldn't have a tail for this long," Dallas said. "What's happening back there?"

"I don't know. There's multiple incoming pings. I haven't seen this many since I was dropping bombs in Saudi."

The DAS illuminated red, and the growl became a solid tone, target locked. Fuck. He caught a flash off the left side of the aircraft, a missile leaving its tube, glaring into the night.

"That's a confirmed launch, Cam, I need some help up here."

"I've got radar lighting us up from all around. We need to get lower." Cam's voice increased in pitch.

Weaving between the growing structures was becoming increasingly difficult, his gloves soaked through from pulling steady hard g's. Another launch flashed off their right wing. "That's two. This is getting serious, Cam." He felt a bump as Cam deployed countermeasures from their tail.

"You're not gonna like this. We're being pinged from the tower tops," Cam said.

That's creative, Dallas thought. He banked hard left. "Can I go up?"

"Mate, if you climb it won't be two missiles; it'll be a hundred."

The *Arethusa's* stealth tech was working to a certain degree, the missiles' targeting systems cycling in and out of lock. He caught a flash of light from behind, and the tone of the first launch went silent.

"Countermeasures worked," Cam said.

New growls became new tones, and another two missiles launched ahead. "This feels like a trap," he grunted, cranking the jet right, the aircraft's skin popping as it strained under the heavy load.

Cam's hand braced against the canopy. "Agreed," he said, struggling for breath.

"Sure is getting tight down here," Dallas said, weaving the machine back and forth between towers.

"It's not far, Dee. Thirty seconds till we're out of this."

"OK, leave me to it." They could run silent off the batteries over flat terrain, then slink off into the night once they were past this construction zone.

Dallas pushed the thrust levers to the stops, intakes hauling in air, the engines giving everything they had. Maximum power. He couldn't afford interruptions; there were too many threats and all of them at once.

Another rocket launched ahead of them, in close, the DAS wailing red. He cranked the jet hard left to avoid it and then came back right, flying behind a half-built collector, its double helix structure climbing skyward above their altitude. Eyes on the tower, he followed the moon's light glinting off the erector's titanium arm, "Coradyne Technologies" shining in silver Helvetica, and watched as it swung clean through the *Arethusa's* wing, a shower of polycarbonate shards spraying into the still desert air, moonlit reflections off disintegrating composites creating a momentary chandelier of light, like curtains of white fireworks detonating in the pitch-black sky.

38.

Opiyo watched the metal shadow fly past with disbelieving eyes, the tip of its wing reaching out, digging deep into the soil he had walked so recently with his herd. The sound was of mzungu, of shrieking banshees. Burning fires trailed the spinning black ghost, and Opiyo felt fear for a thing that his blade could not possibly protect him from.

He kneeled behind it, shielding himself as the thing fell from the sky, his arm up against the night, lit by fire and bright as day, its heat fierce on his skin. He looked up as it swept past, saw it break into pieces, saw the hand of a mzungu, fingers splayed across glass, his arm up, perhaps also trying to protect himself.

He felt the hot air pulled along as it passed and raised his red shuka over his head as a shield. It was wise. Sand, stone, and pieces of the thing clattered past in a great wind and then stopped. Opiyo glanced out from under his cape.

39.

The *Arethusa* snapped inverted.

Shit.

The right wing, now an obliterated trail of polymers, dusted the sand below. Dallas braced himself with a hand on the glass canopy, looked up at the dunes directly above the aircraft, caught the red robes of a Maasai warrior staring up at him, their eyes meeting for a split second of mutual disbelief. The *Arethusa*, travelling a mile every eight seconds and now unresponsive, listed and knife-edged lower as it bleated warnings of altitude and terrain. Dallas watched in helpless disbelief as the jet dug the raked tip of one anhedral wing deep into the cold, beige desert. The nose caught ground, popped a g-load limit, and the flight deck airbags exploded with instantaneous violence, pinning him into place, his body rendered immobile. The rotation accelerated, his vision blurring from the spin. They were saving his life, the airbags, right this instant, better than an ejection seat, but god*damn* it was uncomfortable. The sound was like a car crash, a ferocious tearing of metal. A flash of searing, harsh blackness burned the back of his throat, a blistering heat engulfing him for a moment, then it was gone.

The rotation slowed, and the bag system deflated, easing the deceleration as they bounced to a complete stop. The bags hissed, emptying themselves around him.

Dallas took a long, laborious breath.

The dark quiet of the desert was distressing.

Dallas pulled without success against a venous entanglement of wiring, the *Arethusa's* entrails suspending him upside down above the desert floor, his face so close he blew dust with each breath. The air smelled of hot metal, burnt kerosene, and dark, acrid smoke. Something fizzed in the background.

"Cam?" he yelled.

"Mmmp."

Dallas wiggled his toes, flexed his fingers. Everything seemed attached. "You OK?" he asked.

"No idea. Let me check."

Dallas yanked on a bunching of cables wrapped around his shoulder and armpit. It snapped free, and he piled into the ground with a thud.

"Everything's bruised, but nothing's broken," Cam said from somewhere close.

Pain radiated up Dallas's left side and down the length of his arm. It was wet to the touch. He wasn't on fire though; that was a plus.

He stood up, wiped his eyes clear of sand and took in the scene. They'd rolled it ass over teakettle for what looked like half a klick, coming to rest in a grove of acacia bushes. Behind them trailed a black carbon-fibre stain along the sandy desert floor. The airbags that saved their lives lay deflated and lifeless on the ground. Fire-retardant dust covered him head to toe.

On the horizon the erectors continued their work, AIs blindly completing their tasks. Cam crawled out from under the blown airbags, spitting out dust and patting himself down. Dallas felt his own body for damage and found a fist-sized shard of jagged carbon lodged in his left side, blood pooling through his shirt.

"I'm gonna need some med attention," he said. "Got a puncture."

"Anywhere serious?"

"Bleeding from the ribs. I'll be fine. Just get me the kit."

While he listened to Cam rummaging for the med kit, a naked woman dragged herself from the shattered Pyrex lid of the cryo tank they'd been hauling, dangling monitor leads taped to her arms and legs. Her wrists were bound in steel, her body dripping with a thick gelatinous goo that twinkled in the moonlight.

Kit's brain felt shaken. She wiped blood from a nostril, her hands moving in unison, cuffed.

Right.

She'd managed to pull herself out of the tank, staggered in sand, barefoot, bare everything, the metal around her wrists tightening somehow, her body still coated in the high-tech snot that had been keeping her alive in hibernation.

Hibernation. Right, that too.

She'd been cooled for a long sleep. She'd woken plenty of subjects from the same enclosures. They didn't pop out easily, not like this. She ran through the possibilities, followed her tracks in the dirt. The tank's lid had split open along its glass covering like a pastry, steaming, still leaking the same warming fluids that covered her skin. Emergency cryonics protocols would have brought the temperature up rapidly and to the limit of human tolerance. Pumps would have heated and flushed the amorphous gel out of her veins, replacing it with her own blood stored in the tank, dumping stims into her bloodstream, violently reversing the anesthesia. A process meant to take hours completed in minutes. She'd have permanent organ damage. Her brain was foggy, her neurons stuttering. Tank drunk. She wobbled.

A tall, somewhat Asian man stood beside what looked as though it had once been an aircraft. He wore blue denim and a tight-fitting, white T-shirt, blood streaming off his fingers into the sand. He had a strong jawline and the beginnings of a light beard, his face illuminated by the whiteness of the full moon. His dyed dirty blond hair fell over his eyes, shaved up the sides. He had tattoos climbing his neck, but she couldn't make out what.

"Who the fuck are you?" she asked, folding her cuffed arms over her breasts.

"Name's Dallas."

"Any chance you can get these cuffs off me, Dallas?" She fidgeted inside them. They weren't normal. Seamless metal links shaped in a figure-eight that self-tightened, like an over-complicated finger puzzle. Tech she'd never seen. She pulled against them and felt them slowly constrict, shining steel boas cutting into her softened, pale skin.

"I wouldn't even know where to start," he said.

She huffed, looked around, then back at him. "You planning to sell me for spare parts?" she asked, wincing as she gingerly pulled a catheter tube from her urethra, looked it over, then threw it at Dallas with her bound hands. Figured these guys had to be mercenaries running tissue. Was the only explanation. Bootlegging cheap, vat-grown human body parts out of Africa into East Asian labs.

Just like hers.

"It's not like that." He picked up the catheter and looked it over, then tossed it back at her. "People pay me to deliver product. Today, you are that product."

"So, are your people going to come and rescue us?" she asked, trying to swipe the cold gel off her arms.

"Our employers are not exactly known for their tolerance on undelivered product," he said, looking over his shoulder where a short, bald, and beer-bellied man extracted himself from the wreckage. He was bleeding as well, quite hard from his temple, blood running down the side of his face and dripping off the stubble of his chin. Some had coagulated there, becoming a cinder-brown cake, like a beard, she thought, a lovely brown cake-beard.

"Where the fuck did she come from?" he asked, handing Dallas a white tin box.

"Crawled out of the tank."

"That's a fucking problem."

"You fellas got something I can borrow to cover this up?" she asked, motioning her cuffed hands in circles around her naked crotch.

"And she speaks. Fucking great."

"Name. What's your name?" Dallas asked.

"Name's Kit."

Dallas reached behind his neck and peeled his bloody T-shirt off, tossing it at her. She bent down to pick it up, acutely aware of her nudity, and popped her head through the neck hole leaving her arms under the shirt. Beer-belly took off his pants and boxers, handed her his underwear, then put his pants back on.

"Since we're all getting to know each other," he said with a smile. "Name's Cam."

She pulled the underwear up, then flipped the waistband down to try and reduce the size. "Would either of you be interested in uncuffing me? These things get tighter every time I move."

"Like I said, those things are above my pay grade, *Kit*, was it?" Dallas said her name as though he was about to spit. "Can you walk? Gonna be a long night if you can't."

"Yeah, I'll be fine." She looked back at what she realized now was an actual plane crash. "Was I on that thing?"

"Yep."

"In that tank?"

"Watched you crawl out of it myself."

"How did you survive?" It was a catastrophic wreck, the kind she'd seen on news feeds. No one ever lived.

"Airbag system. Like those Mars landers. Better than ejection seats. Bigger question is, how did *you* survive?"

"This fluid is non-Newtonian. Shear thickening, it's called. Hardens on impact. Reduces the instantaneous g-load. Could stop a bullet. I guess it works on people too." She wiped at her legs from under the shirt, slinging the fluid to the ground.

Dallas popped a gauze from its plastic sheath, grabbed hold of something black sticking out from his side, and grunted, yanking it out. Blood ran from the hole, and he patched it with the gauze, wrapping it around his midsection.

"So, what did you do that got you strapped and tanked for transport in a contraband-hauling, ground-effect jet? In what used to be my *Arethusa*?" Dallas reached up into the crumpled remains of the aircraft's dangling flight deck and pulled out a grey hoodie, covered in zips, thick in the neck. He pulled it on over his still-bleeding tape job. "What's so special about you?"

She looked at both of them, stared at her cuffs, blood trickling from the newly sliced skin there. She was still tank drunk, mostly naked, kidnapped, and bound. *What the hell? Might as well come clean. Can't get any worse than this.*

"I write augments. I wrote all the big ones. Sight, speed, those were all mine."

"Oh, she's an editor. One of those," Cam said, unimpressed.

"Didn't think there were many of you left," Dallas remarked.

"There aren't," she said.

"Explains the kidnapping, I guess," Cam said.

"Hey, my lab buys the organics you guys are moving, and my team endeavours to make humanity better through their use." She was wringing her hands, the cuffs constricting further. "Last month I finished a new one. Thought I'd kept it secret. Never told a soul. Kept the data private." She reached for the locket, just then realizing it wasn't there. She touched her nail, thought against showing them. "Then all this happened."

"What's the big deal with the edit?" Dallas asked.

"You know how telomeres work?"

"Telo-whats?"

"Never mind. I've figured out an edit to the human DNA sequence that's really fucking important, and it appears that some wealthy and powerful people knew what I was working on. Which is impossible. Or," she waved a hand at her surroundings, "completely fucking possible."

"So, you're not a test subject, is what you're saying," Dallas said, tearing off the gauze and taping it against his midsection.

"I'm the person who orders the things that come in those containers."

"And we're the people who bring them. We're all monsters then. Welcome to the club, lady," Dallas said. "Got any friends out here who might want to give us a ride?"

"Last place I saw with my own eyes was the Gambia. Where the fuck is 'out here'?"

"Good question. I'd put us a couple hundred klicks west of the Somali coast. Fucking GAFA is where we are."

"What's that?"

"The Great African Fuck All. Nothing out here 'cept us."

"And him," Cam said, pointing.

She caught the outline of a robed man crouching, not wanting to be seen. In the distance she heard the soft tinkling of bells, a rudimentary tracking device, but it was all anyone would need out here in the silence. Maybe a Maasai warrior; she'd read they still lived out here.

"You see that?" Cam whispered.

"I hear goats or cows or something," Dallas replied. "Thought I saw a man crouching there."

Dallas nodded. "Yeah, me too."

"Me too," Kit offered.

"Shut it," Dallas said, turning to Cam. "How's your Somali?"

"It's total shit, like, not even a single word."

"I can speak some Kiswahili," she said. "He looked like a Maasai."

"I think he's gone anyway," Dallas continued as if she hadn't said a word. He was right. When she looked where the man had been, he had disappeared into the night.

"Look, we need to get out of sight in a hurry," Dallas said, "and I need you to figure out where we are. And Cam, look at me, I need you to focus on getting us a ride off this continent." He enunciated his words, spoke at a reduced pace.

Cam thumbed at the remains of the flight deck and chuckled. "Nothing viable in there we can use." Something was burning inside the remains; she could smell it, like melting plastics in the lab.

"How do you feel about flashing up the satcom?" Dallas asked.

"If it's functional, it'll broadcast our whereabouts immediately. Won't take long for someone to notice we're missing. I mean the data won't be hard to find once they know to look, but not knowing to look could buy us some time." Cam nodded, gears were turning in there. "I figure we've got twelve hours to get non-local, maybe twenty-four to get to the coast. Somali drones are quick, man. They can sweep fast once they figure out there's a salvage out here."

"We don't have a ton of options. We need to get this," Dallas put his arm around her shoulders, "out of sight before the sun comes up. Gives us maybe two hours till daylight. I need a village, a town, anywhere we can bribe someone to put us up for a day." He kneeled, tearing a Velcro strap from his ankle. He pulled a wad of cash from it, stuck it under her nose. "No need to go selling our cargo just yet."

"Satcom's in the tail. I'll see if I can find it." Cam walked over to a heap of bent, black wreckage and reached his fingers into a tear in the metal, stepping a boot into it. He reefed hard, hauling off a panel and revealing an equipment bay that housed the box he was after.

"Voilà. Looks like it did pretty good in the crash."

"We got any friends in Addis?" Dallas asked. "We're gonna need a ride outta here. Pronto."

"I know a guy who works out of Addis. He moves contra like us, only on land, but he works for the same people as us. We call him, they're gonna be up our ass so fast," Cam said.

"We're out of options. We don't need all the solutions, but we need the first solution, and we need it now."

"I'll call him, see what's up."

He unravelled a small headset from a hollow in the box, jacked it in, and put the headphones over his ears. The headset made Kit think of her audio beads. They'd be gone along with the rest of her things. But her sub-dee. She wondered if she could get out a call of her own.

Cam spoke for what seemed like seconds, took off the headset, and unplugged the box from the wreckage.

"It's bad news, good news. He's in Mogadishu. That's bad news. He's the better part of six hours away. But he's in Mogadishu, not Addis, that's good news. Addis would have been a twenty-four-hour drive. Says there's a city not far from us, Beledweyne, maybe a hundred klicks north of us, up by the demilitarized zone. That's bad news. Says someone out there may have seen the crash. Big military base out there. That's bad news too. Said there's farms all over where we are, Maasai country. Said to be careful, get some cover, and call him in five hours with a position update. He'll be in the truck."

"What's the truck?" Dallas asked.

Cam smiled. "You'll see."

40.

He had been watching them, untrusting, two men and a woman, crawling out from the tangle of twisted metal. They were mzungu, not from Africa. They bled like Opiyo, and that they were alive surprised him. He had never seen such a thing, so much fire and speed. The woman looked as though she had just been born, dripping like a newborn calf. They were hurt. Opiyo wanted to offer help—his home was not far—but he had to look for his *mbuzi*, his herd. These mzungu and their crash had terrified them, made them run from this place, this place that was his land, his herd, which was his family's livelihood. Would his wife and child believe him? That a fiery ship came down from the stars and scared off the animals? Mzungu magic?

He watched them, listened for his mbuzi, crouched silent and still. They were speaking in mzungu, which Opiyo did not understand. The woman was bound. The men were not helping her.

He heard the low bell of his oldest goat. She was not far; perhaps she was looking for him. He watched the mzungu as he moved away toward the sound of the goat's bell, crouching down deeper into the shadows.

41.

"Probably a farmer, Hiroki said there were lots around here." They were whispering to each other, though it felt like screams in the quiet.

"Who's Hiroki?" Kit asked.

"Man taking a drive to save our asses. That includes yours. You ready to move? We need some cover."

"Be easier without these fucking cuffs on," she said.

"You're stuck with those for now. That's some expensive tech you're wearing."

Cam shoved the satcom inside a backpack he'd pulled from the aircraft, motioning toward where the Maasai had been. "Might be some trees that way, down the hill. Anything's better than being out here right now."

Dallas stuck his head in the wreckage, took one last look at the jet, then ducked as he exited. "Let's head. I'm getting that feeling we're being watched."

42.

He found them pressed against one another, sheep and goats together, nestled under a large *mgunga*, a safe place from anything but elephants. He looked back at the mzungu. They were in distress, trying to hide in a small cave. Like his mbuzi, they followed and flocked, hiding from danger. Perhaps he could offer them food and somewhere safe to sleep, be a good man, as his wife often told him to be.

He heard a buzzing, looked up at the night sky, and listened but saw nothing. More mzungu magic. This time there was no fire. Perhaps this was what the woman and two men were hiding from. Should he be afraid? He was not. But the herd would not move. They too were afraid. He drew his blade and placed it in the ground before him, waiting for the quiet to return.

43.

"There's no way yer gonna get the three of us in that hole, Dee. No fucking way," Cam said.

"Kit get in there first," Dallas said. "You're the smallest."

They were standing in front of the first cover they had found, a giant rock pierced with a slender crack running diagonal to the ground.

"You *have* seen your friend, right?" Kit asked. "He's like five foot nothing."

"Just slide in there, and let's see if we can all fit. Sun'll be up soon."

Cam was right. There was no way, but he had to get at least one of them out of sight. The faint, high whine of small, ducted fans was in the air. Drones were near, and the options in front of them included wedging one of them into this metre-wide crack in a house-sized stone or burying themselves in the red sand beneath their feet.

"Cam, get digging. See if you can get underneath enough of this stuff to cover your heat signature."

"With my hands?" It was a bad option, but they didn't have many. One option at a time.

"Just dig. We make it through this, and maybe we got ourselves a ride."

They came in fast, not what Dallas had expected from a third-world military. Dozens of them, buzzing like an approaching locust swarm.

"Fuck it. Get in the crack. Suck it in. Right now."

The three of them squeezed in hard against one another, Dallas's shoulder up inside Kit's armpit, Cam's belly deforming around Dallas's hip. He felt their breath against his cheeks. He caught a glimpse of one on his way inside the rock. They were flying together, spiralling on a hunt cycle outwards from the crash site, maybe thirty, forty of them, four-holers, insectoid, curled electric stems housing thrusters sprouting from a body that held a swivelling camera. They wouldn't have much range, maybe thirty minutes tops. If the three of them could survive a single pass, the swarm would be down to recharge before they'd make a return trip, enough time for Hiroki to get in and out with the three of them in his truck.

Dallas became still, their breathing shallowing at once, listening like bats for motion. Cam had talked about the robotics division when he was in the service in the America, and these looked similar. They moved as a single unit until an object of interest crossed their field of "vision," a combination of heat and motion sensitive optics, 360-degree sight. Now there was an augment he'd consider. If any of the drones got a positive hit, one of them would peel off and investigate. Anything that gave a secondary would bring in Tactical. Dallas wondered what that would look like. These things were top of the line. If the Somalis were spending on autonomics, they may have AI weaponry or even Neurals.

The trick here then was to remain unseen.

He felt a rustle from the rock, Kit moving against him, trying to get out. He made eye contact, glared a "Do not move" at her, and went back to stillness, breathing shallow, trying his best not to give off any heat, whatever that looked like.

The din of the swarm quieted as the last of them departed, they left no stragglers. These were not stealthy machines. If any were doing further investigation, he would have heard them.

"Let's get out of here before they come back." He glared at Kit. "And before our cargo tries to get us killed again."

He scraped his way out from the crack in the rock. The horizon had a faint glow of approaching sun. In silhouette, under a large acacia tree, he saw the motion of livestock and the unmistakable sight of a Maasai herder leaning against his blade.

Behind them, a kilometre up, hung a dual-fan drone, its contrarotating blades spinning in ducted silence. Through tactical optics dangling like a jellyfish's trailing tentacles, it watched. Like the Maasai, it was not part of any herd or swarm, its camera's zoom sufficient to read the time on Dallas's wristwatch and the fear in Kit's eyes.

Hunted by robotics. Not how Kit had envisioned rounding out her work week.

"Is that the Maasai?" she asked, pointing with both hands.

"Looks like him and some goats," Dallas said.

"I can talk to him, maybe get us some help."

"You can speak Somali?"

"If he's Maasai he speaks Kiswahili. Like I said earlier, I can help." The two men exchanged a look.

"At this point, lady, I'm all ears," Dallas said.

It was a short walk into the grasses where the Maasai stood with his flock. Kit approached him with a slow, submissive gait.

"Takwenya," she said.

"Iko."

"Kai Ikijiai?"

"Opiyo. Kai iloito?"

"Tunahitaji makazi."

"Lazima unifuate."

She turned to the others. "His name is Opiyo. He says he can help. That we need to follow him."

"I trust a man with a blade that long," Cam said.

"Unahiatji msaada mama?" Opiyo asked.

"Na hizi tu."

She held her wrists up, blood running down her arms.

"Mm. Niamini." *Trust me.*

Opiyo led her to a bare patch of ground. He swept away the dirt to uncover a large, flat stone and then pointed at it. "Niamini," he said.

She bent to her knees, laying her wrists against the stone. He placed the blade against the intersection of the metal bands, and then with two hands swept the sword up and down, severing the cuffs into two segmented and rigid pieces of metal. She picked up one of the fragments. It was warm to the touch. "Fucking finally." She turned to Opiyo. "Asante sana, Opiyo." *Thank you.*

He bowed his head. "Hakuna shida." *No problem.*

"You got any of that gauze left?" she asked Dallas.

"Fill your boots. But let's get out of sight. How far is it to shelter?" He tossed her the remaining roll.

She turned back to Opiyo. "Ni umbali gani?"

"Sio mbali. Kabla ya jua."

"He says before sunrise."

"Nifuate."

"And to go with him now."

44.

They'd waited out the morning in Opiyo's circular mud-and-stick hut. The roof looked and smelled like cow shit. Not ideal. He'd offered them wool blankets and beds of stretched cowhide and then left them to themselves inside. Once the morning's heat arrived with the risen sun, the hut baked like an oven. Kit had been quiet, scheming, Dallas thought, and since there was no physical door to lock, no way to keep her from running, he'd snagged the zap straps from the med kit, grabbed her by a bloody arm before she had a chance to react, and run it around her wrist, joining it to his. Zipped it a little too tight, displacing some flesh there.

"You're bunking with me," he said.

"You're fucking joking."

"Not fucking joking. Get some rest; you're gonna need it." He pulled out his duster, dropped a down into it, and gave it a whir and a hoot, left nostril this time, strictly for the change. Figured he could use a serious rest. Getting off the continent wasn't going to be easy, and neither would sleeping the day away in a hut built with dung. The pill knocked him out cold, clean through the heat and the smell.

Cam's Casio beeped, tearing Dallas from his induced slumber. Their five hours were up. Cam was already on the sat phone to

Hiroki arranging the pickup. Ten minutes, a kilometre away. *Don't be late*, was the message.

"You snore like a motherfucker," Kit said, holding up their plastic bound wrists.

"I didn't notice," he responded.

"Me either," Cam said, smiling as he popped audio beads from both ears.

What a couple of assholes, Kit thought, poking her head out of the door into bright African sunshine.

Opiyo stood guard outside. They had slept in a single hut in a field of waist-high green grass. His herd grazed nearby.

"Asante sana, rafiki. Wewe ni mkarimu sana,[1]" she told Opiyo as they filed out of his home, grateful for her father's Tanzanian heritage.

"Hakuna shida mzungu. Safari njema." *No trouble. Travel well.*

They scurried through the grass to a dirt road, the only road he could see. The afternoon heat scorched. Dallas was soaked in sweat, each step aggravating the hole in his side. He felt the gauze. It was sticky and wet. Not good. He couldn't keep the pace, and the cuff was beginning to burn. He stopped to catch his breath, leaned forward, rested his hands on his knees. "Cam, cut this thing off me."

Cam took off the backpack, removed a small pocketknife and sliced through the plastic restraints. Kit rubbed her wrists.

Dallas scanned the sky for surveillance. He had no interest in finding out what else the Somali's had in their bag of tricks. He looked ahead to where the heat haze blurred the horizon at what

....

1   *Thank you, friend. Your kindness is very generous.*

looked like smoke twirling off the road in the distance. "Cam, you see that?" The dust devil crept closer, a whirling cloud of debris growing skyward.

"Better be Hiroki. If it isn't, we're gonna be down deep in it."

"You say that like we aren't already." The sun reflected with a diamond sparkle off the approaching vehicle. Dallas had to shield his eyes; the flicker was strobing. "What's wrong with his truck?"

"It's easier to see up close," Cam said. "He's usually added to it."

It was the tusks that Dallas saw first, long and upturned, protruding from either side of the semi's engine grille. As it got closer, he could see they were scrimshawed with delicate hand-carved designs, mammoth maybe. In this part of the world, could even be ivory.

Angled octagonal pipes framed its exterior, jutting ahead, shading the truck's windshield. Every square centimetre had something cosmetic affixed. The detail was intricate, ornate. Hand-sized rectangular mirrors glued disco-ball style to its side panels reflected daylight from all angles, too much to take in all at once. As it slowed, Dallas could make out Japanese writing inscribed into its polished chrome bumpers, tassels that encircled the doorframes bounced under whining regenerative brakes that brought the rig to a halt.

The passenger window lowered, and deep East African beats thumped from inside the cab.

"Heard you guys might be looking for a lift." Hiroki grinned under a thin black moustache, visible from beneath his visor, his body moving with the music. He wore a faded black Easy Rider T-shirt with large Japanese characters below the flaking and worn print of a motorcycle.

Dallas looked at Cam, pointing at the truck. "You can add to this?"

"Trust me, there's always something."

Dallas stepped up and opened the door, pulling at Kit. "Get up here. Jump in the back and strap in."

Her legs were unsteady, and she stumbled on the step. He gave her a gentle shove and then went in with her, pulling Cam up with his other hand, the truck in motion before they'd finished closing the door.

Inside was somehow busier. Every millimetre of panelling and a good portion of the windows were covered in a three-dimensional landscape of minutiae. It had a depth to it, layered thick, Kansai style. Gundam replica military switches decorated the instrument cluster. Manga-star, bobblehead, pigtailed, girl dolls bounced back and forth on the dash. A miniature chandelier dangled from the ceiling in the middle of the cab, its tiny mirrors vibrating with the music, pure Japanese subculture. Postcards wallpapered the headliner above. The whole thing was an exercise in clutter management. It had a movement to it, everything bouncing and dangling in a sort of Brownian dance, like each individual item had some inanimate form of rhythmic movement disorder. Samurai sword scabbards protruded from the rear of the driver's seat. The chair floated, gyroscopically stable, the truck's structure in motion around it.

"You got belts in here?" Dallas asked, digging into the folds of the seat.

"Airbags," Hiroki responded, his eyes on the road, pointing at a symbol on the dash. Pathfinder Airbags. Same brand that had saved them in the *Arethusa*. They didn't come cheap.

"How long you had the rig?" The interior had an old smell to it, like memorabilia.

"Many years, Dallas-san. Almost thirty now. Before then my father had it, forty-eight years."

"Jesus. Multi-generational."

An augmented-reality headset dangled from a retractable bungee above Hiroki's head.

"You use the AR while you're driving?" Dallas asked, wondering how different it was from the tech in his jet, the wreck that was now buried in the sand.

"Of course. It's hacked into the local data streams. Intercepts the wide-band. Struggles a bit in the trans-border zone. Some jamming happening up there. Picks up the interesting stuff though. Crimes in progress, ASF locations, ongoing conflicts. I see what they see. Go ahead, try it on."

Dallas pulled the set down from the bungee and slipped it on over his head, its elasticized rear harness self-tightening. Hiroki flipped on the data feed, and the world outside became a generated image.

"This is some nice tech."

Instrumentation for the truck lay below the dashboard coaming. All the expected data was there: engine temps, speed, fuel status. Ahead was an illuminated overlay of the feed off the cameras. Similar to his own helmet's tech, he could see through the vehicle, a 360-degree augmented and unobstructed live video. Layered on top of the feed were translucent graphics. Police code scrolled upwards off his peripheral, displaying distances and vectors to selectable targets.

"You run into ASF out here?" Dallas asked.

"They patrol with tilt rotors."

"I would have thought we'd be fine in this rig," Dallas said. "Not like we're moving any obvious weaponry."

He wondered how infamous Kit was, if she'd been listed as missing yet.

"Long as we keep this a 'by the books, stick to the speed limit' run to the coast, we should have no issues with the ASF," Hiroki responded.

Dallas looked up through the skin of the truck at a visual representation of the night sky. Tags appeared beside aircraft showing publicly available air traffic control data feeds. He caught the distant amber flash of the belly of a suborb in early re-entry, a cyan tag illuminated beside it, WorldWide flight 868, New York to Sydney, overhead Addis, his old route. They'd begin to catch atmosphere near the coast, flames stuttering off the heat shield as the ship slowed off the air's friction. He took a moment. That life seemed like a memory that belonged to someone else.

"The problem is our location," Hiroki said. "We're still in disputed territory. The demilitarized zone is north of here, but the Ethiopian border isn't well defined. If they feel like there's something down this way worth their time, they'll investigate. Not much out here to stop them."

"Yeah, the Ethiopian ASF run a lot of airborne assets," Dallas said swiping, still toying with the visor's interface.

"What's the ASF?" Kit asked from the back.

"African Standby Force," Cam said. "It's an aggregate of militarized police and civilian agencies joined by most of the African nations. Lots of hardware, but they're light on training. Tend to shoot first and not ask any questions. Not to be fucked with."

"We're not fucking with anyone on this trip. We just need to get to the coast as fast as possible. Was a lot of antiaircraft equipment on the Ethiopian side of this border. Like a fucking war zone. Wasn't what got us, but we had more than a couple of missile launches aimed our way."

"What happened to the plane? And what was the cargo?" Hiroki asked.

"She's the cargo." Dallas pointed to Kit. "Wrecked the jet on an erector arm, big one. Sliced through the wing. Didn't see it coming."

Hiroki's eyes stayed on the road. "Lucky you guys got out OK."

"Got the same airbag system as this thing. Guess it works at speed."

Hiroki paused. "Gonna be a problem Dallas-san, you don't make this delivery."

"Tell me about it."

Dallas felt the silence building between them, the weight of that statement settling in. He popped off the set with a thumb on the rear straps, offered it back to Hiroki, then looked back in the sleeper at Kit. "Starting to feel like all four of us might work for the same people."

Something glowed green in Kit's wrist. Her eyes went bland and defocused. Dallas had seen it before, people wandering into the ether, but not from her. He grabbed her by the arm, held it up so he could see.

"She's got a sub-dee," he said.

Sub-dermal silicon grafted into her nervous system. It was like mainlining data, used her nerves as wiring. Simple day surgery for people who could afford it, electoral implants to enhance convenience. Meant she was traceable, and that was a problem for all of them.

"Motherfucker," Cam replied.

"Hiroki-san, you got a knife in this rig?"

"Under your seat, Velcro flap, for hunting. I keep it just in case." He smiled across the truck at Dallas, then snapped the visor on like a mask, went back to driving.

"We're gonna need to cut that thing out of your wrist, like right now." He reached under his seat, pulled a serrated blade from its Velcro pouch. "You want me to do it?"

Kit glared back; her squinted eyes refocused on him. "No, I do not want you to do it. Or anyone to do it. What's the problem here?" she asked, her volume increasing. "It's a fucking phone. We might need it."

"That thing in your wrist is both identifiable and traceable, so it's coming out. I'll ask the question one more time. Do you want me to cut it out for you, or do you want to do it?"

She looked from Cam to Hiroki, then back to him. She held out her wrist, nodding. "It's gonna hurt, isn't it?" More a statement than a question.

He popped a down in his grinder, dusted it, and offered it to her. "Give this a go. The knife is gonna pinch." She did as he said, stuck the nozzle in a nostril, and sniffed. He held her arm against Hiroki's driving seat for stability. She didn't resist, her eyes fluttering as her body buckled beneath her.

Dallas put the blade in where the holo's dim green light was still illuminated, cut a straight line down her forearm, lengthwise, not too deep, like he was scoring drywall. Blood flowed around her arm. In the incision he could see tiny silvery lines protruding from the device. He kept cutting until the visible, dark lines of surgical steel wool came to an end, halfway to her elbow. There was an abundance of tech, much more than he'd expected, running both directions.

"That's weird. There's one that goes forward, up into her hand. Thought this was all meant to be one way, back to the brain. Like it's pulling data from her fingers or something. Look at this. It's been woven into her nervous system." Cam had his nose in close, expanding the opening, inspecting.

"Is that possible? Like it's a neural?" Hiroki asked.

Cam shrugged. "Could be, I guess. Doesn't matter. It's all coming out."

Neural holography. High-test tech. That'd be giving her more than simple audio through that wiring. Wasn't like they could ask her, she wasn't conscious. Her head lolled back and forth from the pill. Dallas handed Cam the knife, holding Kit's arm palm up. Cam popped the small cylindrical holo unit out of her wrist with the tip of the blade, then, squeezing it between his finger and thumb, tugged at the hair-like wires, like he was untying a string tied in a bow. He pulled until the entire entanglement of whiskers popped out of her arm at once, splattering the interior with blood.

"Hey, don't make a mess of Enriko-san," Hiroki said, handing Cam a well-used hand towel from his door's pocket. She bled onto the floor, snoring in short burbles. "I need some glue. I don't think there's any in that med kit we brought. Hiroki, you got any medical supplies on board?" Cam asked.

"Should be a white box on the wall back there, passenger side, big red cross."

Kit was motionless, her weight dead against the chair. Cam was holding her flaps of skin together with his free hand's fingers, in his other he held up the sub-dee and its dripping entrails for a clear look at it.

"Need the glue now, Dee. She's really starting to bleed." Dallas propped her against the seat, dove into the sleeper, and rummaged for the kit.

"I found some. Looks pretty old though. Give me the knife. I need to cut the end off it," Dallas said, moving into the cab between the two forward chairs, a small tube of QuickStickIt in his hand. "Hold her still." He trimmed the end of the tube with the bloody knife he had used to open her up.

"Dee, she ain't moving anymore. What did you give her?"

He checked her pulse. Still there. "Gave her a down. Only the one but it was probably too much."

Dallas squeezed the glue into the incision, ran a single bead the whole length of it, following with a finger, like he was caulking a bathtub. Used his forearm to provide pressure against Cam's, squeezing the wound closed. They held it for a minute, then let go, checking it had stuck.

"There. Good as new," Dallas said. "Let's see the hardware."

Cam held it up, still bloody.

"I've never seen one this close. What's with the metal strings?" Dallas asked.

Cam slid his fingers along the slender metal fibres, burgundy body fluids collecting along them. "They splice it into your nerve endings. Some fancy code sets up the routing. But I wasn't into biotech. Preferred robotics, and I've never seen operational cabling that thin."

"Maybe it's a tracker. Antennae? Either way we should get rid of it."

"Could melt it on the engine block," Hiroki suggested.

"Or tie it to the exhaust pipe," Dallas said. "Could just shove it under the hood and roast it too. It won't work without her biosig so we could toss it out the window as well."

Cam gave her a nudge. "How long she gonna be like this for? Gonna need her walking and functional later."

"Not sure. One of those puts me down for three to four hours. But I'm a heavy user. Could be worse for her."

"Not good, Dallas. Not fucking good."

"I've got some ups left. Could push one of those up her nose."

"Gentlemen, we have a bigger problem ahead," Hiroki interrupted. "I'm seeing a lot of chatter on the ASF network."

He stayed under the visor, his hands swiping at data, their pace and purpose increasing.

"ASF has deployed assets. Someone called in your crash. Got some military choppers in the air. Tilt rotors. They're heading for your wrecked machine."

"How far till we're clear of the trans-border zone?" Dallas asked.

"More about distance than time. We can't outrun the military if they target us, not before we reach the border. We need to ditch this heat sig and hide. Hide very, very well."

Dallas wrapped the metal lines around the holo cylinder, squeezed the resulting ball into itself, and shoved it in his pocket. "Don't let me forget to melt this fucking thing," he said to Cam.

"Can we talk about the tilt rotors?" Hiroki asked. "I've got a visual, three of them, at our six o'clock. Looks like they're touching down at the crash site. How do you want to play this?" His head moved back and forth behind the AR set, his fingers engaged in an invisible dance of data, the automatics taking care of the driving.

"Depends. How long do we have until we find a paved road?"

"Dallas-san, we are in Somalia, in a disputed border zone. This is the only pavement we will find until Mogadishu," Hiroki replied.

Their heat signature alone from a fossil-burning engine would give them away. They'd be searched and imprisoned. Thrown in a Somali jail cell and forgotten about, Dallas figured. No thanks.

"We need to park this thing, hide it, and hide us. They'll be searching hard for us if they think we're on the run. What if we make it look like this thing is busted down on the side of the road? Is there any terrain other than rock and sand in this fucking country? Somewhere we could leave the truck and hide ourselves?"

Hiroki did not answer right away, his hands circled, swiping at air. "There's a river, ten minutes from here, looks like a structure. Abandoned perhaps. We put the Enriko-San against a wall, go lie by the river. Maybe they won't see us on the infrared."

"Best option in my opinion. We're done if we stay in this thing. They'll catch us for sure," Dallas nodded, agreeing with himself.

"I disagree," Cam said. "If they come looking for her, they'll have a ground team doing the real hunt, bots and drones. Neurals are way better at the scan than any human, no matter how augmented."

"So, what then? We going to keep cruising like nothing happened?" Dallas asked. They'd passed vehicles driving in the opposite direction. Like Hiroki had said, it was the only road, and they weren't out there alone. It wasn't out of the question for them to simply continue.

"Hiroki, you use this rig for smuggling, yes?" Dallas asked.

"Hai."

"All by itself? No trailer?"

"When there is a trailer attached, it is for the purpose of distraction," Hiroki replied.

"So, where do you hide the contraband?"

"Ah. Good thinking. Under the bedding in the back is a metal plate. It's held in place by an electromagnet. Thousands of kilos of force. Has its own electrical system, fails on. The only way to switch it off is in here." He tapped the AR set on his head. "Underneath the plate is a container. It has holo imaging on its walls. Shows up as a fuel tank on the X-rays. Fools them every time."

"Big enough for the three of us?" Dallas asked.

"Tight squeeze for three. But one? No problem."

Dallas shared a look with Cam.

"Open it. We can figure out the rest."

Dallas pulled off the bedding and shoved it against the back of the driver's seat. The metal plate underneath was shining aluminum, a filler cap tucked in the corner. He pointed at the cap. "This thing work?"

"Sure does. Carries about a litre of real fuel. Thin walls." Hiroki smiled.

Dallas pointed at Kit; her body folded against the wall of the sleeper. "She's not gonna notice anything that happens to her for a good while. Let's get her inside, nice and cozy, see how much room we've got left. Hiroki, does this thing have an air hole?"

"It's well sealed, Dallas-san. Never had to haul a person before."

"That's a fucking problem," Cam said.

"Only once we close it."

45.

All around Woo, Hong Kong glittered beneath its reflective neon rain.

He dangled his hands over a thick iron railing, looking down a steep stone alleyway with a staircase that descended into Central. Thick, hypnotic beats of Singapore tech house filtered their way outside from the club next door, a fine layer of damp affixed to every external surface from the tropical evening's heated mist. It was how he liked it, muggy. Couldn't have stayed another minute in that arid desert, Mongolia. Couldn't have left soon enough.

He busied himself with individual flakes of tobacco, dribbling them into the folded paper he held in his fingers, his most delicate creation, his quiet indulgence. He didn't need to; he had an auto roller in his pocket. But he enjoyed the process. It allowed him to think, to drift away with the data, allow it to coalesce into a story, a suspect. At this point, he thought, even a lead would do.

"You gonna smoke that or just keep playing with it, soldier?" The question came from a young Eurasian with blond cornrows, a single dread snaking its way down a shoulder, colourful tattoos coating both his arms, none of it obvious triad ink.

"It's not what you think, kid. Nothing but a cig." Keen boy was looking for a hit on some green. He didn't seem jacked on any kind of stims, but his body was moving in step with the muffled sub emanating from behind the club's door.

"Hey, that's not easy to find around here either. Mind if I share it with ya?"

Woo nodded and then sealed the cigarette, running it through his lips as he always did, lighting it with a squint and a wince before passing it off to the stranger.

The kid dragged on it, long. "Don't see a lot of tobacco smokers around these days, bru. And this is smooth. Where you find this stuff?" He had a slight accent, Kiwi perhaps.

"I know some people in Europe. They bring it back on the suborbs for me whenever they're in town."

"Mmm...Amsterdam Shag. Great stuff. Is that legal?"

"You a cop?" Woo asked. For fun.

"Ha! No, bru, just trying to bum a ciggy outside the club." He smiled, motioning for another drag. The nightclub door opened, deafening beats spilling out onto the curb along with a couple, arm in arm, eyes wide, tweaked. They staggered past, engrossed in each other.

"You ever see anyone in there with a face tattoo? Chinese numbers?" Woo motioned toward the club, Drop, triad owned and operated for decades. Wo Shing Wo, if he remembered correctly, the oldest of the surviving triads.

"Depends who's asking, eh," the kid replied.

"I'm trying to steer clear of that kind of action these days. I've seen a few of 'em hanging around the mid-levels, and I don't want any trouble, if you catch my drift."

"Gotcha, bru. Yeah, I seen a fella in there tonight with a lot of face ink. Could have been a number, I guess. My written Chinese isn't as good as it used to be. Bit of a statement if you ask me. But he's not dancing, more like he's working, kind of patrolling the floor. I wouldn't mess with him. Scary-looking dude."

Bingo. Found you in your home base, fucker.

To walk in there would be a not-so-subtle form of suicide, strolling solo into the heart of the hive. Drop was well known to the precinct. Being a cop in there was a serious liability. Woo was here to get a sense of it, see who was coming and going. Not a good time to have a look inside. Good time to leave and do some more digging.

"Appreciate the info, kid. Not the kind of night I'm after." He took a long, deep drag, the cigarette only half finished, then offered it up. "Rest is yours. I know where there's more," he said, turning for the stairs and the escalators home, to solitude, an unopened bottle of scotch, and perhaps even some answers.

46.

"All three birds are in the air again," Hiroki said. "Heading directly toward us. I'm only picking them up on night vis. They're not running any lights. They're on the hunt."

"They got any reason to stop us?" Dark birds in the sky hunting them was a major problem.

"They don't need reasons out here, Dallas-san."

"How much time?"

"Maybe a minute till they reach us. They're in forward travel."

Those coax twins could do almost six hundred kilometres per hour, then stop on a dime and heli down to the road. They'd have a drone squad descending on them in seconds.

"Time to get inside, Dallas-san. I can toss the mattress and bedding on top once you're all in."

"Not gonna be nice in there," Cam offered.

"S'what I'm thinking. You first."

Cam got in, lying sideways, trying not to step on the crumpled heap of Kit beneath him. There was no way Dallas was going to fit in there as well.

"Cam, I hate to do this," Dallas said.

"What?"

He closed the lid. "Seal it," he said to Hiroki, who tapped the air ahead of him. There was an audible thump as the magnet energized. Dallas tossed the mattress and blankets on top, then jumped in the passenger seat.

"There's drones up, swarm of 'em out already ahead of us," Hiroki said. "Night vis is catching an occasional glimpse."

The AIs were casing the truck, trying to get a facial recog off either of them. Hiroki handed Dallas a pair of black-framed, clear-lensed glasses. "Put these on. Tricks the ID scans."

"How's that?"

"Intercepts the incoming scan and sends back a false image. According to those glasses, you're nothing but a dew farmer catching a ride with a goods transporter. They're hunting for runners, trucks hauling trailers. This should be all the distraction we need to get out of this mess."

Dallas felt the rotors thudding deep in his chest before he saw the aircraft. Tilt-rotor blades clawing at the air, slowing as they approached the truck. There were two, one on each side, hovering a metre off the surface, moving in perfect formation with them. The prop wash hit from both sides at once, the truck wiggling in their wake, the rattle of road detritus bouncing off Dallas's door, reminding him of the crash. The third copter would be farther back, running quiet, targeting. He felt corralled, like hunted prey.

The left helo matched their speed, flashed a brief and visible laser scan over the truck's hood and windshield. The second helo climbed, facing them, flying backwards, its blades increasing pitch, twin rotors digging hard into the air, its signature double whups driving deep into Dallas's bones. An instantaneous and intense white beam bathed the truck, blinding him. Neither of them spoke, neither of them moved. The helos' rotors continued to beat. The truck drove on. The world paused around him, the copters in perfect sync.

Dallas remembered to breathe.

They would be analyzing the data from their flight decks, hunting by proxy, letting the AIs do the heavy lifting. As his eyes adjusted once again to the darkness, Dallas caught a glimmer of moonlight off the rotor disk of the third helo orbiting above them, a silent monitor of the hunt.

47.

Woo's precinct band warbled on the bedside table, Fong's voice asking through the ring tone if he was there. Slivers of light crept from behind the blinds. The interruption irritated him. His head pounded. He let the band warble a little longer, then picked it up and flicked it to voice only.

"Boss, you need to come in. We've made a discovery."

He looked at the time, nine a.m. Really not that bad. Beside him in the bed, the bottle was half empty.

At least the lid was on.

"I'll be there in twenty."

He snapped on the band and watched as it self-adjusted around his wrist. Then he swiped for a Ryde, dreading the trip.

48.

The truck bumped along beneath them, the automatics perform-ing an occasional swerve as the system lost navigation cues in the dust kicked up by the marauding tilt rotors that hung motionless in the air, synchronized in flight at their ten and two o'clock.

"They're gonna leave. Transponder's not being pinged anymore," Hiroki said from under the visor.

The low birds moved off first, the copters' twin spinning discs getting fat with pitch, biting hard and peeling vertically, disappear-ing behind blinding ground clutter into the black night sky.

"That third one up high is gone too. They're done with us." Hiroki swiped into the air, took off the AR set, and put his foot on the dash, turning to face Dallas. "Told you, no problem." He smiled.

"We good to bring those two out of the hole?" Dallas asked.

Hiroki pointed at a signpost leaning away from the road. "That's the end of the border zone."

"You can pop the lid on the compartment back there. I'll get them out. Then we need to figure out a way off this bullshit continent."

"You bastard," Cam said, shielding his eyes against the dim cabin lighting as Dallas slid the metal cover off the tank.

"Had to be done. We were out of time. Good news though, the ASF has decided we're not worth further investigation." He reached in with an arm. Cam grabbed him by the elbow and yanked himself up into the cab. Kit snored down below.

"Still, hey?"

"Man, she never stopped," Cam said, looking at her. "Feel like it might be my turn."

The road had gotten better, smoother.

"*Our* turn." Dallas got back into the passenger seat. "Hiroki, you got this? We could use some down time."

"We got three or four hours to the coast, Dallas-san. You got time to nap."

Dallas snagged a blanket from the sleeper, then angled the seat all the way back. "I need an hour, tops." Hiroki nodded. Dallas closed his eyes, feeling a rare natural sleep sweeping over him.

Dallas woke slowly, like the mind was meant to, he supposed, to the jolt and rumble of East African roads. He watched sand peeling off the top of a ridge, like ocean spray off the lip of a wave, a wind farm's spinning turbine blades whipping along the edge of the road beside them. Ahead, a melon-coloured sunrise glowed. They passed water harvesters a hundred metres tall, illuminated in the morning light, patchy green grass surrounding their bases.

The interior decor of Hiroki's truck jiggled and swayed in a hypnotic dance, threatening to put Dallas back to sleep. The motor's fine purr vibrated the cab, the constant speed engine cycling in and out of sync, the transmission resonating as it adjusted to the ever-changing load on its drivetrain. It was soothing, rhythmic, like children's laughter, a lover's sleeping breath. He rested his forehead against the glass, his gaze drifting along with the shifting sands where he saw the spectral eyes of his Persephone, her bouncing golden curls, her infectious giggle, her unconditional love. A dream, his mind not yet woken. It didn't seem possible that she was so long gone, back in a previous life that seemed so distant it couldn't possibly have been his own.

He heard a groan from the sleeper that wasn't anything motorized. Pulling his grinder from an arm pocket, he dusted an up. Inhaled. His brain warbled and woke. Not many of those left, he noted. He looked over at Hiroki, who had the AR set on, oblivious to the rest of the cab, his head following a slow repeating arc, like a blind man's motion, left to right and back again as he scanned the data feed.

"Hey…" Kit mumbled.

Cam was awake and staring out the opposite side of the sleeper. Dallas looked down into the smuggling compartment at Kit writhing against herself, flailing. He'd been there. She was waking up from the pill he'd dusted for her earlier. Her first time. Never pretty.

"Let's get her out of there," he said to Cam. They pulled her up and into the sleeper cab, closed the lid, and replaced the bedding. They laid her down on top of it.

"What did you g-give me?" she asked.

"Might have been a little much," Dallas said. "Don't fight it. You'll come out of it quicker than you think."

"Someone back there on wheels just did a major U-turn, kicking up dust, catching us fast," Hiroki said. "You got Somali friends, Dallas-san?"

Dallas shook his head. "Not out here." They were on the outskirts of Mogadishu. The road was better, and there was an occasional streetlamp. Dust particles danced in their headlights as they passed, an industrial haze illuminated in the beams against a darkened backdrop, the city's background taint.

"Then we have some problems. Because right now, *we* got Somali friends."

Alongside the truck, matching their speed, came a silver Mercedes, longer than it should have been, the rear doors elongated like a limo, a tinted side window lowered halfway. Loose stones cracked off the side of the truck. Dallas wondered if the Enriko-san would be shedding some of that glued-together junk collection hanging off her outsides. Behind the Benz's lowered window, he saw a sun-darkened Asian face, a white cowboy hat perched atop his larger-than-normal head. Along the man's hairline, above the eyebrow, he wore a Chinese number six, tattooed in red, outlined in black ink.

Cam was watching too. He stiffened and moved out of sight of the window. "That ink, that six on his temple, that's an assassin right there. Yazi."

"The fuck's a Yazi?" Dallas asked. Kit sat bolt upright without warning, wiping drool from her lips.

"Some dark-voodoo, Chinese folklore, dragon-worship shit, I dunno. Call themselves the Nine," Cam said, pressing his back against the rear of the sleeper.

"What should I do?" Hiroki asked.

"S'long as he's not shooting, keep driving. Cam, who's the Nine?"

"Look, this is just some shit Montoya told me at Thieves, so grain of salt and all that. Guy named Chen Rong, mainlander, made his money in mining. Got into the asteroid rush when it was getting started. Pioneered the catch and sling and was the first to snare one out past Mars and get it back to Earth. Thing was so full of precious metals, he let half of it burn up on re-entry. There was that much of it. Destabilized the world market for a while there. Guy still made a killing though. Built himself an island out of the leftover regolith from the asteroid impact out in the South China Sea, west of Manila. Decided it was going to be a rogue state, named it Atlantis. His own country, fabricated out of this imported land mass from space. Apparently had half the world's dredgers working on it at one point.

"So now he's got an island country and decides he needs protection. But he's old world Chinese, right? So he decides on ninjas and assassins, nine of them. Sounds absurd, I know, but it gets worse. China starts harassing him, surrounds the island with navy ships, constant flybys with bombers and drones, telling him he needs to assimilate, give up his little island and come home to the motherland. This crazy fucker says no. China laughs and says they could take his island in minutes. Chen Rong maintains it won't happen. Says they should book a meeting in a few weeks to discuss. China says fine and leaves him alone. Probably bought himself some time with all his money. So, over the next few weeks before this meeting they'd set up, major fucking heads of state in China start going missing. Gone, never seen again. By the second week, it's the health minister. She's found dead and bloated in the Xiangxi River. Did her with a weapon of mass destruction. Had one of the nine put sarin in her veins. Authorities find no trace of the assailants, and I mean *zero* fucking idea how this shit is going down. In the third week, it's high-ranking PLA officers disappearing.

"While all this shit was happening, the chairman did nothing. Hadn't put two and two together. Figured it was the Americans, and it all got real fucking serious between the two countries for a while there."

"I remember that," Dallas said. "Was before the Wall. Press said it was a cabinet shakeup, that they were all being replaced."

"Right. Thank you, state-controlled media. Then a couple days before this meeting with the chairman, his entire security detail dropped dead. Ten of them. At once. Poisoned. They were being hunted, man. And then it went quiet. No more killings.

"So, the meeting date comes up. Chen Rong asks the chairman how his security people are feeling. Chairman heads over, this time by himself, sits down with Chen Rong on his island of fucking Atlantis and says, 'Whatever it is that you would like, we can help. The PLA is at your disposal.'

"So, at the end of it all, this guy gets anything he wants. Anything. And what does he do? He gets them to build him a lab, up in Ulaanbaatar, Neg something or other. Starts pumping out edits. Making even more money. No government interference. No interference at all."

Dallas pointed at Kit. "You're an editor. This story starting to sound familiar?"

She shook her head. "It doesn't make sense to me."

"Sense. NegSense," Cam said, snapping his fingers. "That's the name of the company."

Kit nodded, looking out the window at the Benz beside them. "I work for NegSense."

"Christ."

"In a pancake," Kit added.

"This is a big problem for all of us," Hiroki said.

"What kind of augments did you say you were working on in that lab?" Cam asked.

"Nothing any organized crime syndicate should be looking for," Kit said.

"Word is that same guy with his own country, he's running the Shing Wo," Hiroki said.

"Like he's the Shing Wo Dragon-Head?" Dallas asked.

"Like that Dragon-Head."

Dallas looked at Kit. "Why's the head of the Shing-fucking-Wo running a lab in Mongolia?"

"How am I supposed to know?" she said.

"I'd say this asshole, Chen Rong, who has a team of marked assassins, his own country, and a private augment lab in Mongolia, is not only our boss," Cam said, pointing at Kit, "but hers as well. We've been running tissue on this route for years. Been hauling more and more full-sized tanks lately. Did I hear you say earlier that you were working on something special?"

"But why kidnap me?" Kit asked. "I was in Mongolia two days ago. He could have had coffee with me, for fuck's sake."

"To begin with, we—and that includes you—ain't going to Mongolia," Cam said. "You were to be dropped in Hong Kong."

"Still doesn't explain why this particular asshole is shadowing us," Dallas replied, rummaging in the footwell. "We got anything to shoot with in this heap? Preferably something with a bolt action and a functional projectile?"

"I don't think it would help," Cam said. "That car looks bulletproof."

"He's put the window up," Hiroki observed.

Dallas looked out. The car window's cloudy tint obscured any view of the interior. With no warning, the vehicle accelerated away from them, twin plumes of dust climbing from behind its rear wheels as it vanished into the dawn ahead.

They sat in silence, the truck bouncing around Hiroki's gyroscopically stabilized seat. "You ever get the feeling you're being urged along like a child?" Dallas asked.

Cam nodded. "Yeah, that's twice now. Somebody in power knows we're here."

"You think it's possible they want us to know?" Kit asked.

"Might be an easier delivery than we thought if that's the case," Cam said.

"Without a doubt if it turns out we all work for the same people," Dallas added.

Kit shook her head. "I still don't get why they wouldn't just take me."

"Something to do with face. They paid for a service. It's our job to deliver, not theirs."

"Could be they're protecting their investment?" Cam asked.

"More like they don't want any of their people crossing borders,"

Dallas replied. "We're the specialists, believe it or not. Speaking of which, we need to get her on a ship to Hong Kong. And for that we're gonna need paperwork. On *and* off the boat. Hiroki, you got anyone that can help?"

"I can make some calls. I have people at the market who do passports."

49.

Woo chucked his filterless butt end into the street, blowing the smoke from his lungs before opening the door to the precinct lobby. Fong was inside, waiting.

"We found a dump site, up in the New Territories, Tai Po, on the Fortune Garden beach. Multiple bodies, and boss, there's a survivor."

"A survivor?"

"That's right. She's got no ID, no implants. We think she's a mute. Won't talk to us. Doesn't seem to understand Cantonese, English, not even Mainland."

Woo knew Fong meant Mandarin, but no one called it that anymore. "Where's she now?"

"Paramedics weren't sure what to do with her. She's dehydrated but uninjured. They dropped her at the morgue, put her in the containment cell, keeping her under surveillance for now."

"How many vics?"

"It's a messy scene, boss. I've got a broadcast for you to watch. Maybe not here though, I'll put it on the holo upstairs."

Fong cast the video from the scene as soon as they walked in the office. It looked like a plague pit, naked, discarded bodies stacked on top of one another, eyes open. Some were fitted with zippers, some of which had been left open, organs and dark stains dribbling down their bare, exposed flesh. Woo was grateful for the lack of smell.

"How many?" he asked.

"Got seven plus the Jane. Total is eight."

"Are those zippers?"

"Yes, boss."

"That's organ trafficking. And the zippers, Jesus, that's war crime stuff. This is so much bigger than the TKO victim." He walked in a tight circle. "Where was the survivor in all this?"

"Buried with the rest of them. Shallow grave. Woman walking her dog on the beach came across the site. Dog started digging."

Someone got sloppy, Woo thought. *Careless*. "I want to meet her."

"You willing to catch a Ryde?" Fong asked.

"Just today, and only to see her."

"Anyone tried giving her food? Water?" Woo asked. The woman was curled up in a fetal ball on the concrete slab bench in the morgue's translucent quarantine cell, a sealed airlock between them. She wore a hospital gown, bunched up around her waist, her long, brown toenails twisted around her ankles.

"That's worth seeing, boss."

Fong opened a holo and played a feed of the girl in the cell. "This was right after they brought her in." The mortician handed her a bottle of water through the cell's feeding slot. She struggled to move her limbs with any sort of coordination, her motions clumsy and random. She knocked over the bottle and lapped up the water like a dog.

"That is not expected," Woo said, nodding his head.

"Hm, yes detective," the mortician replied. "I have some information about this Jane for you. It's like you said, *unexpected*."

The mortician didn't look well. Bags of fluid had built up under his eyes, and his skin looked paler than before, which, Woo thought, was a difficult thing to achieve. "You get any sleep last night?"

"These data are quite irregular, so no, detective, I did not. I've been working on her since she arrived." He brought up a data sheet on his desk display. "We sampled her DNA. You can see here, in the Jane's sequence where I've highlighted. Look right here." He zoomed in, down to the nanoscale, and pointed at a section of the double helix where there was print. "That's a molecular tag, a trademark symbol on her strand."

"What does that mean?"

"Can you read it? It says Regrowth™," the mortician said. "This Jane was augmented up in Mongolia by NegSense Labs for regrowth. They owned that trademark you're looking at until it was outlawed."

"As in she's been genetically labelled? Like a product?" Woo asked.

"That skin job from TKO had the same augment," Fong said. "Now we know where it came from."

"That one wasn't molecularly labelled," the mortician said. "I looked for it."

"Could be a bad copy. Not like the triads haven't ever tried their hand at copying something. Is that why you would label someone like this? Copyright protection?" Woo asked.

"If you ask me, boss, it's so you know which one is which."

"And that would mean there's more than one person to label."

"A lot more, boss."

"Well. Fuck."

"Hm, yes. I don't think I need to remind you, detective, that regrowth was outlawed many years ago as an augment. Its use is internationally regulated. Specifically, to stop people exploiting it in circumstances not unlike these. I'm convinced there's more edits in her sequence; I just haven't found them yet."

Woo looked over at her. She was sitting up on the slab, quiet. Her head was tilted to one side, watching them talk. Listening. Like she was trying to learn. "Let's get back to why she's so uncoordinated. What language does she speak? Do we know?"

"Detective Woo, this child has, in all probability, been edited further. She moves as though she's an infant. It's possible that she's been in an induced sleep since birth. She may have reached consciousness for the first time in her life when the officers found her last night."

"So, we've got NegSense for organ trafficking at the very least."

"I'd say at the least," Fong agreed. "Who knows what other human rights violations are hiding up there, boss."

Woo had not enjoyed Mongolia. "Who's bankrolling that lab?"

"Good question, boss."

"If we have to go up there to make arrests, we're going to need cooperation from the local Mongolian police force, which means we're going to need some assistance from Beijing with the warrant process."

"That'll be complicated," Fong said.

"And unpleasant. I don't want to head back that way unless we have something concrete to follow. Like processing the other victims." Woo pointed at the Jane in the prison cell. "You need to get someone in there and clip her fucking toenails; they're disgusting," he said to the mortician. "Fong, let's head up to the office. I need some time with the holo to piece all of this together."

50.

"So, we just planning to walk her through security cuffed and gagged and hope no one raises a fuss?" Cam asked, fidgeting with a piece of black Lego he'd managed to pry away from the truck's interior.

"As long as it isn't her making a fuss, we should be alright," Dallas said, looking at Kit.

He was struggling with the why. Why had the military let them drive away? Why had the man in the Mercedes done the same thing? If he was in fact part of this Nine, why not simply take Kit from them and transport her themselves?

Hiroki's face wore the glaze of online communication. He spoke inaudible words into the AR set. Nodded. Flipped the visor up. "My people are at Bakaaraha. Passports will take five minutes to produce once we arrive. They'll need some mug shots and bio scans. Be twenty minutes or so until we get there."

Cam looked unhappy. He flicked the Lego piece against the window, glaring outside, frantically chewing his lip.

Dallas turned to Kit. "We're gonna need some cooperation from you." She hadn't been paying attention. He didn't like it. It was like she was casing, looking for a way out. Like she thought she had some chance of escape.

"Do I need to cuff you again or are you gonna behave?" he asked.

She rubbed her red and inflamed wrists, ran her finger along the glued incision Dallas had cut along her arm. Her wrists looked infected. He popped open the tin lid on the med kit, handed her an antiseptic wipe.

"I'm not sure what other options I've got." She tore open the packet and wiped her swollen wounds.

"Seems we're all running short on those," Dallas replied.

She looked him over. "You're still bleeding from that wound in your ribs. I can clean and dress that properly if you give me the med kit. I promise not to beat you to death with it."

He felt the bandage. She was right; the blood stain was growing. He nodded.

"Might be worth trying that glue you used on my arm," she offered.

"Not a terrible idea." He pulled off his hoody and unwrapped the bandage. Warm fluids oozed down his side. He reached across himself to touch the wound, got two fingers clean inside the hole. She flicked the crust off the end of the tube of QuickStickIt and applied a generous blob, squeezing the skin together to seal it. She taped a patch of gauze over it, then snapped the tin shut. *Stuff really does harden fast*, he thought.

"There, good as new," she said.

He put his hoody back on and then fiddled with the grinder, popping its lid open and closed.

Passports. A boat ride to Hong Kong. The woman seemed more or less compliant. He wasn't sure returning was their best option, but for now it seemed like a much better idea to come home with the package than not. There was a name for mercenaries who fled and tried to disappear with undelivered cargo.

Dead.

And Dallas wasn't ready for dead.

Hiroki pulled the truck into a gravel parking lot, waved in by a man in a collared shirt and slacks who clutched at his straw hat against the dusty wind.

Dallas stepped out of the vehicle with Cam and Kit, stretching and squinting at the daylight. He was still whizzed from the pill and more than a little paranoid. Hiroki paid the attendant. Dallas took in the scene. Where the parking lot ended, the market began, a dense procession of temporary wooden stalls covering their owners under linen tarps. They sold vegetables, caged poultry, clothing, ammunition, and automatic weaponry. Most everyone was openly armed, and the market was busy.

They walked along makeshift sawdust-covered alleyways of tarpaulin shade, not talking, Somali hawkers catcalling at them for sales. Dallas was hyper-alert. If anyone from Hong Kong was following them there, an Asian face would stand out against the foreground of African skin. The market around them was mesmerizing, hypnotic, no visible tech, Somali shillings changing hands with a magician's speed. Contrasts were wide. Ancient wooden wheelbarrows overflowing with beautiful ripe apples lined the dirt path. Bright and colourful African textiles hung from racks of rebar. They followed a young shirtless boy, pubescent stubble peppering his upper lip. On his head he balanced a two-metre swordfish, blood still dribbling from the bullet hole that had ended its life.

Hiroki led them to a stall that was walled in bamboo, a tan canvas sheet pulled taut, making a roof. Beneath it sat a middle-aged Somali man, saliva the colour of hot tar collecting in the corners of his swollen lips, an afternoon's worth of khat rammed in his cheek. He was surrounded on his white plastic lawn chair by produce. Lettuces, carrots, onions, potatoes, limes, bundles of herbs, fat, luscious mangoes by the dozen. Dallas could smell the coriander and the faint bite of freshly cut lemon on the breeze. The man smiled from behind his boxed garden. "What can I find you, bucktee?" *Stranger.* He'd heard that one before. It wasn't a nice word.

"We're looking for baasaboorka. Spoke to our friend Indisi. You know where we can find him?" Hiroki asked.

"Ah, Indisi, yes. He down at the special special. All the way to the end of the market. You gonna find what you need there, ajnabi." *Foreigner.* Still derogatory but a kinder version of the word.

The path narrowed to a tunnel, and the breeze disappeared, the temperature noticeably increasing. The sky was no longer visible, the lane had been sealed in opaque plastic sheeting that snapped in the desert wind. They followed Hiroki to a doorway slashed through the poly, a decades-old, hot-pink neon sign blinking "Special Special" from inside.

At the entrance stood a tall, olive-skinned man in an almond-coloured Moroccan dishdasha, a Russian AK slung across his chest, his finger on the trigger, red and tired eyes watching them, one black combat boot tapping in the dust.

"We here to see Indisi. Make some baasaboorka. Need for these three." Hiroki stated in his best broken English.

"Ya, ya, no problem. You go inside, Indisi expecting you." The guard urged them through one at a time, his hand on each of their backs.

Inside, a wheeled air conditioning unit hummed, blowing dusty particulate through thin beams of sunlight that cut through gaps in the textile ceiling, which looked like it was made of rugs. The conditioned air cooled Dallas's moist skin. Incense burned, swirling and silent, filling the room with rose petal smoke.

"Indisi," Hiroki said.

"Hiro-san. Konnichiwa, my friend." He stood from behind a polished aluminum desk in the shape of a wing, "Piper" embossed along its curved leading edge. His robe was Maasai, an arterial-red, armless cloak that fell below his knees. A string crown of multicoloured beads lay across his forehead, his stretched earlobes contained large white hoops. Dallas knew that behind that smile and underneath that cloak was a recently sharpened machete that the man would be unafraid to use.

They bowed to each other. "You got some paperwork for my *saaxibo* here? We in a bit of a rush." Hiroki's smile came with a plea for help, using the local word for "friends."

"Yes, yes. We can help your saaxibo, Hiro-san." He looked Kit up and down. "You from East Africa?"

"Zanzibar." She shivered in the aircon.

"Hm. Tourism." He sneered as he spoke the word. "Looks like you could use some clothes, Zanzi." He handed her the suit jacket from the back of his chair. She put it over her shoulders. "There are many clothing shops here. Be kind to yourself. Have these men buy you some pants." He waved at Dallas and Cam, nodding, and returned to his chair. His fingertips came together into prayer, touching his nose in thought as he addressed them. "Now, these baasaboorka we can give you, they are short expiry date, three days left, no more. You may leave Somalia with them, but where you take them you cannot use." He opened a drawer in a flimsy steel filing cabinet behind him, pulled out three rectangular, credit-card-sized pieces of carbon fibre, China and South Islands passports, photos blank, ready for printing.

"Works for us. Not exactly gonna be clearing customs in Hong Kong," Dallas said.

"Over here then, one at a time." The man motioned at them to come around to the side of his wing desk, where he had a camera and a bio-scanner set that looked like it was fifty years old.

"This gear seems outdated," Dallas said, putting his index finger on the green screen of the fingerprint scanner. "We got any sort of guarantee it'll work?"

"Not to worry, ajnabi. First we take your photo. Then we take your fingerprints, scan your eyes, and your beat, and *then* we take your money. After that we can put you in the system and book your tickets with the IDs. You will see. It will work. Don't worry." Something about the statement made the man smile as he nodded to each one of them. Their data, their now forgeable identities, would be worth much more to him than the money they were about to pay.

The aircon droned away in the corner of the room while they fed their bio-sigs into Indisi's ancient computer system, an illuminated apple on the back of his display. None of them spoke as the poly wrap blew in the afternoon's increasing breeze. Kit hadn't said a word for hours. Dallas couldn't tell if she was terrified, plotting her escape, or both. He wondered what she was augmented for. What sort of superpowers was she hiding behind that compliant face? What would *he* do if could write his own augments?

"We also need tickets to Hong Kong. Something private, away from other passengers, something *easy*," he said. This job had become anything but.

"Everything is easier with *money*, my friend," the Somali said.

"Money is something we have," Dallas replied, removing the roll of Bank of China notes from his ankle wrap.

"Then easy is something *you* have, ajnabi."

51.

Woo stood inside the holographic display, all the data from the case displayed at once, projected as a globe, interlinking items and people with dotted red lines like pieces of string. He and Fong were the only two in the office, and the projection filled the room. He grabbed the image of NegSense Labs with his hand, moved it to the centre of the holo.

"So, we've got three identified vics plus another seven in the pit." He linked the TKO murder and Avery to the lab with a pinch of his fingers and a tap. "One alive with some sort of global amnesia." He circled the Jane's image, bolding the ring, and linked her to the lab as well. "Like she's forgotten everything that's ever happened to her, including language." He tapped the NegSense image. "It's possible these assholes are dumping genetically modified bodies in Hong Kong during typhoons. We've yet to find a motive." He tapped the skin job from TKO. "How many of those haven't we found yet?" He reached for his only image of the cowboy hat with the face ink, then linked it to the lab. "Shing Wo is up my ass warning me to 'look inside,' whatever that means. Again. We have no idea why." He took a step back, outside of the globe. "It must be related. Like we're getting close to something. The tissue runners…" He had no images of them, wondered if anyone did. "They must be related too. What are we missing here?"

"The bar, Nailing Thieves, boss." Fong cast an image of the sign that hung outside the bar into the globe. Woo grabbed it, linked it to the cowboy. He preferred actual red string to the virtual kind.

"We go back in there, gonna be inviting trouble," he said.

"Agreed. Buckyball guy was a mob hit. Could link him to the Shing Wo." Fong tapped the image of Avery Hill. Woo linked it to the Shing Wo, gave it a long red line to remind him that it happened in West Africa.

"Triads don't do hits outside of the Greater China area. This guy must have done something heinous."

"Snitched or something maybe?" Fong said. "Boss, I've been thinking about that girl, the one with amnesia. The mortician said she moved like an infant. What if he's right about her? That she only just gained consciousness for the first time. What if she's a test subject? What if all those cosmetic augments coming out of the lab aren't exactly ethically sourced?" Fong sat on the edge of his desk, staring up at the holo.

"Testing for augments. Human test subjects." Woo nodded with him. "Let's call that established, Fonger." He circled the lab several times, bolding the ring. "NegSense keeps coming up. It's front and centre. Who runs it?"

Fong's fingers bristled through data on his personal holo. He swiped his hand up, casting an image of a woman in her early thirties, straight dark hair and light brown skin, into the data globe in the middle of the room. "Kit McKee, lead geneticist," the text said.

"Fucking genetics. I'm starting to understand why the America shut it all down. Let's give her a call."

Fong swiped for a call to the lab.

"NegSense Labs, this is Fiona. How can I help today?" a smiling female voice said.

"This is detective Fong with the Hong Kong Police Force. We're investigating a case and would like to ask your lead geneticist, Kit McKee, a few questions."

"You're not the only ones, detective. She hasn't been seen on the campus for a few days now. We understand she took a last-minute business trip with her friend and colleague, Avery."

Woo looked at Fong.

"Was that a mister Avery Hill?"

"Yes, detective, that's correct."

"Thank you very much, Fiona. If Miss McKee does return, please have her call us at this number."

"Have a nice day, detective."

Fong swiped the call closed.

Woo grabbed the image of Avery Hill, attached it to Kit McKee, the process illuminating the circles around NegSense Labs, the Shing Wo, and all three of the victims.

"Someone very big is behind all of this," Fong said, looking at the holo.

"So, what is happening all the way out here," he pointed at the murder scene in the Gambia, "that's got the Shing Wo so wound up they send an assassin to take down a geneticist? What assets do the Shing Wo have in West Africa?"

"Tissue, boss."

Woo tapped twice to create two circles. Inside each he wrote "Runners.""The bartender at Thieves said a couple of mercenaries were doing contra runs. Is it possible that in addition to running contraband tissue, these guys are moving fully grown humans out of West Africa so they can be used as test subjects up at NegSense?" He linked the runners to the Shing Wo, the bar, and the lab.

Fong nodded. "Makes sense to me, boss."

Woo tapped for a new circle, wrote the number seven inside it. "Like those seven genetically modified human victims found in a pit?"

Fong grabbed a photo of the crime scene on the beach, cast it at Woo. He tapped the photo into the same circle.

"So, where is Kit McKee?" Woo spun the globe to the image of Avery Hill. "That woman on the call, Fiona, said she was travelling with Avery. There was no mention of her in the homicide report in the Gambia." He spun the globe back to Asia and tapped her image, the links pulsing in red. "She got family?"

Fong's fingers blazed. "Mother's deceased. American. Father's alive and, get this, lives in Hong Kong. South Lantau, near the launch centre."

"Got a number for him?"

"Calling it right now." Fong cast the call into the central holo. Kit's father answered, coughing. "Hello?"

"Hello, Mister McKee. This is senior detective Woo from the Hong Kong Police Department. How are you today?"

The video feed showed an aging cocoa-skinned man. Tightly wound coils of coarse, white hair thinly covered his head. He coughed again into a tartan handkerchief, pausing to look at the sputum. "I'm doing OK, detective. What can I help you with?"

"Sir, as part of an ongoing investigation, we would like to ask some questions of your daughter, Kit, but we're having trouble locating her. Can you tell us when and where you last saw or spoke to her?" Woo asked.

"Well, we were meant to have dinner when she was in town last, but she had her flight bumped up, and she couldn't make it. That was almost a week ago now. Is she in some kind of trouble? I can give you her number."

"That would be helpful, Mister McKee." Fong took down the number. "Did she seem stressed in any unusual way?" Woo asked.

"Nothing out of the ordinary, just that she was having some issues with work."

"Did she tell you anything about it?"

"She said she was being stonewalled. Not sure what that means. Can you tell me what this is about, detective?"

"We aren't able to discuss the investigation with you, but we will notify you if we get in contact with her. We appreciate your help. Have a nice day, sir." He swiped his hand down, ending the call.

"She's missing, boss."

"These two mercenaries." He highlighted the rings labelled "Runners." "Is it possible these guys are bringing the test subjects into Hong Kong?"

"Sure, boss."

"And possible they pick them up in West Africa?"

"Makes sense."

"The fucking Gambia?"

"You think they have Kit?" Fong asked.

"Shing Wo followed her to West Africa with a magnetic weapon and murdered her colleague, Avery Hill. He would have had that buckyball inside him for days. That's a premeditated assassination. I don't think the killers expected the trip west, but they went anyway, which means it was last minute, means it was *required*." He selected a map, a detailed image of the planet exploding into view. He spun it to the Gambia, then around to Hong Kong. Drew a line between the two.

"Is that even possible? To do a flight that long and have nobody notice?" he asked.

Fong slid off the edge of his desk, walked over to the projection, his hands on his hips. "It's a lot of water to cross. Could probably do it without too much interference if you had the right equipment."

"Getting somewhere, Woo?" Superintendent Lee asked, startling him from behind.

"Sir, I think it'd be wise for us to connect with the Customs and Excise Department. We've got this lab in Mongolia connected with the Shing Wo on what looks like cross-border human trafficking of some kind."

"Some kind? What kind? I don't need to remind you C and E are not our biggest fans," Lee said. He was talking about "the attack." The Anti-Terrorism Squad had been staffed entirely with customs officers, all but one. All had lost their lives, and all had lost their families, all except Johnny Woo of the Serious Crimes Division.

Woo pointed at the circles labelled "Runners." "Whoever these guys are, we think they have this woman." He pointed to Kit.

"Kidnapping?"

"How it looks to me. Puts the Shing Wo over in Africa to do a hit on this guy." He pointed at Avery, illuminating the links to his avatar. "That's not something we see. Ever."

"I'll make a call. I don't think they'll work with you, Johnny, but they may work with Fong."

52.

Kit fidgeted with her fingernail, careful not to let it pop while she waited her turn to donate her biosig. She'd decided there was no point in trying to run. These kidnappers were not violent and running would get her nowhere. She stood out in this part of the world, a quarter Asian with mocha skin, identifiably foreign.

She ran through escape scenarios. If she could get to Addis, it might be possible to get Doudna to come to her. If she could get out of their sight, she could maybe beg for help, but at what cost? She had no money, no subdermal, no way to purchase anything. All she had was the holomem in her finger, and she could never let that go. Her most viable option was to ride this out, get on Chinese soil, and find a way to contact her father, or Doudna, even Grandpa Rong.

Grandfather.

Was it possible that she was being kidnapped by her own family? *Better the devil you know than the one you don't*, he would have said.

What would he say in this moment, to her face?

She decided to play along, wait for an opportunity. She'd gotten close to Dallas, helping him with that bandage, close enough to smell. If she was going to ditch these guys with any genuine hope of escape, she would need to get much closer than that.

She was the last to scan her biosignature, the printer ejecting their passports in seconds. Dallas exchanged the bills he'd waved in her face at the crash site, the cash disappearing into Indisi's clothing with remarkable speed. "Ajnabi. It has been a pleasure. Safe travels," he said, holding Hiroki's hand from behind his Piper wing-desk.

The man with the AK led them outside, his hand on their backs once again. He pointed to a stall with colourful clothing hanging from bamboo lattice. "Over there, ajnabis. They can help you with something to wear for the lady."

Dallas bought her linen pants, a sweatshirt, even underwear, grandma style. They'd be sweaty in this climate. She wore them anyway, straight out of the change room, a treat after Cam's over-sized and well-worn boxers.

Hiroki led them out of the market toward the truck. "I can drop you in Old Mogadishu. The ferry port is there."

As they approached the port, the ocean vessels rose into view. Great, hulking hybrids of boat and aircraft. They'd seen them while crossing the ocean at night, travelling at speed, their furled wings extended above and below the surface. Foils that lifted the massive structure out of the water's drag, taking advantage of the same ground-effect mechanism the *Arethusa* had used, achieving speeds that would take the boat ride from a week down to a manageable twenty-four hours.

"This is it for me, friends," Hiroki said.

"Wish we could say the same," Dallas replied.

"You deliver the package, things should be OK," Hiroki said, nodding. "Take this." He offered Dallas a wrist holo, placing his free hand on Dallas's shoulder. "It's like a walkie-talkie. Encrypted end to end. Case you find any trouble on that boat."

"We appreciate it, Hiroki. Safe travels," Dallas said, leading Kit away by the elbow.

Kit had never been on a ferry this size. Standing at the dock looking up at it gave her vertigo, her vision obscured by its walled hull. It was massive. They ducked through a small door to board. It led them into a corridor, where were herded into a large elevator by Somalian staff dressed in pressed, short-sleeve, naval whites. The doors opened to the first-class deck, its tinted windows reminding her of the Mandarin Oriental, the typhoon, of her lunch with Avery. She steadied herself with the railing, wobbling as she thought about him.

Through those windows she could see the main deck of the boat. It was impressive. Had to be thousands of people down there. A floating city block about to launch on an ocean-crossing voyage to a destination that terrified her. She wanted a glass of wine, her purse, a pair of pyjama bottoms, and more than any of it, a shower. Dallas and Cam (she hated that she was now referring to them by their first names) had hurried her through the ship all the way to their cabin, as eager, it seemed, as she was to get somewhere they could relax for a moment without being followed or noticed, where a shower had become a very real possibility. They were filthy, hadn't slept, and had survived a fucking plane crash. She needed some serious rest.

Dallas closed the door, latched it. "How are the incisions?" He was the first to speak. If he was legitimately concerned, it didn't show.

"Itchy." She held up her left hand. "It feels infected. I should probably go see the doctor on board." It wasn't. The glue had sealed the opening well. Was worth a shot though. She hadn't spoken much. "My wrists are worse." They hadn't healed, and if they weren't infected they would be soon.

"Yeah, that's not happening. I should have glued those closed as well. My fault. Go take a shower and give it a good cleaning.

I brought the QuickStickIt, so we can seal it if we need to." She wasn't surprised, but the shower was a gift. One step at a time.

The suite was pristine, minimalistic, a long way removed from the trucking nightmare she wanted to forget. The room was decorated with stark white plastics and polished steel, first-class comforts. The bed would comfortably sleep all three of them.

She closed the sliding door to the bathroom. Locked it to solitude, privacy, to a peaceful moment. She breathed.

After, she thought. After she washed and after she slept, she would consider her escape.

The shower was blissful. Warm water made tiny rivers of heaven down the back of her neck, along her shoulders, and down her filth-ridden arms. She scrubbed, rinsed, then leaned against the wall, letting the water run over her as she considered her situation. Someone had gone to an enormous amount of trouble to have her shipped unconscious to an unknown location to an unknown purchaser for an unknown reason. It had to be for the Zeus data. It was the only explanation.

Fuck.

She reminded herself that it couldn't have been Avery. He didn't know. The lab was centred around her. If she was being spied on, her data could never have been safe.

She turned off the water and dried herself with a clean, white towel, eager to be horizontal. There was a remote chance that staying with the two smugglers was a better option than running but leaving her life to chance had never once been an option to consider.

She stepped out of the shower and tied the soft belt of a white terrycloth robe around herself, hair still dripping. "What's going to happen to me when we get to Hong Kong?" she asked through the door as she towel-dried her hair.

"Hard to say," Dallas responded, "you're not exactly our regular cargo. And I've got some large and unusual expenses to cover."

Fully dressed in the new and clean clothes from the market, she slid the door open. Dallas was waiting outside, glaring at her, his eyes a deep turquoise, rimmed by a thin ring of navy. They were bloodshot, sad, and lonely. "And we gotta get you there first. We might have company on this boat, and no easy way to hide from them."

"What do you mean by 'company'?" she asked.

He looked nervous, making fists with his hands, and for the first time she saw him messing with a wrist holo.

"I mean Hiroki just messaged me on this thing and said he saw what looked like government assets moving toward the dock. *American.* A handful of drones, surveillance hardware he's never seen outside of militarized zones." He tossed the wristband on the bed, looking through her to where a faint whine of spooling turbines filtered in through the single window to the outside. There was a woof of light-off as the ferry's engines started. The smell of burnt kerosene drifted in, and the boat nudged its way out of the harbour. "Says there could be American agents on board. They have no jurisdiction here, so they might not be armed, but anything's possible."

As he reached behind her to close the porthole, she caught a sense of his odour, days unwashed and pungent. She glimpsed his ropey triceps as he latched the window shut, surprised to find herself flushed. She considered telling them about Zeus, about the edit, but they didn't seem in any way interested. She'd never disclosed the details. Not to anyone.

"Those drones will be neural. Autonomous," Cam said. "Probably gonna watch this tub all the way to Hong Kong, report when we get there. If there's agents onboard, they'll link up and find us for sure. They'll have her voice, her heartbeat. She's an American *citizen,* man. Her vitals will all be on record. You can't hide that stuff when the government's looking, like really looking. Only a matter of time till we're made." He was right. American records on her would be exhaustive. She was educated, endorsed, registered. That beacon they'd cut out of her arm wasn't the only way she could be tracked.

"They didn't like your kind in the America, as I recall." Dallas remarked.

"Let's say they disagree with my ideology in a broad sense."

Cam joined them on the bed, all three of them sitting along its edge, side by side, facing forward.

"We may also have some people on this boat who are interested in seeing our delivery through to completion," Dallas said.

"Be nice to know who they are," Cam replied.

Kit considered the consequences of confessing the edit buried in her fingernail. So what if she told them? It wasn't like they'd be able to do anything with the data other than deliver her to whatever horrible fate was waiting on the other end of the voyage. As she sat there between her two captors, she ran her hands along the clean, white sheets, felt the grain of the fabric. She thought of Avery, of his horrific murder.

Come what may.

"I can show you what the people who are trying to kidnap me are interested in," she said, sweat beading at her temples. The two of them stopped talking, turning to face her.

"Aren't *we* the people who kidnapped you?" Cam asked.

"Not unless you were there when they tanked me. Listen, this is complicated. The human genome is full of design flaws, genetic disease, faults or weaknesses that we've been editing out. We've solved so many. Saved so many. The list is endless, and we've been accelerating the evolution of our species as a result of our successes."

"Let's get back to what they *are* interested in you for, because we're not huge fans of editors in a broad sense," Dallas said.

And so she decided.

She flicked up her false fingernail and depressed the holomem there to release it. "Be a lot easier if I had my implant," she said, both of them looking at her finger with surprise.

"That's a neat trick," Dallas said.

Cam nodded. "S'what I'm thinking."

"This is what these people are after. It's the Zeus edit. It's the answer."

"The Zeus edit." Cam laughed. "Whatever."

"Zeus is the name of the test mouse," she said.

"The answer to what?" Dallas asked.

She held the holomem between her finger and thumb. "If you guys are willing to help me out of this mess, I'd be happy to share this with you. But I still need a holographic reader and a lab to make it."

The two men shared a look. Dallas shook his head. "Can't help. We don't deliver you our lives are on the line."

"This would change your lives."

"Not delivering you would end our lives, so no thanks. Put that thing back in your finger, and let's focus. First of all, on how we're going to hide you and then how we're going to get you into Hong Kong."

She put the chip back in her nail bed and flicked it closed. She knew better. Bribery had never been her thing.

Delivery was nonnegotiable. They were being paid to provide her alive, preferably tanked and sleeping, which, with her stasis tank and the *Arethusa* scattered in pieces across the Somalian desert, was becoming increasingly unlikely. It also made his and Cam's lives expendable, which was going to be a problem on delivery. Dallas felt like they'd been tracked to the ferry but not located, not yet. They were safe only as long as they remained in the berth. If Hiroki was right, and government eyes were monitoring the boat, there would be a welcoming committee to meet them as they sailed into

Hong Kong's waters.

He looked at Kit. That false fingernail. He figured if anyone knew about that holomem she was hiding in there, none of them would be alive. There had to be a reason they were being allowed to run. He tapped her hand. "Best keep that thing a secret."

"Whatever she's got in there, someone is going through an awful lot of trouble to get it," Cam said.

"Agreed. And it's our job to deliver it. We mess this up, there's gonna be trouble for you and me." Dallas felt guided, manipulated, trapped in the room. "We need a way off this ship." He pulled out his handset. "I'm calling Maneli."

He unwound the wire wrapped around the phone, fit the bead in his ear, flipped it open, and called.

"Maneli, it's Dallas."

"'Ello, Dee, my friend. Been awhile. What is it you need today?" she said in a deep, smoked-all-her-life Israeli accent. Straight to business. Never was any bullshit with this woman.

"I'm in some profound, extensive shit, and I need an extraction. Three of us. We're on a foil. Just left Mogadishu. Got about fifteen hours until Singapore, another seven to Hong Kong. Government eyes on us, and something else, something odd." Right to the point, she'd appreciate it.

"Which government?"

"Looks American."

"That's particularly bad news. What's odd about it?"

"Hard to describe. I'd say our employer has a good idea where we are but isn't taking any action."

"Your employer is my employer, Captain. Makes this a tricky conversation." She sounded like she was chewing on the end of a pencil.

"Can you help?" Dallas asked.

"Depends. You want me to pull you out before the boundary?" She was talking about the border between the Greater Bay Area and the South China Sea, where the government paid attention only when the tides of politics demanded.

"That would be ideal." The sound of her fingers tapping keys was cut silent by mute. The seconds dragged. She unmuted.

"It's going to have to be just me. Solo pickup in the sub. Where's the Arethusa?"

"I left her in Somalia. Bit of an ugly breakup."

"Sorry to hear that." He listened to more typing. "You on the China Ferry 828 to Hong Kong?"

"That's the one."

"Drop a marker when you get off. Do it as soon as the ship slows. Call me when you're wet." That meant they'd need to jump unseen into the open ocean.

"We left everything but the cargo in the Arethusa. We don't have any markers. I can call you right before we jump, but don't expect a hello."

"I understand, Dee. I'll be there."

"How long we gonna be in the water?" he asked. The waters of the South China Sea had not been kind to swimmers over the years.

"When your foil comes off the wings, I can get the sub on your six and keep pace. I'll be waiting for you when you drop."

"Looking forward to the towel."

There was a method for delivery of contraband to Hong Kong, and to a greater degree the nation of China, that dated back centuries, to the 1700s and the East India Company and their British boats carrying large shipments of their own government-approved and quality-controlled opium. They would bring their cargoes to Hong Kong's offshore islands where local dealers would meet them with smaller, faster boats to bring the product inland for distribution, circumventing detection by an underwhelming Chinese navy, which at the time struggled to operate in open waters.

Today's detection methods far outweighed the naval capabilities of the eighteenth century. Sonar buoys and drones encircled the surrounding waters in perpetual surveillance. But farther out, at the boundary where the ocean met the Greater Bay Area demarcation line, the Chinese had no further ability to monitor than existed back then. The gaps were too large to observe with any kind of effective efficiency. The modern method of delivery, which Dallas had been utilizing on a regular basis, involved flying low level in whisper mode, aiming for those gaps in surveillance, then dropping temporary locator beacons from the *Arethusa's* modified weapons bay along with the shipment. A small but effective covert flotilla of triad fishing vessels along with state-of-the-art, triad-run submarines would coordinate, retrieve, and submerge. The premise was the same as it had ever been—divert, distract, then deliver—only this time, it was Dallas who was going to do the swimming.

The problem was they would be jumping off a large, fast-moving vessel into rough seas, hoping for a quick pick up from a friend. Not an ideal moment, Dallas thought.

He closed the handset, ending the call.

"Did I hear you say we're going swimming?" Kit asked.

"We need to find a way off this ship without anyone, and I mean *anyone*, noticing," Dallas said to Cam. "The good news is the water's warm, and we shouldn't be in it for long, maybe a few minutes. Maneli's gonna pick us up in the sub."

Cam took a deep breath. "Not that I don't want to join in your little plan to have a frolic in the South China Sea, but if I stay on the boat I can give you a distraction, block a camera or two while you jump."

"What have you got in mind?"

"Sorry, did you say jump?" Kit asked.

"I can do a quick recon of the ship. Find a good spot without too much security, off the backside where the survival gear is housed." Cam walked into the bathroom. "I'll take the shampoo, squirt some on the camera lenses, take them out long enough for you to get overboard."

"Did you say overboard? Because I think you're talking about leaping off this giant boat, which sounds insane," Kit said.

Dallas thought for a moment. "Gonna need to get as low as we can. Bottom decks. Even then, it's gonna be a hell of a drop."

"You know I can't swim," Kit said. Deadpan.

Cam looked at her. "Could give her a floatation device."

"No, that'd be visible. She's gonna have to swim. Her life depends on it." Dallas looked her in the eyes. "Right?"

"This is nuts. You know that," she said.

"Go get the recon done. Then we sleep until Singapore," Dallas said to Cam, yawning.

The ferry slowed, coming down off the foils to traverse the Singapore Strait. Dallas felt it happen, the pitch change of the impellers waking him from the deepest sleep he'd had in weeks. Seven hours to go. He'd been out for eight. The other two were still unconscious beside him, head to toe in the king-size bed, Kit with her same gentle snore. He put his head back down into his pillow, savouring the doubling of his four-hour mark. Just a couple more hours, he thought, a tiny bit more peace before the certain storm coming for them.

Kit woke to a symphony of the two men snoring. Sat bolt upright in the bed, looking at their feet. The cabin door invited. The threat of Americans on the other side of it, however, kept her in place. There was no real way out of this mess without Dallas. If they'd wanted her dead, they'd have done her with Avery. That cowboy hat. She shuddered.

She walked to the bathroom and closed the door, then sat on

the toilet for a long, drawn-out pee. They had hours to go. The wall display showed them sailing past Singapore. She should get some more rest; she was going to need it.

They ordered room service, so they could stay out of sight, Cam paid the waiter with the small roll of bills they had remaining. They ate dim sum off the metal cart. Kit excavated the shrimp from inside a dumpling with her chopsticks.

"Weird how you dig it out like that," Dallas said, shovelling one into his mouth.

"It's a thing I do. I like the way the shrimp pop between my teeth, no wonton."

The hull bounced beneath them in the ocean swell, just clearing the wave tops, like the *Arethusa* on landing. Outside it was midday, sunlight poured through the porthole.

"Might be awhile until we all get to eat like this again, so I will take that." Dallas plucked her discarded dumpling from the cart. "Thank you."

"That's not funny," Cam said.

"You given any thought to what's going to happen to us after we turn her over?" Dallas asked, chewing.

"You could always choose not to," Kit offered.

"Trust me. If that was a viable option, we wouldn't be sitting in this room together. Our boss is going to want some restitution for that jet we wrecked in the desert. We bring you back in one piece, that's significantly in our favour."

"Not gonna be good," Cam said.

"S'what I'm thinking." The display showed thirty minutes remaining. They'd be off the foils in ten. Dallas put his chopsticks down, wiped his mouth clean. "Ten minutes till we jump. Time to get this shit show rolling."

Outside the safety and confines of their first-class suite, Dallas felt naked, observed, under surveillance. There were six passenger decks below them, then three vehicle decks full of transports.

They were walking as three, Kit between them, making their way to the rear of the boat through the cafeteria on deck four when he first noticed the tail. Long ginger hair to his chin, flattened straight, shaved on one side like his, ripped blue jeans and a pair of jet-black Doc Martens laced over the denim. He had Asian skin and green eyes, intense and aware, no obvious augments, but he looked like the kind, tall and lean, wide at the shoulders. He was wearing a casual navy suit jacket unbuttoned over a plain white T-shirt, grey patches on the elbows. He couldn't see the bulge of a weapon, but Dallas was certain something was hidden under that jacket.

Their pace slowed as they weaved their way through cafeteria queues of passengers. The man matched their pace, picking his way through the crowd, sun-darkened hands sliding between the backs of strangers blocking his way. Dallas maintained a good distance between them, but the narrow hallways of an oceangoing vessel were a difficult place to lurk unnoticed.

"Think I've made our government man. White shirt, blue jacket with grey patches, ginger hair," Dallas said under his breath. He stood tall on his toes, up above the sea of heads. "Cam, you need to drop back, get between us and the tail. Bump into him, distract him, whatever it takes. We'll head down to deck two, meet you at the rear of the ship. See if we can pick up his partner."

"Or *partners*," Cam said.

Dallas grabbed Kit's hand, interlacing her fingers with his, like lovers. She glared at him. "Hey, it's better than cuffs," he said.

He led her to a stairwell entrance and watched as Cam, his head down, plowed into the ginger-haired man's chest. Dallas and Kit slipped into the stairwell and hustled down to the second deck, no one followed.

Cam met them a few minutes later, alone. "I didn't see another tail. He was some unimpressed though. Don't think he knew who I was."

Dallas plugged the wired bead in his ear, dialled Maneli.

"Ello?"

"It's Dee. Jumping in two."

"Right behind the ferry and ready when you are."

He snapped the phone closed, spun the wire around it, and handed it to Cam. "It's time."

They quickened their pace, Cam in front. He led them rearward, his eyeline up, hunting for electric lenses floating in the dark. They ducked a sagging rope, ignoring the "No Access" signage, as the noise of the ferry's motors grew.

"Here." Cam stopped under a metal overhang, reached above him to a camera, and smeared its lens with shampoo from the room. "One more over there." He moved between rescue craft bundled into car-sized containers to another camera and smeared it too. "Go."

The sea churned and bubbled in a violent white froth that trailed the ship below. Dallas held Kit by the shoulders and looked into her eyes. "We need to run fast and jump together to clear the prop wash. Follow my lead. Ready?"

She shook her head, her eyes wide. "No."

"One." He held her hand tight, pulling as he ran for the edge. "Two." She kept up. It was two more steps. "Three."

53.

Superintendent Lee's fingers moved with surprising dexterity, swiping through a virtual holodex for a number. He picked one labelled "Officer Lam" and swiped for a video call. The holo displayed a short-haired, local woman with jowls that drooped below her jawline. On one cheek she had a dark brown birthmark in the shape of a comma.

"Officer Lam. Jou-san." *Good morning.* "This is Superintendent Lee of the Serious Crimes Division."

"Mister Lee. Yes, we know exactly who you are." Her disinterest was impressive. "What can I help you with?"

"I have a pair of detectives working a case involving the Shing Wo, and they're requesting assistance from the Customs and Excise Department. Possible trans-border human trafficking offences."

"Is it Johnny Woo?"

"It's Detective Fong, and yes, he is partnered with Detective Woo."

"This better be good, Lee."

Woo stepped into the feed. "Officer Lam, we've been following this case for about a week. We have links with the Shing Wo, as Superintendent Lee mentioned, plus multiple local homicides and one abroad linked with a gene lab up in Mongolia. We believe they've been dropping contraband in Hong Kong waters for transport through Chinese territory. Have you witnessed any unusual border activity that you think could be connected?"

She looked off camera, swiping. "We've been monitoring an operation in the South Islands." She read from her holo. "Caught a foil-jet heading north with contraband meat on board. Beef and pork. Nothing living, mind you, and not that we were thinking to look, but nothing human either."

Those foil-jets were slick as shit, Woo thought, winged watercraft that skimmed the surface of the sea. Powered by turbofans robbed from aircraft, they could travel at speeds of over a hundred knots. No regular boat could hope to catch them. Must have been a well-coordinated sting to snare it.

"Where'd you pick it up?"

"En route northbound abeam Sai Kung."

"Any idea where they picked up the meat?"

"Somewhere in the South Islands. We're watching a group of derelict barges moored off Lidou Bay." She ran her finger along a string of text. "South side of Erzhou Island. It's a functioning fish farm, but we're seeing some heat sigs there that don't make sense for such a small operation."

"That'd be a good spot to do a drop off, boss," Fong offered. "Remote."

"S'what I'm thinking."

Woo turned back to the holo. "With your approval, of course, we'd like to investigate those barges ourselves."

"All the surveillance we've done has been with the drone squad. We haven't observed anything criminal, but there's a lot more activity than we traditionally see from a farm of that size," she said.

"Detective Fong and I would be investigating in person."

She rubbed her forehead, then nodded. "Send me a req form. I'll have it back to you in an hour, and detective," she paused, "believe it or not, it's good to hear from you. We look forward to a future with more cooperation between our departments."

"Thank you very much for your time, Officer. We'll be in touch."

Lee swiped off the call.

Woo grabbed a precinct wristband off the chargers and snagged his tobacco pouch off his desk, giving Lee a "that was weird" look.

"Thanks, boss," he said.

"We going to Lidou?" Fong asked.

"Yeah. And we're taking a boat."

54.

The fall felt endless. Kit screamed the entire way down. She hit the water feet first and alone. It churned and spun her in a thousand directions. She opened her eyes into a stinging, saltwater blur, then starfished her arms and legs, slowing her rotation. She swam for the lights. More unending panic. The surface was madness, froth then sky then sea. She gulped for air, gagged on bubbles as unrelenting waves smacked her in the face. *This must be what drowning feels like,* she thought.

She spent long, unbearable minutes treading, sputtering, and choking on seawater in the chaotic boil of foam and turbidity in the vessel's long wake. She sipped for air between pursed lips, keeping most of the water out. A trick she had learned surfing on the east coast of Long Island. Montauk. She wondered what it was like there now, behind the America's wall.

As the ferry pulled away, the sea eased. Froth became foam, and foam became water. Kit lay on her back with her arms outstretched, adrift in the ocean's rolling swell, the Hong Kong skyline a distant ripple of shadowy mountain and blazing neon against a backdrop of South Asian starlight. She bobbed, a strange moment of silence after so much clatter and noise. Beside her floated a sealed blue plastic drum, large enough to fit a small man. She swam to it, clutching its rim for floatation, wondering if it contained the same human biogenetic contraband she had once ordered on a weekly basis with such indifference.

The ferry's turbines dopplered into the distance, and for the first time since the drop, she saw Dallas bobbing in seesaw waves against hers.

"Quite a ride. Looks like you're not a bad swimmer after all," he said over the top of cresting swell.

She took great care with her next words. "I'm scared, Dallas. Legit fucking terrified." He was doing the breaststroke toward her, taking care not to splash or panic. She guessed there were sharks.

"There's always sharks," her surfing friend used to say. "You just have to hope they're not hungry."

Her wrists had been bleeding for days, something a hungry shark would smell. Dallas closed the distance between them, oscillating above and below the swell. "We'll be fine. Relax, and try not to fight the waves. Could be worse. Water could be cold." He was right; it was a nice temperature for a swim. But not like this.

"I'm ready to not be in this warm fucking water," she said.

"Don't worry, Maneli should be here soon. But don't splash around. There's probably sharks."

Just no hungry ones, Mister.

She lay afloat on her back, fingertips holding the drum, staring up at the low and disorganized cloud base, her body rising and falling with the sea. She took long breaths to soothe and distract her from the situation.

Dallas was treading water, scanning the horizon and saying nothing, perhaps so as not to disturb the sharks that she assumed were nearby and hoped were not hungry. She watched him, allowed his presence to calm her. She wasn't alone, she reminded herself. He stopped his scan, staring in one direction, away from the harbour and all the nautical traffic there. She saw a disturbance in the water heading straight for them. Her first thoughts raced to *shark!* But Dallas swam toward it. A periscope. Right.

She had expected some gargantuan warship to rise from beneath them, but it was a much smaller vessel that came to their rescue, a personal-sized submersible, painted a dolphin shade of grey. It looked like it had been carved out of the inside of a coffee pot, a glass ball with twin propellers flanking a small, enclosed hull. The bulk of it remained submerged, like an iceberg, only its hatch and ladder clear of the surface. It nestled alongside her with surprising precision, and she followed Dallas up the ladder and inside. A dark-haired, ponytailed woman handed them both towels, then sealed the hatch above. Without speaking she returned to the yoke and submersed the vessel below the surface.

Dallas had never been inside it. From the three seats, they had a 270-degree view of the suspended murk and filth of the South China Sea. Without the holo that was projected onto the glass, there would be no hope of any form of navigation; the haze of the harbour's water was that thick. The visuals looked similar to the software package he'd had in the *Arethusa*. He recognized the tags: Coast Guard and military hardware displayed as orange triangles. Alongside the tags were three numbers preceded by a plus or minus denoting relative depth to the sub. Airborne civilian targets came up as blue circles.

"Why is this tag so bright?" he asked, pointing at a blue circle shining brighter than the rest.

"Airborne target flying below a thousand feet. Normally it's helicopters. Macau and back, that sort of thing. But they're also potential Coast Guard sub hunters. They mess around with their transponder codes, show up as civilian aircraft most of the time. I have the software flash them brighter than the rest so I can keep an eye on them, take a closer look, or you know, run like hell for the bottom." She laughed.

"And the red square out there behind the cruise ship?" Dallas asked. In visual terms, it was co-located with the cruiser. Its tag showed zeros.

"That's a problem, that's what that is," Maneli said. "Chinese navy follows around those big cruise liners with military subs, a little bigger than this, for reconnaissance, making sure there's no American assets down here. I don't think they're even armed. They're not looking for a fight; they're like informants, passing on the intel so the PLA can send in the big guns to chase off any foreign military subs down here. They cozy up close thinking they can't be detected, but as you can see…" she swept her hand through the air in front of the holo to show the navy submersible's obvious detection.

"So, if we can see them…" Dallas said.

"Then they can see us."

"What does that mean for us?"

"We're close enough to the surface to pass for the small junk we're pretending to be. But if they notice our hull and send out a ping, we'll be diving and hiding."

"I don't get the feeling this thing can exactly make a run for it," Kit chimed in.

"No, but we've got a few tricks up our sleeve to buy time, and at the end of the day, they're not looking for us, and we're not going very far. You just buckle up and enjoy the show." Maneli gave her a hard "Do as I say" stare. Kit obediently buckled into the five-point harness.

"Anything I can do?" Dallas asked.

"Nah. We're clear right now. Like I said, our tag shows as a small junk. I'll turn it off before we descend." Maneli snapped her shoulder restraints one at a time into the buckle at her waist, reaching down between her legs for the last one. "Strap in, Dee. The real excitement is under the sea," she said smiling as she dimmed the cabin lights.

Submerged and inverted with his cargo strapped to the seat

beside him was not how he envisioned this delivery's completion. There was a tranquility to it though. The hum of the electric motors driving the sub's twin screws made a slight change in pitch as they rolled upside down, but otherwise Dallas enjoyed the maneuver. Kit's arms had splayed out wide in a manic grasp for railings that weren't there. Maneli pulled on the yoke for positive g's, maximizing the craft's down capability. The hull creaked and popped like the *Arethusa* under load as the depth and pressure increased.

"We going to the farm?" he asked, looking up at the rapidly approaching sea floor.

She rolled the sub out level, metres above the seabed, then pushed the throttle up, the blades cavitating under load. She backed off, and the props smoothed. "We've got a secure mooring location in Opposite Corner. You've dropped in there before." She was referring to a watery, half-kilometre gap between two rocky outcrops in a thin grouping of rugged islands ten kilometres south of Hong Kong.

"I've never even seen so much as a single light flying through that pass," Dallas said. He had always loved that drop, tearing through there at thirty feet and the speed of heat, dropping his cargo for money between rocky cliffs in the pitch of night.

"Yup, it's where we keep the toys, but you never needed to know that," Maneli said as she flattened out the sub's path along the rocky bottom, flicking off the floodlights in favour of the synthetic vision displayed onto the window ahead.

"Got any smoke?"

"I thought you might ask." She tore open a Velcro pocket on her black tactical vest and handed him a Ziplock of pre-rolled cigarettes. "You can light that in here. The air scrubbers are solid, Israeli design," she said with pride. "We could have half the cabin on fire, and there'd be clean air coming out of those." She pointed at venting above and behind their heads, where the glass dome met the steel hull, her eyes never leaving the display.

The depth gauge showed 225 metres. *Not that deep,* Dallas thought, but it was sure dark out there, the only light outside the bubble coming from the interior of the vehicle itself, catching the odd reflection off curious aquatic passersby. No further tags of nautical traffic were displayed, and the rear camera showed a solitary ocean liner chugging west for her nightly booze cruise.

Maneli engaged the autopilot, then swivelled in her chair to face Kit. She carried herself like a man, her back wide like a swimmer's, her forearms in perpetual flex, ropey muscles strung from wrist to shoulder. Her nose had a kink in it, like it had been broken sometime in the distant past. She had dark amber eyes that penetrated from deep-set sockets. A short scar below her left eye, something she could have easily had removed, gave her a further air of toughness. She wore black, skin-tight, polyprop leggings. Thighs like a cyclist's bulged underneath, augmented for strength; Kit was certain of it. From another pocket on her vest, Maneli produced a lighter and offered it to Dallas.

"Tell me what happened," she said to Dallas, her eyes fixed on Kit.

Dallas took a long drag, the ember canoeing up one side of the cigarette. "Clipped a water collector construction arm north of Mogadishu—bunch of new builds that hadn't shown up on the holo. Went clean through the wing. Spread her pretty even across the desert. Be a nice salvage for someone." Smoke exhaled from his nostrils in streams that spread, forming a layer in the confined space above them. He was back there, at the site, his eyes glazing over as he relived the nightmare of the wreck.

"That's not like you."

"Somalis have gotten smarter. Put surveillance radars on top of those water collectors. We had a series of missile locks and a couple of actual launches. Guess I got distracted." He thumbed at Kit. "This girl's the cargo. We think she's got the America on her tail. Plus, we're pretty sure we saw a triad operative on the road outside Mogadishu, though we haven't seen him since."

"Is it a good idea to be smoking in here?" Kit asked. "I mean, isn't there a limited amount of air? Don't you have some gum you could chew instead?"

Maneli gave her a look. Spoke to Dallas. "So you've got triad heat on your tail?"

"Pretty sure we lost them in the jump. But look, if they followed us that far, they're gonna know where we're heading right now."

"That is true, my friend. But it's time to give over this cargo, is it not? Finish your contract? Collect your payment?" She rolled her tongue on her r's.

"You know I'm right here," Kit said, frowning. "I'm not cargo. I'm a living fucking human being."

Maneli took the cigarette from Dallas, ignoring Kit, drew deeply and exhaled at the ceiling with a feminine flourish, adding to the layer. She leaned in, the cigarette still in her hand. Kit felt the heat of close contact. She smelled of metal and motor oil, of hot, melted insulation and the sweet scent of tobacco. "And what is it that you have that is so very important?"

Kit felt claustrophobic for the first time in her life. This woman was somehow surrounding her from all sides, her thick, black, wavy hair crowding, her aroma strengthening, enveloping. She backed away into her seat. "They're after this." She produced the memchip, flipping up her index fingernail and removing the thumbnail-sized sliver of memory that held all the secrets she had left to tell. "It's the Zeus edit." The holomem between her fingers shook with her hand. She flipped the nail back into position.

"And what exactly is a Zeus edit?" Maneli asked, one eyebrow raised.

Dallas took back the cigarette, smoked at the two of them. "Go on," he said, waving his hand. "Tell her."

"It's the most important genetic discovery of our species. And these people you're delivering me to don't seem to want anyone else to have it." She was feeling the reality of her situation, held hostage in a submarine designed for smuggling with mercenaries delivering her back to the kidnappers who had abducted her in the first place. There was nowhere to run to. The smoke had her gagging. The walls of the submarine closed in, nausea rose in her stomach. Subduing panic was never something she'd been any good at, and when her abductors gave her an identical perplexed look, she recognized that she was hyperventilating, falling helplessly to the floor.

55.

Through wind-whipped waves crested by waterfalls of spume and spray, the bow of the *Gau* rose and fell with a repetitive thud. As they exited Victoria Harbour, the circus of laser light that ignited Hong Kong's downtown core each evening grew dimmer, the night's display disappearing into the ragged bottoms of a low stratus layer shrouding the territory's mountains.

Chen Rong stood at the helm, one hand on the ship's wheel, the mainsail snapping in the gusting winds. It was sheeted in tight, and this main hull that could make seven knots on the gauge made nine on the downslope of the increasing swell. *How appropriate,* thought Chen of the number nine. *Always you appear when I am on the correct path.*

Beside him stood one of his Yazi, Nine, clutching at his black cowboy hat in the buffeting wind. Chen judged him for wearing it, having never understood the fascination with the *gweilo* pastime. His loyalty though was unwavering. He could find no fault in that.

Chen thought back through his more than ninety years, to a less complicated time. A time of less automation. Artificial intelligence controlled so many of their transports that he seldom had the opportunity to operate such a vehicle. So it was with great pleasure that Chen eased out more sail, to run with the wind at their backs. He felt a connection to the boat, to his distant past, to stories recounted on parchment of his great ancestors sailing their wooden junks from dynasties long ago, making trades with the white men of the west, though this modern hydrosail bore little resemblance to her Song dynasty predecessors. She carried wings in her undercarriage, long daggerboard foils that would unfurl deep below the surface to assist in raising the hull out of the water, enough to propel her along much faster than any ship. As they rounded the corner at Pok Fu Lam, he extended her legs, making for speed. He hoisted the spinnaker, the sail inflating in the wind, and she lifted off the surface to make forty knots as her belly skipped along the undulating water beneath.

The distinctive silhouettes of Lamma Power's cooling towers grew in the distance, taking shape in the island's reflective glow. The city's lights illuminated the low cloud, giving the white-capped crests an artificial, ethereal warmth. They sailed in solitude, not speaking, a quartering tailwind gusting at their backs, the ocean's roll and frothy salt sprays providing a rhythmic nautical soundtrack.

There had been plenty of opportunity for failure on this delivery; it had been rushed. He thought Dallas was up to the task. He had always been their best. *If you want a job done right, best do it yourself*, his father had taught him all those years ago.

And so, they soldiered on, two men, wordless, under a neon-reflected pastel sky, sailing toward Hong Kong's southern islands, to ensure this job was done right.

56.

Woo stood at the Aberdeen Marina Club, the island's mountainside city climbing high at his back. The South China Sea rose and fell at his feet at the end of a long, thin, and slippery wooden dock, its seams thick with green algae. He handed a stranger a week's wage for a ride to Lidou Bay on the tip from Customs and Excise and a strong feeling that he was on the right path. The stranger had disappeared with the money to retrieve his boat, which left him standing alone with Fong, moored to this floating extension of Hong Kong Island, waiting, anchored to the end of a long chain of small mistakes made by the people he now found himself hunting.

He'd expected a small junk, even an old fishing trawler, not the outboard skiff that peeled out from behind rows of polished, multi-million-dollar yachts. The stranger he'd hired kneeled in the boat's stern, steering the motor with what appeared to be a bamboo broom handle lashed to the engine with nylon strips. It was unmuffled, loud, and obnoxious, a petrol burner. He pulled up beside Woo and Fong with precision, gentle on the gas, one eye shut against a burning cinder trailing from a half-smoked cigarette dangling between tobacco-stained lips.

"Jau la! Jau la! Fai Dee La!" *Let's go! Hurry!* The man yelled, waving at them to join.

Woo stepped with caution into the long, thin boat, allowing it to settle from his added weight before taking a seat on the splintered wooden bench beneath him. He motioned for Fong to get in.

They motored out of the wharf, past multiple hundred-storey walls of concrete housing, shrouding the treed hills of Ap Lei Chau behind. The wake of transpacific vessels slapped against the boat as they passed through the shipping lane into the open sea. Woo clutched a metal handhold bolted to the wooden hull, trying to gauge the craft's age. It was older than him, descended from at least one generation back, maybe more. Modern watercraft were made with printers and quick-hardening resin, like so many things these days. They rode alongside a cargo ship's vast wall of iron, containers rising above its deck toward the evening's low clouds. Its hull was emblazoned with the red and white logo of the China Shipping Company. He had to move his head to read it and the view gave him vertigo. He steadied himself against Fong.

"You OK, boss?"

"Yeah, I'm good. Just need to stop looking up at these things."

He focussed on Tsim Sha Tsui's pulsating light show reflected off the mountain tops of Tai Tam as they made their way out of the harbour. Thinking ahead to the possibility of armed conflict, he wished for modern weaponry, noting that if he was going to meet members of this as-of-yet undisclosed triad, they would be equipped not only with ballistics, but blades. While he felt he was well-equipped to handle a gunfight—even his boxer-briefs could absorb a bullet— he lacked any type of defensive training against sharpened steel.

The motor droned on, and the three of them sat wordless, a steady rhythm of South China spray misting across their knees with each drop of the bow, the city's night sky glowing with a synthetic dusk against the illumination of humanity.

As they exited out past Lamma and the protective custody of Hong Kong's inner islands, the wind and the rolling swell had Woo reconsidering his choice of transport.

"Can you remind me why we needed to take *this* boat, boss?" Fong blurted, hot vomit spewing from his lips. He aimed it downwind, chunks ricocheting off the inside of the boat.

Woo had to yell over the heaving seas. "They see us coming in a patrol boat, and we'll never find them. No one's expecting a couple of detectives in a skiff this size out this far."

Fong nodded, continuing to retch.

Woo held his hand against the wind. There were no more well-lit ships giving comfort in the dark, the lights of Stanley disappearing and reappearing farther in the distance behind each rolling wave.

The fisherman navigated off a wrist holo, similar to the precinct band that Woo wore. He flicked a switch on a lamp tied to the side of the boat, piercing the dark with its beam. Like an aircraft's high-powered landing lights, it turned the sea into a blinding reflective surface.

Woo motioned to the man with a finger. "No lights."

The man nodded, flicked off the beam. They'd need to proceed unseen, using the weather to cover their approach. There would only be one chance at achieving surprise. They continued south. Somewhere out ahead of them was Lidou Bay, "*here bay.*" An uninhabited collection of rocky islands and abandoned reclamation mines out on the border of the Greater Bay Area. A perfect location to reel in a smuggler.

57.

Kit awoke feeling beat up, like she'd been clubbed in the back of the head. She was cuffed again, plastic zips that sealed tight, her wrists bleeding and raw. The smell of Dallas's tobacco burned the inside of her nose, way up into her sinuses. Her right eye was swollen, not quite shut. Her vision was blurred, and everything hurt.

"Princess is awake," Maneli announced, reaching to touch her face. Kit pulled back. "You went down hard. Fainted. Banged your head on the railing. Gave yourself quite a shiner."

Kit managed a grunt, her head hung low. Her thoughts were of defeat, of stinging rage, and bitter, angry resentment.

"I'm just a fucking scientist," she spat. "What have you done to me?"

"Neshama, you did this to yourself. I'd have stopped you if I could have. Delivery of product is something our superiors take very seriously. Wouldn't want them to think we roughed up their prize now, would we?" She was back at the sub's helm, the control wheel extending up into her hands from the floor.

They surfaced in what appeared to be a cove, a dome of unlit darkness with no sign of sky. Kit scanned the rocky walls, determined to find a way out, a way home, any chance to escape this carpet bombing of her life.

Dallas opened the hatch. Outside air wafted in, heavy with the reek of seaweed. He climbed out first, followed by Maneli.

Kit offered her shackled wrists above her head to Maneli. She sighed, lifting her out with a single arm. *Augmented*, Kit thought. *Without question.*

The sub was moored alongside a sailboat. *It's beautiful*, she thought. It looked like a falcon, like it had been designed for aerodynamic speed. The mast rose high above, its sails stowed like a bird's wings. The slim, low, navy-blue hull was punctuated with eyelet portal windows. They gazed out, dark apertures like dilated pupils looking gently on.

On its deck stood two Asian men, one of which wore a cowboy hat like the man in the Gambia, though this hat was black. Images of Avery, confused and bleeding, flooded past, her eyes stung with the approach of tears. He carried a gun larger than any she'd ever seen. The other smiled, an older man. He gave her a parental stare through circular glasses, an unnecessary accessory from a time before augments. A mole under his bottom lip was familiar. His pants, the colour of late-September grass, hung low off his hips, the cuffs rolled high, dangling below the knee above tanned and sandalled feet. He wore a traditional Chinese, drab, olive chemise, buttons laced up to a loose-fitting Mandarin collar. He looked as though he had been out for a picnic at the beach. It made her think of her father, his colleagues, and his friends; there hadn't been many.

"Intelligence alienates," her father had said to her when she was a child. "So be ready, Kit, because you are *brilliant*."

She'd spent her life living up to those lofty words. He had been right. She'd done it, and she was not prepared for this shit show to be the end result.

"Well, well, not our best pilot after all, Mister Dallas," said the man with the mole, his Hong Kong accent heavy, splintered syllables and a lazy lip, far too familiar.

"Hey, if we'd been provided with better data, we would have avoided Somalia. It was like they were ready for us. Waiting. We had multiple missile launches. Like it was a setup," Dallas said.

They moved off the sub onto the rear of the sailboat, toward the two men, the boat rocking with their added weight. Dallas steadied himself on a rail. "We're gonna need some sort of payment before we hand her over." His teeth were clenched, his eyes locked on the man wearing the cowboy hat.

Kit was outnumbered, panicked, searching for any opportunity out of this cluster fuck.

"Well, I have a small payment for you. We shall discuss the disappointing loss of the Arethusa later, Mister Dallas. We had our eyes there with you, watching. We watch with our drones and our Yazi." He put his hand on Cowboy Hat's shoulder. "We keep the Americans just far enough away. A spectator sees more than the player in the heat of the game. You understand? Better to watch from a distance, you see. We help ensure our prize comes home, but no one ever sees us, Mister Dallas, they only see you." He smiled. His eyes widened, and he gave her a nod.

That nod. The mole. The lazy lip. The accent. Those horrible hairs growing from that cancerous growth on his chin. Memories flooded in. She remembered him from high school, judging at genetics contests. He had spent so much time with them growing up, stood at her mother's bedside as she succumbed to ALS, then vanished. She hadn't seen him since. She felt like vomiting and stifled a retch.

"It's not possible," she stammered, staggering as her knees buckled beneath her. Maneli caught her by the arm.

"You are so smart, Kit. Your father, he is a proud man, so proud of you." He was walking toward them now, down the prow of his boat, hands locked behind his back in a cultural display of respect and trust. "With his permission, of course, we have guided you along all these years. Long time now. Since your mother passed." He shook his head. "There is nothing worse in life than to outlive your own child. She was so young, your mother. Her disease so preventable now, with your research, of course." He nodded.

She recognized him, he was her grandfather, her mother's father. He had aged, and the years had been unkind. "You look much older, grandpa Rong," she said, fighting the stinging tears she was determined not to allow to fall.

"That's because I *am* much older. Something I believe you may be able to help me with, my dear."

"I can't make people younger," she said.

"Oh, I believe that you diminish yourself, young Kit."

58.

Woo opened his wrist holo so he could track their progress on a map. Erzhou was the middle island in a chain that ran from east to west. They came around its western shores, approaching Lidou from the south. Fong had stopped vomiting but held tight to the side of the boat. He didn't look well, and Woo wondered how much use he would be when they reached whoever it was they were chasing. The seas were worse south of the islands. It was open ocean all the way to the Philippines, and the swell had doubled in size. They stayed outside the surf, where the waves weren't breaking. There was a light in a cave up ahead where Officer Lam had guided them. He closed down the holo and tapped Fong on the shoulder with the back of his hand.

"Get it together, Fonger. Looks like a sailboat in the cave there. Get the bot up."

"I can't launch it in this wind, boss. Too strong." He retched over the side.

"Gau cho aa," Woo said, shaking his head. *Fucking kidding me.* He motioned to the fisherman driving the boat. "We need to approach quietly, so we can get on that sailboat. So nobody sees us. Understand?"

"Ming baak," he said. *I understand.*

59.

Cowboy Hat hadn't been paying much attention to the conversation. His head was on a swivel. He was alone and looked uncomfortable about it. A single weapon dangled from his right hand. It appeared cumbersome, heavy, like a wide-barrelled shotgun, but it wasn't. Dallas had seen them on the streams but never up close. Kinetic Energy Projectiles, military issue. Fired an entire magazine of cylindrical rods from a ring of magnetic rails, some kind of heavy, depleted uranium or tungsten slug. Left the barrel at hypersonic speeds, vaporizing anything that got in its way. Precision handheld violence. The target tended to implode with the force of impact, its insides exiting out its back, heavy mass and extreme velocity creating a maximum energy dissipation on contact. Weaponry not easily attained.

"Hasn't exactly been a standard delivery day," Dallas said, helping Kit get her legs back under her. He pointed at the KEP. "He planning on using that?" The sailboat listed in the steady lapping waves, rocking back and forth along its length, nudging up against the sub's stealthy grey exterior. He reached for a railing to steady himself.

"Kinetics carry expensive ammunition, Mister Dallas," the old man said. "As with you, there needs to be a very good reason to deploy them."

Kit was fucked. Altogether and without question. They were midship, starboard side, the sailboat in motion below, rolling with the incoming tide. Rong had strolled to the front of the boat, away from the group, he picked up a briefcase there, holding the handrail to steady himself. Cowboy Hat approached her, his free hand outstretched and ready to grab. Dallas held her firm. "Not until I say so," he said to her under his breath.

She focused into the distance, her vision blurring as her pupils dilated into low-light sensitivity. Colours became varying shades of grey, illuminating the heat signature of a small skiff approaching in the dark, its exhaust pipe glowing white, three luminous figures sitting low in its insides. *Backup*, she thought, blinking back to normal sight. She said nothing. Not like it was possible for this moment to get any worse.

Come what fucking may already.

60.

Woo could see the backs of five people as they approached the sailboat, a woman cuffed and bleeding, wearing baggy clothing. Perhaps Kit McKee. A man in a cowboy hat, who reminded him of the Shing Wo operative who had paid him a visit in Central, held a weapon he'd never seen, a large, flat cylinder at the end of a short barrel. Looked like a tommy gun but all wrong.

Woo, Fong, and the fisherman crouched low in the skiff, the engine revs low, motoring in shallow water toward the cave. Fong was leaning over the rear beside the fisherman, breathing but not retching, a step up from earlier. Along the side of the sailboat ahead of them was the Chinese character for nine, *Gau*. He watched the exchange on the boat between the three men. There was talking, but the weapon remained at ease, swaying in Cowboy Hat's hand. He was witnessing a transaction. A kidnapping in progress. A shackled scientist handed off to a triad. He removed his Glock from its holster, held it low. It had been years since he had last fired it.

"Boss." Fong pointed, retching, waving his finger ahead. He turned back and saw the approaching hull. His focus had been on the exchange. The sailboat filled his vision. Their closing speed was way too fast. "Lidou! Lidou!" he whispered, waving his hand at the fisherman as the skiff broadsided the *Gau*.

61.

The deck lurched in a sudden and violent motion. Kit fell to her knees, her bound hands helping to absorb the slip. The man in the cowboy hat stumbled, confused, his free hand out beside him to break his fall. The gun fell toward her. She grabbed for it with both hands, snatching it from his unsteady grip with ease. She was astounded by its mass, her entire body compressing as she cradled it, falling backwards, her finger reaching for the trigger. Cowboy Hat hit the deck hip first, sliding with professional skill, righting himself into a one-knee crouch to face her. The weapon, now in her hands, upside down and awkward, was aimed directly at him. She clutched it tight and fired.

The sound was unexpected. A thud that Dallas felt in his chest, like a magnified, errant heartbeat. His ears rang from it. A blast of blistering heat came and went in an instant. Pink mist swirled where Cowboy Hat had stood a moment before. His dismembered legs sheared clean off at the knees, the man's boots still laced to his feet. One severed arm dropped to the ground. A short section of shoulder belt holding rounds for the railgun went with it. Dallas wiped his eyes with the palm of his hand, flinging blood and flesh to the deck. There was a smell of boiled chicken, a metallic flavour in the air. The boat continued to rock back and forth from whatever had hit them.

He reached down and removed the weapon from Kit's grasp. She sat motionless, stunned, staring straight ahead. "Why don't I take that?" he said, aiming it at the old man.

"Mister Dallas, please, it's not even loaded. Put it down. Don't you know who that woman is?" The old man pointed at Kit.

"She's the cargo, which is now officially delivered," Dallas said, motioning at Kit with the weapon. It was buzzing in his hand, recharging its coils. "Now we all need to walk out of this mess, you with her and us with a safe ride out of Hong Kong."

The old man moved toward Kit. "This young woman has some information we will *all* want eventually. He pulled her up to her feet by the wrists. "Isn't that right, Kit?" He kept her in front of him. Protection.

"That information you want her for, it's in her fingernail, left side, index," Dallas said. "Now can we all get the hell out of here?"

"You total and complete prick," Kit said.

Dallas shrugged. "Just doing my job." He lowered the gun. "Nelly, fix this thing for me," he said, tossing it to her. Maneli one-handed the catch and then kneeled, one boot on the dead man's belt while she pulled off the remaining clips. They were held by Velcro, each one tearing into the strange and awkward silence. She pressed a button on the stock, popping the old clip out, then snapped in a new one, the weapon auto-populating its barrels one after another, each with a perceptible *snikt*.

It was now or never.

"I can see two men in the back of the boat, Dallas. They're hiding over by the helm," Kit said. She was standing in front of Chen, who held her tight by the wrists. The pain was atrocious.

The two men standing in the recessed area of the wheelhouse were armed with handguns, their heads and weapons visible. Behind them, a skiff powered away at high speed, a rooster tail of water shooting out from its rear.

"Hong Kong Police! Put the weapon down and get on your knees!"

Police. She didn't know if that was good or bad.

Christ in a pancake.

Maneli popped a Glock from a vest pocket, slid it along the boat deck toward Dallas. He picked it up and stayed low.

"Nelly, I'm not ready to shoot at police," he said.

Maneli took a step toward Chen, lifting the KEP to her hip. "What a fucking disaster," she said, pointing the weapon at the cops. "Put your guns down, or I'll dust all of you!"

Chen stood behind Kit, his back to the police.

"We doing this?" Dallas asked, inching toward Kit. Chen held her tight, pulling her against his chest.

"We have a choice?" Maneli lined up one of the cops with the KEP. "Are you deaf? Guns on the ground! Now!"

The police put their weapons down in front of them, kneeling.

"Let her go," Dallas said to Chen.

"Dee, we don't have a lot of time here. Get her clear and inside the sub."

"You're making a mistake, both of you. We're not the only ones interested in her," Chen said, backing away from Dallas.

Maneli stepped from the boat to the sub's small deck. The police moved forward, both at once. Collaborating. She shifted her aim. "Nah ah, gentlemen. What did I say? Get on the ground, face first. Don't move."

The police did as they were told. She trained the gun back

on Chen.

"We been in business a long time, you and I," Chen said to Maneli.

"No reason it can't continue," she responded. "But whatever it is that's so special about this woman, it should be worth something extra, no?" She re-cradled the weapon, its weight resting on her hip. "So what is it? What is this Zeus edit?"

"Grandpa," Kit said, her wrists throbbing.

"Grandpa?" Maneli asked.

Kit's head ached. "Why don't I just tell them."

"Yes, yes. Tell them. We want everyone to put their guns down, so we can put your little secret to good use. Maybe even give them a taste for themselves," Chen said.

The world slowed around her. She took a long breath. "I found a way to regulate the braking system on telomerase. Synthesized it."

"English lady. Explain it quickly," Maneli said with some urgency.

"At the end of every strand of DNA are these things; think of them like shoelaces. At the end of your shoelaces are these caps. Telomeres are the caps. They're like protective caps." The madness surrounding her paused, all their eyes on hers. "If you didn't know better, you'd say they were put there on purpose because they are ticking clocks. Every cell replenishes by copying itself; and every copy of every cell takes a little tiny piece of that telomere with it. As each cell in your body divides, telomeres shorten. Eventually, they reach senescence, meaning they run out of telomere, which is when the cell dies, unable to replicate itself further. This is called mitosis. It's aging, and it's happening to every one of you right now.

"In there with that DNA strand is an enzyme called telomerase, a regulating mechanism. Too much of it and the cell's division runs away; you get cancer and die. Too little and you get wrinkled, old, and die. It's the natural order, and it gives us all a finite shelf life. What my edited telomerase does is allow each offspring of all replicated cells to replace that lost bit of DNA, meaning your cells get to continue replicating. They never reach the Hayflick limit and senesce, which is about seventy cell divisions, which means you never die. It's the fucking fountain of youth. It's been working in mice, on Zeus in particular. It has worked on humans, and it has also worked on me. Genetically, I'm younger than I was last year. My telomeres *grew*; they got *longer*." There. It was out. She breathed.

Her grandfather nodded. "You see?" He looked at the police, then back to her.

"So you *kidnapped* your own family and *stole* the formula for everlasting life," Maneli said, lifting the weapon off her hip.

"Not entirely true," Chen said. "We had to keep her safe from the America. Her secret was out, leaked. Someone in Mongolia must have known. The Americans were hunting her. She needed to be hidden, brought to us with discretion. She is *ours*, after all."

So that's why they'd tanked her. She'd been protected the whole time. Her family had always had connections. How deep they ran, she could never have imagined. "What exactly do you mean *yours*?" Kit asked, looking over her shoulder at him.

"Your father come to me so many year ago, asked me to help guide you to success. Told me about your gift for mathematics, for genetics. Do you remember writing edits to the human sequence when you were twelve years old? Twelve!" He shook his head. "Children your age were editing *plant life*. You were changing the colour of people's skin! So, we make a deal, he and I. We both agreed to guide you like the valley guides the river. Make you curious about the mechanisms that control aging. We sent you to private school. Paid them to keep you in genetics class. Keep you interested. We set up a whole company. Built you a lab, Negligible Senescence in Mongolia. Get you making commercial edits and show you the path that brought you here today. We even set you up with Avery. He was always on your side. So sad about him. He was good for you." He shook his head again. "We sent you so many parcels. Dallas here, he brings you pretty much all the biomass you order. Straight from West African labs, we brought you the finest farmed human tissue. Even brought you fresh human test subjects to work on, so you could make this beautiful edit *in vivo*. Kit, your father, he doesn't want to die. *I don't want to die.* He's scared and near the end of his life, as am I. Don't you see? You made this thing not only for me; you made it for him. You made it for us. You made this edit so our *whole family can live, maybe even live forever.*"

Kit's head was spinning. Was this possible? That her own grandfather had been watching her for this long, for decades? She ran through so many moments in her life. Graduation: he had been there. She remembered him sitting beside her father. They'd been friends for as long as she could recall, but she'd never considered that they were conspiring against her. Such a long time ago. And for such a long time. She'd been manipulated her entire fucking life. NegSense. Negligible Senescence. *To not exhibit evidence of biological aging.* They'd suggested she pursue longevity edits, her father and grandfather. She'd studied it and had found it intriguing, even defended her doctoral thesis on the subject. She'd never once considered the lab name's possible meanings. Christ. It was all there, right in front of her; she'd never seen it. She was horrified. Ashamed. Embarrassed.

"So, that's the cure for aging?" Dallas asked, pointing at her hand. She nodded. "Yes."

"Like, no more old age?"

"Technically, yes, that's correct."

"And it works on anyone?"

"Synthesis of the telomerase is a lot more complicated than that. It's not a 'one size fits all' type of edit. It needs to be coded for each individual's sequence."

"That's why we need more than the data, Kit. That's why we need *you*," Chen said. "Please, come with me. We will look after you. Keep you safe in our Hong Kong mansion. There's more protection there. Better lifestyle. Come." He had his hand out, his skin coated in a fine and slowly browning film of coagulating blood.

Dallas had always been able to see a path forward in his life. From every fork in the road, he could see a future forming ahead of him. But not now. Not from this moment. He'd run this well dry. The *Arethusa* was gone. His career of running contraband for the triads was now a rapidly disappearing part of his history. He had done so much wrong in his life and never been caught. Always somehow gotten away with it. But right now, he felt his run of successes had come to a definitive close. The right path, he had learned, was often the most difficult.

"Nelly."

"Yeah, Dee."

"That thing loaded?"

"Yeah Dee."

"Take him out."

Maneli levelled the weapon at Chen. He released Kit from his grasp and held up his hand, facing Maneli. "You don't have to do that. We can all have the edit. We can all live long, happy lives." Dallas grabbed Kit by the ankle and pulled. She fell hard on her backside and slid toward him across the boat's blood-damp wooden slats.

"No, hey, he's family! You can't kill him!" Kit yelled, reaching back for Chen.

"The fuck I can't."

Maneli fired.

The blast caught Chen below the waist, his legs vaporizing into a bloody fog. The slugs had left a metre-wide hole in the side of the boat behind him, the deck splintering into shards of carbon. It reminded Dallas of the *Arethusa*, her wing exploding beneath him. Rong's torso fell to the deck, his arms flapping, blood seeped from the clean cut the projectiles had left halfway up his thighs.

"Fucking missed. I never miss." Maneli reloaded the weapon, this time with speed and precision, and levelled it at Kit. "What else are you hiding that's so goddammed important?"

One of the policemen crawled forward, moving for his gun. She trained the weapon on him. "Stay out of this, both of you! No need for anyone else to get unnecessarily misted!" She shifted her position, putting Kit between her and the cop. "I get a two for one if you take another step, chai low."

Kit flipped the fingernail up, depressed the holomem there, slid it from her fingertip, and held it out to Maneli. Tears flowed over her cheeks. "He wants this. Just take it. All the data is there. It's the Zeus edit. Long life. Give it to him and get me out of here."

Maneli took the holomem from Kit's fingers, looked it over. "I've got a reader for this." She slid it into a pocket on her vest. "Might be worth something to us later."

The old man moaned. Pulled himself along the boat deck with his hands. He picked up one of his boots, his calf exposed, his face despondent. "Regrowth, Kit," he rasped. "Please, take me with you. We can fix all this with your regrowth edit."

"How is he still alive?" Dallas asked, moving Kit toward the sub.

"The slugs get so hot it cauterizes the wounds. Bit of a design flaw in my opinion. Leaves the target alive if you fucking miss like I just did," Maneli said, holding the KEP on the police.

"Is he right, Kit? About regrowth?" Dallas asked.

"Yeah. The augment can regrow limbs, major organs. Takes a few months, but it works," Kit said, wiping her eyes.

"And you can't buy it at the market?"

"Those are copy edits. They have too many off-targets. Usually cause more problems than they solve. Can I ask what we're still doing here?"

"These chai low are a problem. A 'there's gonna be more and soon' kind of a problem. Maneli's right; we need to get out of here now," Dallas said.

"Take me with you," Chen begged. "Help me, so I can help you. We are yat kuo ga-ting." *One family.* He was dragging himself toward them.

"He gonna live?" Dallas asked, his gun aimed at the police.

"He has access to the lab. Any one of the techs there could spin up an edit for him in hours," Kit said. "But he definitely needs a hospital."

"OK, we're done here. You two get in the sub." Maneli shoved Kit into Dallas. "I'll follow you both down." She took the handgun from Dallas and walked over to the two cops, a weapon in each hand. "You two, I don't know how you ended up here with no backup, but you need to leave. This gift right here is the dragonhead of the Shing Wo, and he needs a hospital. I'd say you don't have a lot of time." She handed one of them her Glock, grip first. "Don't fuck us around. It won't end well for you, chai low."

The woman handed her weapon to Woo, its barrel facing her. Glock subcompact, a nice gun. He could have squeezed the trigger and killed her in an instant. But to be given the dragonhead? It seemed impossible. The man was pulling himself along the deck, his leg stumps wiggling, in a slow chase after his granddaughter. He took heed of the warning. There was no possible conclusion to this that was going to end well for *any* of them.

"Get him below deck," he said to Fong. "Put him in a bed or something, and if there's any alcohol down there, bring me some."

Fong stood up and walked over to the flailing old man, picked him up by one arm like a monkey, and carried him down the stairs into the belly of the boat.

Woo holstered the gun and stayed put. They were aiding criminals in their escape. Chen was a bonus prize, but they weren't here only for him.

"And add the Coast Guard to that call for backup. That sub is gonna be hard to tail with a police boat."

The skiff and its driver had long since vacated the cove. Woo had never sailed a day in his life, and he wouldn't be taking this crime scene of a sailboat out in any weather, let alone the seas they'd crossed to get there. He picked up their handguns from the deck then took a seat at the rear of the boat and watched the group of criminals he had come here to apprehend climb into the submarine and disappear below the surface.

They piled back into the sub, Maneli sealing the hatch above. "Can someone take these fucking things off me now?" Kit held up her wrists, blood running down past her elbows. Maneli grabbed a hunting knife from her belt, held her by one hand, her grip like a vice, placed the blade between her wrists, and swiped up, bisecting the plastic straps.

"Where are you taking me?"

"First things first. We need to get into a room in the back of that cavern." Maneli dove the sub, aiming it nose down. It sank like concrete, making a vertical path down to the ocean floor. "We're going to wait here until those two cops figure out how to get that boat with Chen Rong on it out of our harbour. Then we'll sneak back up."

"What's in the cavern?" Kit asked.

"Gear."

They sat in silence. Maneli had her chair tilted all the way back. She stared up into the holographic display, the white circle around the sailboat sitting static, unmoving. Her eyes adjusted fast to the darkness. That edit was her favourite, Dark Adaptation. The sub's interior was unlit. There were no running lights outside. An inquisitive sea turtle nosed up to the glass bubble. A school of slender, translucent fish swam past, taking no note of them.

"I need bandages. That med kit still in here?" Kit asked.

Dallas stared at her. "Your eyes are shining," he said.

"Huh?"

"Your eyes are shining like a cat's. Only ever seen that once before, a bartender I know. Guy's got a lot of edits."

"It's an augment, Dark Adaptation. I grew a thing called tapetum lucidum, behind my retinas. Got eyes like a cow's. Increased low-light sensitivity."

"That expensive?"

"Probably cost you more than this sub to get it done."

"Not if you know the editor though, right?" Dallas said, leaning toward her.

Maneli sat upright and pulled on the yolk, advancing the throttles. The sub angled up like an aircraft, pushing Kit back into her seat. The white circle had moved off. Maneli brought them to periscope depth, then displayed its feed across the glass bubble. The sailboat was gone, the cave empty. She brought the sub up out of the water, gentle as a fish, nudging it against the wooden dock.

Maneli unbuckled and spun the latch mechanism on the hatch above. "Time to read your little holomem."

62.

They followed heavy-gauge cabling sheathed in black polyprop from the water into an unlit corner of the cavern.

"I can't see a fucking thing," Dallas said. "Guess the editor's not having any trouble?" His pace was slow as he felt his way forward. He was right; through Kit's augmented eyes, the entire cavern was illuminated in shades of dark, adapted grey, everything edged with a wavering blur. Ahead of her, two wooden chairs sat upside down against a desk layered in tarpaulin. An overwhelming odour of ammonia grew stronger as they approached the desk, a thick layer of guano bathed every surface.

Maneli snapped on a flashlight, blinding Kit with its beam. She blinked long to reset, listening to the sounds of flapping wings, scratching, and the faint clicks of echolocation, bats in flight scanning the cave's upper void. So many species had evolved sonar; why not humans? Something for the future, she thought, something for after this. "What's under the tarps?" she asked.

"The gear," Maneli replied. She yanked off one of the sheets of plastic, turned over a chair, and sat down. The cables terminated in the backs of several large displays, code scrolling up them against a translucent black background. She flipped a keyboard guano side down and began typing, the flicker of screen reflecting off the cavern's dark and uneven rock walls.

Maneli took the paper-thin holomem from her jacket pocket,

gave it a once over, turning it between her fingertips. "This is nice tech. No wireless." She tapped it against the tabletop, waved it in front of a display. "Whole thing's a faraday cage. Government issue?" She slid a thin, black, metal cover off its end and snapped the exposed gold contacts into a slot on the front of one of the displays.

"That's compressed crystal-lattice-mem in there. I'm surprised someone like you has a reader," Kit said.

"So, not government issue is what I'm hearing."

Dallas paced in the glow from the displays. "We literally have minutes here. If those cops called in the Coast Guard, they're gonna be on the way in a hurry."

Maneli leaned into the display in front of her, reading the code.

"What am I looking at?" she asked.

"Well, to begin with, it's encrypted. No way you're gonna crack that crypto. It's quantum. Take you decades."

Maneli glared at her, then sat up straight in the chair. "You can walk over here and let this reader scan you for the key, or I can bring you over myself. Your choice."

Kit didn't need to think it through. It was a good reminder that she was being held against her will. She walked to the screen and allowed the reader to scan her biosig, providing the crypto's genetic key to decrypt the holomem.

"What are you planning to do with the data? It's not usable info to anyone outside of my lab."

"I disagree." Maneli looked at Dallas. "Dee? What we talked about?"

"Yeah," he nodded. "Put it up."

"Up? Up where?" Kit asked.

Maneli sat forward, typing.

"You don't mean upload. You can't upload it." She looked at both of them.

Aquamarine lines of blurred data scrolled up the display.

"That, my new friend, is *exactly* what is happening," Maneli said, her eyes on the console in front of her.

"Keeping this private would be like keeping the cure for plague, Ebola, SARS," Dallas said. "We don't have a choice; it's got to go up."

"Like, to everyone? Are you *insane*? It's the fucking cure for aging, not a flu vaccine!"

"We're giving it away," Dallas said. "It's not a discussion."

"I don't think you understand. I don't think you have any idea what that code is worth."

"Clock's ticking, Nelly. What's the progress?"

"It's a lot of data, Dee. Talking exabytes. We've got fat pipes in and out of here, but I'm working it. Gonna take some time."

"Dallas, please, think this through. If you give it away, it'll change humanity. Change it all. There are consequences. We can't hand it out for *free*. The whole fucking planet will live *centuries*. There is *nothing* in our millions of years of evolution that has prepared us for a change like this!"

She couldn't let it happen. She couldn't be the catalyst for a species-wide alteration of this magnitude. The KEP was leaning against Maneli's chair, barrel down, the cartridge loaded. Kit had fired it once, and she was ready to fire it again. She had nothing left to lose. She reached for the weapon. Maneli reacted like she'd broadcast it, deflected her away from the gun with ease, gripping her bleeding wrists with that terrifying augmented strength, wrestling her to the ground. Maneli dug her knee deep into the back of Kit's neck. She grunted, struggling to breathe. She'd been kidnapped, frozen, bound, robbed, and beaten. She'd fought enough. It was time. She gave in and collapsed under the Israeli's weight.

"Is it up?" Dallas asked.

"It's uploading to my people in Tehran. I'm gonna publish it on a public feed when I'm finished with her, and once that's done, it is no longer anyone's property."

"You've open-sourced my life's work," Kit spat. "You bitch."

Dallas leaned down close to Kit's face. She felt his heat, his warm breath like peaches past due, a hint of ashtray.

"You haven't figured it out yet, have you? You've switched teams. You're on our side now. You wasted a triad operative in front of his boss. Identified and witnessed by the Hong Kong Police. You're a marked woman. Marked, like us." He stood up. "You ready to play nice?"

"Yes," she grumbled. "Now get off me, you whore."

Maneli climbed off her with a purposeful shove. Went back to the keyboard.

"It's time, Nelly."

Maneli tapped the keyboard with a finish. "Done. Help me get these pipes into the water." She yanked the thick cables from the rear of the displays, laying one across each of their shoulders. They dragged them back to the water and dropped them in beside the sub. Kit stood watching as the coiled loops snaked out of the cavern under their own weight, slithering into the sea.

They'd hidden in that horrible, tiny submarine for hours, watching harbour traffic crisscross from 200 metres below. Had sat with its motors off, blending into the sea bottom, undetectable by any means. Dallas had chain-smoked. Maneli had, in time, taken them to the Sai Kung country park in northeast Hong Kong, to an uninhabited white sand crescent beach. Under a half-moon night sky, they'd scuttled the sub, sent it motoring out to sea with the main hatch open, sinking it forever. They'd made a temporary home in a dense and unpopulated jungle in a well laid out camp, its structures buried beneath the soil. Complete with chemical toilets and solar power, it had a lifetime of packaged water and dried food, stamped on the side with Arabic lettering, compliments of the Israeli army. A safe house that few but Maneli knew of.

They had spent an entire week living below ground. Optic sensors above picking up the occasional drone flyby. It was safe but it wasn't a long term solution. Kit had entertained more than one fantasy of running, but she was as wanted as they were now. So, on the day Maneli had declared it was safe to leave, she felt more dread than joy. What could be next for a criminal, American diaspora?

They walked through hours of forest to a concrete road, a faint yellow line running along its centre. Up a small hill, a cement bench sat empty under a tall metal signpost, a bus stop. "Kit, what's next for you?" Maneli asked. "Can't stay here." She had an old flip phone, like the one Dallas had used. She opened it, held it to her ear, and ordered three Rydes.

"They investigate that lab in Golia, I'll be hung," Kit said.

"They get their hands on any of us, and we'll all get hung," Maneli responded.

"I'm not suggesting we stick together," Dallas said, "but it's worth mentioning that we are all criminals of varying degrees in the eyes of the law."

"Let's not forget our friends in the Shing Wo," Maneli said.

"Know any good islands?" Dallas asked.

"Might have been a good idea to keep the sub," Kit said.

Three green Huawei Ryde copters touched down curbside, spooling down their turbines.

Maneli took a small, folded piece of paper from one of the multiple pockets on her vest and handed it to Dallas. "Meet me at this address in a couple of hours. Kennedy Town. Don't come together. Show up ten minutes apart. There's a hot pot down the street, Xiau Yu, second floor on Belcher's. Hang out there, separate tables. I can help us all get out of Hong Kong alive."

She jumped in the Ryde. With the canopy closed, it hovered

while it spun in the opposite direction, then climbed away, its lanky landing legs retracting into its body. Kit looked at Dallas. "See you there?"

"You go now," he said. "I'll be there in twenty. Get the beef; it's good and spicy."

Outside on Maneli's ground-floor deck, the southern Chinese evening air held thick and muggy. Above them, skyscrapers cast their shadows against a manmade backdrop of incandescent sky. They sat around a picnic table printed from pink resin in her postage-stamp-sized backyard, a rare piece of private outdoors encircled in three-metre-high bamboo lattice. A 3D-printed palm tree and a metre-wide square of green plastic grass allowed an illusion of nature. There was even a red child's play bucket and small blue shovel. On the table between them was a bottle of Tanqueray, three glasses, metal tongs in a bowl of ice, and sliced lemons.

Mosquitos buzzed over Dallas's head. "You got any bug spray?" he asked, waving his hands. "Mozzie country out here."

Maneli smiled, "Those are mine. They're edited. Don't worry; they don't bite. Can't, in fact. They're born without a proboscis."

"How's that?"

"They're personal, Oxitech. I bought the eggs and grew them myself in that bowl of water by the sink like Chia Pets. They don't last long, but they help breed out any wild mosquito populations. Germline edited so their babies are born with the mutation. Those can't bite either."

"The telomerase edit I made," Kit said, shaking her head, "it's germline too. The whole fucking species is going to live hundreds of years. Humanity just got a free upgrade to 2.0."

"Evolutionary," Dallas said, squinting as he sipped at his gin and lemon. "When are the two of us getting our Zeus edit then?"

he asked.

"There's a medical printlab beneath that hot pot I sent you to," Maneli said.

"It still needs to be tailored for your specific genome," Kit said, "but I can do that on anyone's holo with a sample of your DNA and that holomem. Those printlabs can synthesize in thirty minutes. Might not be perfect, but it'll get the process started on your sequence."

Maneli went inside for a moment, then returned holding a silver briefcase. She put it on the picnic table, popping the two locks with thumbprints.

"I've got passports for you." She reached inside, putting two plain cards of carbon-fibre on the table. "They're blanks, so we need to scan your biosigs. They're high-test; you'll be able to use them for years. Scrambles your signature, so it won't match any of your previous scans." She slid them forward. "You got a plan, Dee?"

"Get somewhere on a boat, maybe. Stay off the grid a few years. Maybe forever."

"You got a one-way?"

"I've got a getaway case like yours at home, some Amsterdam Shag, and plenty of cash. I'll get a ticket with that passport, somewhere hot, quiet. What about her?" He pointed at Kit. "She can't come with me."

"I'll take her. I've got a plan, and I could use some company to get it done."

"Local?"

"No." She took a pull of gin straight from the bottle. "You know, if Chen Rong lives, he's gonna come looking for you. For all of us. Should have finished him off out there."

Dallas downed his drink, poured another. "Let's get that edit synthed. I want to go home, so I can get the hell out of Hong Kong for good."

"All I need is a sample tube and some saliva, and a holo to do the math," Kit said.

Dallas got up and spat in one of the empty glasses. "Good enough?"

She nodded. "Good enough."

63.

The deadbolt popped as Dallas turned the key, unlocking the door to his home. It opened into the down-sloped hallway, bare walls illuminating with the flicker of warming fibre-optic light. He took a step into his dangling apartment, leaned against the wall, and crossed his arms. Took one deep breath. There was nobody chasing, no data stream monitoring, no low-level aerial firefight to avoid while flying at ninety percent of the speed of sound, dodging water towers and missile launches. This was his zero point; he felt it. The place from where progress could be charted. It was peaceful there, solitary, a place to begin anew. But it wasn't safe any longer. Not from government, not from the police, and not from triad eyes. Another brief stop along another interstitial path. To where, he didn't know. The newscasts he'd seen through noodle house windows on the walk up blazed with a story he'd sown the seeds to himself.

"Shing Wo leader found maimed, arrested on charge of kidnapping."

"Anonymous source claims aging solved."

"Fountain of youth discovered."

"Endless life available for all."

Maneli had seen to it that the world's laboratories had the data. They were making it available en masse, a vaccine against aging, Israel leading the charge.

Dallas lay down in his bed. Took in the silence for a moment. There was a global change in place, a change that was out of the control of the powerful few. A change that perhaps for the first time in humanity's existence rightfully belonged in the hands of all.

The moment passed. He sat up to leave, the injection site on his arm still fresh. He rubbed the warm itch under the bandage, asked himself a question that, right up until that moment he'd have answered without a second's thought.

Did he really want to live forever?

He grabbed his grey, pre-packed getaway briefcase from under the bed. His grinder sat open on the table.

Maybe not forever, Dallas thought, closing the door behind him, *but certainly a few years more.*

Like Persephone used to say, "You're a long time dead."

And Dallas still wasn't ready for dead.

Acknowledgements

Writing is a journey, a series of rewrites, iterations of ideas thought long ago. This I did not know. In recognition of the team required to bring this fictional world from my mind to print, I would like to extend a heartfelt thank you to the following:

Sue Telford for reading an early draft and offering important guidance throughout;

Keith Fong for his Cantonese coaching and accurate translations;

Katie Telford for her contributions to the possibilities of fingernail tech;

Kevin Miller, my editor, for taking on a first-time novelist, for our conversation about "things Dallas would say," and for helping me bring this manuscript from laptop to print;

Jordan Rokosz and his team at FriesenPress, for allowing me to overthink and self-correct, sometimes with a gentle nudge in the right direction;

Geofrey William Karianga for bringing a Maasai Warrior's perspective to the conversations between Opiyo and Kit;

Nimo Abdulla Aden for her help with translations and her husband Gernot Bremermann for bringing the four of us together;

and Ian Telford, for introducing me all those years ago to the world of science fiction.

About the Author

 Lucien is an airline pilot who has lived and traveled worldwide, including places like Hong Kong and Africa. This novel draws heavily on those experiences. He now lives in Western Canada with his wife Katie. *The Sequence* is his first book.

www.lucientelfordbooks.com

CPSIA information can be obtained
at www.ICGtesting.com
Printed in the USA
LVHW050141030522
717729LV00004B/550